FEAR OF FREE STANDING OBJECTS

A COLLECTION

DOUG RINALDI'S

FEAR OF FREE STANDING OBJECTS

A COLLECTION

Mayhem Street Media

Second Edition

Fear of Free Standing Objects © 2018-2020 by Doug Rinaldi/Mayhem Street Media
Cover & interior design and formatting by Doug Rinaldi

Cover Photo Cloud VA Wind Turbine, Saint Cloud, Minnesota by Tony Webster licensed under the terms of the cc-by-sa-2.0

All other photos obtained and used via CC0 Public Domain or by permission © Passing Bird Photography. www.passingbird.com

All rights reserved

The right of Doug Rinaldi to be identified as the author of this work has been asserted by him in accordance with the Copyright, Designs and Patents Act 1988.

No part of this book may be reproduced or utilized in any form or by any means, electronic or mechanical, including photocopying, recording, or by any information storage and retrieval system, without permission in writing from the author and publisher.

This is a work of fiction. Names, characters, places, and incidents either are the product of the author's imagination or are used fictitiously, and any resemblance to any persons, living or dead, business establishments, events, or locales is entirely coincidental.

ISBN-13: 9781650577845

Printed in the United States

Edited by Linda Nagle

*For Those
Who Matter Most*

PREFACE

I'm usually at a loss for words when it comes to writing these types of things, but when it comes right down to it, acknowledging those folks that have either convinced me to get off my ass and put this collection together, or have helped me make sense of the nonsense between the covers has been the easiest part of this process—this time around.

Self-publishing is a scary thing. There is no glitz or glamour. Self-publishing a collection of short stories is even more nerve-racking. Whether the word on the street is that the short story is dead or single author collections don't sell, this is what I do, and it still feels good that there are people pickin' up what I'm puttin' down. With all the honest support I've been gifted, I write these stories for those people.

So, the first big shout out goes to my darling Liz, who gets mad at me when I'm *not* writing. She's always there for a hearty kick in my ass when the depression and self-deprecation reach fever pitch. Or maybe she just wants me out of her hair so she could binge watch more episodes of *Property Brothers*. Who knows for sure?

Thanks go to my buddy, Jared Collins, from my second favorite rock and roll band (sorry, Jared) Mississippi Bones. We discovered each other's work around the same time and it blossomed into a very rewarding friendship. His opinion of my writing is highly revered and appreciated. And he's been an amazing sounding board for when I'm either stuck in a story—or in the process—or to offer that extra boost when I don't feel like writing at all.

I would be remiss if I didn't mention the New England Horror Writers. While I'm not the most vocal or active member, they are an invaluable group of amazingly talented people. Through them, I have made solid connections with some of the most helpful and friendly people I've ever had the pleasure of meeting. For instance, Dave Price has the ability to read my work and add just the right amount of polish to make some passages shine like no other. He's got a gift and has been a wonderful friend and guide. Also from the group is Greg Dearborn. He is my beta reader extraordinaire. His insights and willingness to help have left me humbled and grateful. Thanks, guys!

And thank you to all my beta readers, book reviewers, and readers throughout this journey of mine. You're the best!

TABLE OF CONTENTS

Unfurl	01
Osteogenesis	03
An Incident in Central Village	19
Bequeathed	33
Alchemy of Faith	39
The Yattering	51
Egregore	69
The Sickening	77
And the Hits Just Keep on Comin'	91
Lotus Petals: Liminal Personae	109
The Jatinga Effect	137
Sybarites (Or the Enmity of Perverse Existence)	159
End_Game (Dementia Praecox)	177
A Different Kind of Slumber	205

UNFURL

I've forever known that escaping this place would solve a lifetime of despair. Here, standing on the ledge of the third-floor window to this Gothic edifice I've called home for more years than I can remember, I bathe in the fading warmth of the setting sun. I feel its magical rays highlight the scornful lines of sadness carved in my face from an existence of suffering. Yet, I hear its siren's call beckoning me to be one with it. And I hear the eternity in its majesty... feel the comfort *in* that eternity.

As I gaze down upon the magnificent facade of stonework and artistry, I'm well aware that no one outside of its hallowed halls and impenetrable walls will ever know of the evil and pain held within them. If I'm truly the first to break free from this seemingly inescapable fortress of corruption, no one will ever hear my tale—or learn of my horrid reality. Even if someone were privy to my story, I believe they'd find it absurd, and in a twisted sense of irony, recommend I be put right back inside.

I brace my arms between the window panes, pushing on the cold structure with my hands as if trying to widen the expanse of my escape route. I look up just as twilight begins to engulf the enduring hints of light. Shadows twist and dance across the polished architecture, creating visual murmurs calling me to join them, spurring me on to commit to my plan.

Below, I can sense others staring out through their barred windows, noses to cold glass, wishing they, too, could somehow break free. Yet, their fate isn't their own—perhaps it never was. They had succumbed to the inevitable, unable—or unwilling—to challenge the providence of their keepers.

The time has come. Vestiges of sunlight vanish beyond the horizon as the dark's icy tendrils claim the night sky. I look behind me one last time at the clandestine horror that's taken everything from me, that's wrung almost every drop of will I have left—*almost*. My toes curl over the edge and the cool air soothes my mind. The time is now.

Creeping towards freedom, I lean forward, letting the shadows envelop me. Air rushes by my face in my free fall, and I smile. From my back, wings unfurl, catching fate's windy current and lifting me high above this terrible place.

Sun… I'm coming home.

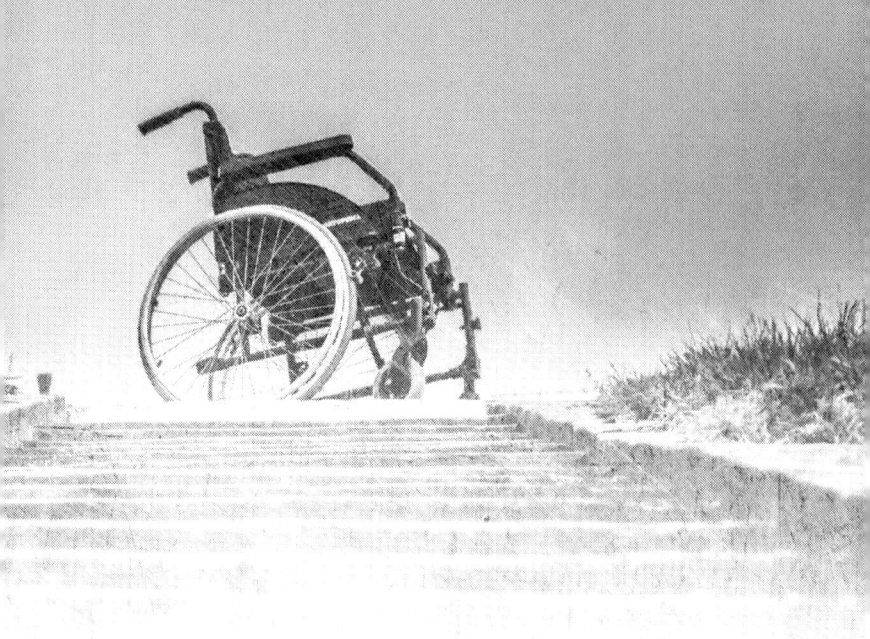

OSTEOGENESIS

It was only mere weeks after my spinal fusion surgery, but something in my back felt wrong around the area the surgeons had magically fused. They'd used titanium screws and rods and bone grafts—soon to heal the vertebra into one solid piece of bone—it truly sounded like sorcery... but I felt a constant, abnormal movement as if something was loose and jingling inside my spinal column.

When I first brought up my concerns to my orthopedist, he assured me that the "radical new" procedure they'd performed on me was a brilliant success and that, based on preliminary x-rays, the donated bone tissue they'd used for the graft looked perfect. Surgeons just love to pat their own backs.

Still, aches and throbbing pains wracked my body. I could barely sit in one place for more than ten minutes at a time, let alone walk without the pimp lean, and when I would finally pass out from exhaustion, I would be tormented by these god-awful, bizarre dreams that something had gone horribly wrong inside me.

I stood in front of the mirror, grateful the surgery had helped me shed most of my unsightly beer pounds. My incision, the soon-to-be permanent treasure trail carved in skin, ran from my navel down to the top of my groin. It looked impressive, and would surely lead to many interesting conversations. I traced its redness with my finger, surprised at how well it was healing, before getting dressed and heading off to my follow-up x-ray.

After I signed in at radiology, a nurse wheeled an elderly woman right by me as I headed for a seat. The wrinkled and sour-looking woman snatched my arm and yanked me down to her level. The nurse made moves to intervene, but I waved her off, as I didn't really feel it was a bother. Luckily for her, she didn't see the cringing wave of revulsion flash over my face when I received a close-up of the old woman's one empty eye socket. The other eye was no prize either, all filled in with what looked like a California roll mashed inside a clear balloon—the cataract having advanced to a disturbing milky hue.

"And what can I do for you, young lady?" I asked. She cupped my hand with freakish strength.

"Tell them to get it out of you!" The fluid of her inner eye bubbled to the surface as she spoke. "Get it out! Now!" She released her grip and slipped into a catatonic trance.

"Sorry about that," said the nurse, embarrassed. "I have no idea what any of that was about."

"It's no problem. Just a bit odd. She usually like... that?"

"Not really. In fact, that's the most I've heard her say all week. Ever since she had her eye removed."

"Hmm. That's not weird at all or anything," I joked.

The nurse shrugged and rolled off with the old woman and I walked to a waiting chair, rubbing my hand and mulling over the experience. What an odd thing to say, not only to a complete stranger, but to anybody—odd and creepy. To add to my heebie-jeebies, my back pain began to flare up, spasming something fierce.

Just as the white-hot pain subsided—as quickly as it had begun, my name was called.

As instructed, I lay on the table in my hospital gown, keeping perfectly still. My mind raced back to the old woman's words—the precursor to my sudden flare up. Was it ominous? Yeah, a bit. But I chalked it up to coincidence as the x-ray machine did its thing, working its age-old magic to ascertain what could possibly still be wrong with me.

Back in my own personal little medical cell, I waited for Doctor Fischer to pop in with the results. Kicking and swaying my feet over the edge of the exam table—just like I remember doing as a kid, I hoped for some good news or, in the least, a reason for all the new pain.

Dr. Fischer's look of complete befuddlement entered the room the same time he did, which didn't bode well. "Um, we may have to take another round of x-rays."

"Really? What for?" I asked, trying to disguise my concern as annoyance.

"There's no cause for alarm yet, but the films show something concerning in the area where we did the fusion. How long did you say you've been experiencing the pain?"

"It's probably been about three weeks or so. Why?"

"Well, I have the techs checking the camera and the film stock to see if there are any defects or smudges and such to rule out equipment malfunction." He slid the films over the light box so I could see what he was trying to explain to me. "You see this area right in here?" He pointed to a darkened, blurry spot around the fused vertebrae.

"Yeah, and?" I had no idea what I was supposed to see aside from a fuzzy looking shape. I just wanted a fucking answer! If I needed another surgery, I would seriously consider running into traffic. "You're killin' me, doc. What am I looking at?"

The doctor circled the general area with his finger. "This dark mass here has me worried. As I said, I don't want you to panic or jump to conclusions."

"Don't want me to panic? Seriously? Because I had so much friggin' fun the first time around."

"Like I said, we're still checking the equipment. But it might be one of those rare cases where something isn't taking - either the materials we used for the graft, or the bone tissue itself."

Tell them to get it out of you... Get it out!

"In fact, it looks like the cage has completely detached and the bone tissue inside of it has started growing," the doctor said, in a hush.

"All the technical mumbo-jumbo aside, this isn't close to normal, I take it?" Panic clattered around the forefront of my thoughts.

"No, it's not," he admitted—realizing I'd heard what he said.

Get it out!

I squinted as I looked at the x-ray. "That's kinda spooky, actually."

"What is?"

"The blurry spot looks a little like a fac—" I keeled over in blinding pain, gripping my back and almost falling off the exam table. The pain was so exquisite, like having your vertebrae shucked like a clamshell. Bright flashes clogged my vision and tears erupted from my eyes. Doctor Fischer bolted over to me, calling out to the technician in the control booth, but neither were able to hold me still as I twisted and squirmed.

I managed to curl into a ball on the table, shaking from the bolts of hot agony torturing my nerve endings. Behind Fischer and his tech, the x-ray film ripped out of the light-box clips and crashed to the floor by their feet. The air rushed out of my lungs and my ears popped. The overhead lights flashed on and off and everything fell into a vacuum-like silence.

"What did you do to me?" My shouts rattled around in my head. I felt the blood in my veins boiling as something started tearing through my back muscles. The pain intensified as the source of that pain seemed to grow exponentially.

GET IT OUT!

The doctor and technician scurried around unable to decide what to do, mumbling to each other about "it" not working. Amidst my throes, I managed to pry open my eyes. On the floor, the x-ray of my spine quivered and warped, turning almost three-dimensional, like looking down a hole or out of a window. Through my glossy, wet vision, I watched two gnarled and emaciated hands reach up and out of the sheet of exposed film, pressing down on the floor and climbing out. My hand shook as I gestured toward the thing.

The technician turned to see what I was pointing at and I saw the confusion on his face. I watched one of the bony hands clasp around his ankle, knocking him off balance and sending him plummeting to the linoleum. A ragged gasp, almost a chuckle of amused satisfaction, burst out from the x-ray and ricocheted off the examining room's walls.

Though tears still blurred my vision, the image of a gray, impish figure climbing onto the technician's back was unmistakable. The tech wriggled and squirmed trying to break free from its grasp. As it wrapped its legs around his midsection and squeezed, the tech's choked scream fought to escape. While all this was happening, I skittered across the exam table. "What the fuck did you do to me?"

Fischer lunged toward me. "Stop! Let him go!"

A knobby-handed fist clocked the doctor in the jaw, dropping him hard to the floor. Overhead, the lights still flashed and sparked, creating a trippy, strobe effect. I watched Fischer scuttle away in terror, his eyes unable to hide his true level of shock.

Then I heard the snap.

The technician crumpled to the floor, his eyes rolling around in their sockets like loose marbles. Through the clenching and intermittent bouts of pain, I could only stare awestruck and overwhelmed as the deformed imp-thing giggled while slowly lurching towards Fischer. I closed my eyes, wishing for the madness to stop. Doctor Fischer mumbled for what I assumed was help—or mercy—between breathless sobs, but all my ears would register was the giggling until....

.... I heard another meaty snap.

I took off.

With the abrupt end of Fischer's cries still ringing in my ears, I made my escape down the hallway of the radiology office, rushing past confused nurses and patients before exploding out into the waiting room. Everyone must have heard the murderous commotion just a few rooms over, because all eyes were on me as if I were some two-headed mutant. It wasn't until I was barreling down the corridor, oblivious to my pain, dodging people on crutches, and jiving around orderlies and security personnel, that I noticed not only was I still in my hospital Johnny, but those same orderlies and guards were after me.

I could see why; I mean, I'd just witnessed two people die before my eyes, but fear was the bigger motivator here. In the process, I hustled around a corner, nearly taking out a man shuffling around in a back brace and tethered to his IV stand. The sounds of bedpans and gurneys crashing to the floor, crash carts and patients shoved into walls, and people shouting, echoed behind me. Complete bedlam. But I kept on going, knowing if I didn't, that goblin-looking freakshow would catch me and snap *my* neck as well.

Up ahead, the emergency room's sliding doors awaited to aid me in my escape. The need to flee outweighed my common sense. Again, the air around me thickened and the fragile tubes of iridescence sputtered overhead. An orderly, a big Hispanic dude covered in tattoos, stood like a Technicolor tree stump obstructing the exit. It wasn't until I was mere feet away that I saw those horribly familiar gray hands reach up from behind him. I skidded to an abrupt and painful stop as I plowed right into him... but it was too late. With a giggle and a slip of the wrists, the orderly's neck cracked and popped.

All around, frightened people shrieked and clamored. More security guards funneled down the hallway towards me, waving their batons and prepping their pepper sprays.

"Fuck this!"

Giggle.

I scrambled up, sensing imminent liberation from this infirmary of terror, and spun around in my hospital-approved, skid-proof socks right into the waiting arms of two cops who took no time wrestling me to the floor. In a flurry of blue and silver, they snapped the metal bracelets on tight and yanked me up by my armpits. I knew struggling would be useless, but it sure didn't prevent me from trying. With my resisting and kicking all the way out the sliding doors, they dragged me towards their cruiser.

Off to the side and barely paying any attention, was the nurse from earlier, chatting on her phone. Parked next to her was the crazy, one-eyed lady, in all her glorious dementia. As the nurse ignored her wheelchair-bound patient, paying attention instead to a cigarette and engrossing herself in digital conversation, I glanced up. Amidst my squirming, I noticed the old crone was coherent again, and glowering at me in displeasure.

"I told you to get it out!" she barked from a distance, hooking her crooked finger at me.

"What's happening to me?" I shouted back, as the officers forced me forward.

"Stop resisting, asshole," ordered cop number one.

The old woman's voice sounded like she had spent half a lifetime gargling with gravel. "Get it out!"

"How?" I wrangled myself free from the public servants' grips and bolted over to her, almost colliding with the wheelchair. "What's happening to me? Get what out?"

She just sneered, drool collecting in the corners of her mouth as her dry, wrinkly lips smacked together. The cops were on top of me and my head hit the walkway, kept there by a strategically placed knee. As they held me prone and embarrassed on the hard concrete, I managed to see the woman jabbing a disapproving finger at me. Her nurse handler, finally aware of the commotion, rushed over to her patient and wheeled her away from the scene, leaving me hollering and asking, "Why?"

I turned away only to see all the curious looky-loos relishing the excitement at my expense, and the arrival of even more police cars all with their blues and reds flashing. In the distance, I heard the old hag shouting as she was wheeled away, "I told him to do it. I told him to get it out."

"Crazy fucking bitch! Why won't she tell me what's going on?" My voice trailed off.

Cop number two, the burliest of the pair, hoisted me up and pushed my head under the car's doorframe and into the backseat of the cruiser. As luck would have it, I ended up dropped to my side so my nose could better acquaint itself with the stink of hooker ass and meth-head farts that were most certainly embedded deep in the fabric of the upholstery. "Shut your mouth, psycho," the cop blurted as he slammed the door. "Goddamn psychos."

My back was screaming from the manhandling I'd just received. I tried to right myself in the cramped backseat, while I overheard the arresting officers outside talking to the detective who had just arrived on the scene. They were throwing around words like murder and homicide. Me, a murderer? That's ludicrous! They had it all wrong!

I bucked in the seat, kicking at the security divider and front seats, my anger and panic surpassing the pain. "I didn't do anything!" I shouted from behind closed windows. "It wasn't me!"

All my nerves turned into rivulets of agony coursing over my skin and through my body until they flooded my brain's pain receptors. I needed to settle down. Out of the corner of my increasingly blurring vision, I spotted that little gray imp fucker snickering and pointing at me from behind a bush. I could almost hear its freaky, childish giggle. As I tried to get someone's attention, to point out the scrawny bastard, I realized I was only going to make myself look crazier. Another crashing wave of pain finally locked up my brain and, mercifully, I passed out.

Giggle.

Strangely enough, I found myself face-down on a wooden surface covered in sweat and still in my hospital gown. My eyes creaked open and the perspiration dripping down from my forehead was stinging them. I reached up to irrigate my eye sockets but the metal clink of resistance prevented me from doing so.

I forced myself to focus, discovering that my newly acquainted cop pals had shackled me to a table in a small, drab room. A monitor straight out of 1987 sat on an old, beat up media cart by the table while a wide mirror covered in fingerprints and smudges graced one of the room's long walls. I'd seen enough cop shows in my time to realize that beyond that reflective portal, other officers of the law stood watching me, judging me, and planning their next move.

Would they go with good cop/bad cop, bad cop/worse cop, or would I get that one detective who felt a moral obligation to show compassion to those on my side of the interrogation table?

As if compelled to delve into complete cliché-mode by those same TV shows, the elasticity of my newly-molested brain reminded me of my current predicament and the fear I should be exhibiting. "Hey! I know you're in there! I didn't do anything!" I pleaded through the glass. Even though I imagined any evidence to the contrary would be damning, I still insisted I couldn't have—wouldn't have—hurt those people at the hospital.

I was just as much a victim. "Please! I didn't hurt those people. It wasn't me. Why does no one believe me? It was—" *tread carefully here, stupid* "—it was a—"

The door burst open. A hardened looking detective with a fiery mop of hair appeared in the doorframe, the chip on his shoulder beating him through the threshold. "A rawny little gray man with big, sharp fingers. Yeah, we know. You were mumbling mad as a box of frogs in the squad car all the way here." I found his deep and gruff dialect rather off-putting.

"Detective, I swear on my—"

He interrupted me again. "You'll be what? Swearin' on your mother's grave will, ya? Or on the life of an innocent wee baby?" A large uniformed officer standing guard at the door snickered, despite his best efforts to resist. "C'mon, mate. Give it a rest. You're already boring me here."

In defiance, I stood up, forgetting about the cuffs still tethering me to the table. My gown ripped and untied, falling down around my forearms and stopping, introducing my ass to the chilled interrogating room. Despite it all, I felt my cheeks burn from embarrassment.

"For fuck's sake," the Detective began. "George, will ya be a peach and go fetch our friend here a fancy orange jumpsuit so his bare ass don't be corruptin' my chair?"

"Sure thing, Detective."

I lowered back into the hot seat opposite the detective. "Thank you."

"Yeah, don't mention it," he said, blowing the steam from his cup of Joe. "Ya muppet."

Great, a dickhead with compassion.

The officer returned and tossed the bright orange package onto the table. "Here ya go. On the house."

I tentatively eyed the jumpsuit as I reached for it, suspecting it was a trap.

Hagan flashed me an I-got-you-right-where-I-want-you smile as he went for my shackles. "Now, if I'm to be takin' these off, you have to promise to be a good lad." He dangled the key between us, treating me like some circus mutant fiending for a treat. "Or I'll be forced to let my equalizer, George here bounce your head off the table."

"Of course," I replied. "I want to comply, cooperate, whatever I gotta do, but I really have no idea what is happening or why nobody believes me." Hagan unlocked my wrists and I immediately started rubbing away the soreness. "I'm not a killer. I'm not crazy."

The officer at the door readied his hand over the sidearm in his holster.

The detective listened intently as I switched into my new clothes and recalled—to the best of my ability—what had happened. "Some weird shit is going on and for some reason it is happening to me," I finished.

Hagan paused and stared at me for what seemed like a minute. He slammed his fist down onto the table, almost knocking over his cup of coffee. "Ya know, I tried to be nice, lend an ear, and perhaps even take your plight serious with the hopes you'd be tellin' me the truth." Anger smoldered in his eyes. "But then your crazy ass starts up again with this little gray monster bullshit."

"Jesus Christ! Why is no one listeni—?"

Detective Hagan raised his finger to his lips, telling me to shut the fuck up without saying a word. I complied. "Come off it, mate. Admit it. There's something wrong with your noodle." As he stood up and grabbed the monitor's remote control, he said, "Watch this." With a click and the hiss of electronic fuzz, the ancient screen came to life.

I had no idea what I was looking at; it just looked like some busy hallway in a building somewhere. "What am I supposed to be seeing?"

"Wait for it," said the detective.

Then, as if on cue, there I was, running down the hallway in my gown, flipping over gurneys, and mowing people down with orderlies and guards on my tail. The screen switched to a different view of the hospital and the large Hispanic fella who I'd witnessed falling victim to that troll bastard. Yet, as I watched myself slip on the floor right into the orderly just as I remembered happening, I saw no little gray demon-man climbing on the man's back. My stomach dropped, and the sour burn of vomit rose up my gullet.

Wide-eyed and shocked, I watched myself on video. Limbs flailing, I scrambled on top of the orderly and snapped his neck to an unnatural angle before he could even react. The assault was so quick and violent that I flinched as I watched. I gulped a mouthful of fear and disgust, my thick saliva crashing into the puke filling my throat. However, what shocked me most was the sick grin on my face the whole time.

"There's your wee gray monster," said Detective Hagan, with a hint of satisfaction.

"No, no, no! That's not right! It's gotta be a mistake. I didn't do that to him." Panic capsized my spirit; I could almost hear the prison cell door closing shut in my mind. I hopped out of the chair and the guard at the door was on me in half a flash. He slammed my face into the table and wrenched my arms behind me. "Wait! This is a mistake! It wasn't me!"

"Yeah. Keep telling yourself that, buddy," said the officer as he hoisted me upright.

Detective Hagan looked me in the eyes. "Ryan Ellis, you are under arrest for the murders of Dr. Alan Fischer, Hugo Morales, and Jason Humphries. You have the right to remain silent…"

As he continued to rattle off the rights I was certain I no longer had, my mind went blank and the only thing I knew was the returning pain.

Like being startled awake while dreaming, I slowly realized they had transported me to a new place. My eyes popped open and I found myself in a large, open holding cell. I was standing upright and somehow out of breath, thinking I'd just exerted myself beyond capacity. Against the metal bars, other inmates stood huddled, calling out for help. The guards were desperately trying to get inside our cell, but a stack of bloodied, orange jump-suited bodies barricaded the cell door, denying them access.

Something—or someone—had thrown the whole wing of the police station into turmoil. I finally snapped out of my daze. Blood marinated the front of my jumpsuit. In my hand, I clenched a long shiv fashioned out of a toothbrush. So much red covered my arm and the handmade shank that I didn't know where it ended and my sleeve began. A quick glance to my feet at the dead inmate with the mangled hand hinted at where I'd acquired the primitive weapon.

There was so much commotion enveloping me that I stood, transfixed, unable to reconcile the multitude of bodies littering the cell floor... all with their heads facing the wrong way. The madness around me meant nothing, becoming only a distant, annoying buzz. On one side of me, guards pushed and banged on the cell door while on the other, inmates, men much larger and more intimidating, eyed me with mortal terror.

I glanced back to the crude blade in my grasp and knew that I had to act before I—and that thing inside me—hurt any more people. No sooner had I made the decision, that everything dropped gear, slowing to a crawl again like wading through molasses. Nevertheless, my hand held fast to its trajectory. The searing pain engulfed me as I dug the shiv deep into my lumbar spine—hoping it was sharp enough—determined to carve out the accursed bone graft between my vertebrae and free my body from the source of this lunacy.

GET IT OUT!

I found myself on the hard floor, unable to move.

All I'd wished for was good health, to not feel like a man broken beyond his years. But that bitch called Bad Luck was calling the shots all along. Positive outcomes weren't in my future. Bad genes, be damned! This nightmare was far beyond any medical or logical rationale. What they had put inside me, unwittingly betraying my trust and my wellbeing, was bountiful chaos, a stumbling block of unnatural proportions.

Did they know what would happen when they melded my body with the tainted tissue? Or were we all just pawns in this twisted mishap?

As I lay floating in a pool of my own blood flowing from the breach in my back, I slowly drowned in my transgressions. With the adjudication of the harsh overhead fluorescents scalding me, I held tight to the cursed chunk of mangled foreign tissue. All around me, I could still hear the cries and shouts. While everyone reacted to what I'd done, my mind reached its nadir.

Within the whirlwind of pandemonium, my thoughts stumbled back to the crazy old woman, the harbinger of my demise. How did she know? *What* did she know? How did this evil invasion of my body propel me to commit these heinous acts against my knowledge?

I felt a sudden pressure, not an internal sensation like the boulder of grief settling on my heart, but a physical tension. I tore my watering eyes away from the blinding lights and glanced down to my chest. Grinning like an idiot was my counterpart, my accomplice to this mayhem, the demon that resided both inside and outside of me. It stared into my eyes, unable to stop another fit of giggling—all at my expense, of course. Its gray hands and pointy, gnarled fingers pushed on my chest as if trying to expedite the crimson flow of life from my body.

I cringed, wishing for death to relieve me of this pain-soaked insanity. The imp walked his fingers up my torso. Between twisted giggles of glee, it hummed "The Itsy-Bitsy Spider" in horrid, wet dissonance.

In my periphery, I could see the people in the police station tending to the victims of my carnage as panic ran amuck. Why would no one save me? With this evil thing sitting on my chest, didn't they understand now?

Though I was unable to move my body, my left hand—which contained the contaminated matter—still retained meager functionality. I squeezed it with all my might. The freakish, little demon flickered like an old television caught between stations.

I clutched the bony tissue tighter.

The thing's jagged face contorted, no longer deriving any amusement from my torment. The harder I gripped the tissue, the angrier it became until its face twisted into a contorted amalgam of malevolence and rage... yet it kept rippling, diminishing in power.

Fist after fist, it pounded on my chest. I felt my ribs cracking, the shards splintering and piercing my lungs. Blood gurgled in the back of my throat, but I refused to relinquish my grasp. Desperation filled its eyes. Ferocious grunts rumbled from its mouth. Confused, it tried breaking my death grip, beating me into submission.

The more I squeezed, feeling the rigid hunk cut into my palm, the more my enemy twinkled, growing more transparent. Now, just moments from passing into obscurity, I finally had the upper hand.

It snarled and clawed deeper into me, panicked beyond reason. But I refused to relent. Its rough, skeletal fingers clenched my throat. Blood foamed to the brim of my gaping mouth. As it choked the remaining life out of me, I infuriated it more and more with my sincere smiles of an impending victory called death. Continuing to dissipate before my blurring eyes, it emitted the metallic stink of electrical discharge. Around my neck, its grip lessened, fading in strength as it quivered between dimensions.

To say I was beyond saving at this point, with mere moments of life left on this rock, would've been a gross understatement. My fate ever so sealed by a surgically vile twist, I closed my eyes before I no longer had the choice in the matter.

The nightmare that was both inside of me and out, fought valiantly to the end, but I could no longer gather the mental faculty to care. However, it was still a race to the end and I had the wherewithal enough to make it a fight; the little fucker was not going to win by a blowout! With its fiendish hands poised for unavoidable certainty, I felt the waves of relief crashing on the shores of my departing consciousness as it giggled one last time in spite of itself... *Giggle*.

CENTRAL VILLAGE
AN INCIDENT IN

I ignited a trail of velocity in my descent down Kinney Hill Road, blazing down the asphalt. But in front of me, the windy day kicked up enough road dust to sandblast my face. Being that it was my first week on a ten-speed bicycle, I figured, what would be the worst that could happen? Besides, I was tired of watching all the other kids on their ten and twelve-speeds while I was stuck riding around on a beat-up old, second-hand Huffy.

Watching all the other kids in the neighborhood whiz on down the mammoth hill with skill and ease, I knew that accepting such a challenge would put me on the cool kid radar for sure... as long as I didn't end up repeating the embarrassing hyper-ventilation episode from a few days ago. Apparently, dropping the bike into the lowest gear and then trying to pedal up an incline was not how one got it done. Dad had to come get me as I sat on the side of the road defeated and barely able to breathe, fearing death.

But that was all in the past as I heard mighty Kinney Hill calling my name and challenging my budding manhood.

The scenery continued flashing by me in color-streaked blurs; the rushing wind pounded against my eardrums. My smile beamed, and I didn't care at all about the road spitting dirt up into my mouth. It felt immense. As I quickly, yet sadly, neared the end of the asphalt giant's path, I felt triumphant, like a genuine badass. First week riding a ten-speed—take that!

At the bottom of Kinney Hill, I merged onto River Street and hit my brakes. I guarantee it would've been the smoothest stop ever had I squeezed the correct hand brake. Before I realized what had happened, my soft head made swift and painful contact with the hard and unforgiving blacktop. I somersaulted with the grace of a buffalo on a trampoline right over the handlebars. Gravel and chunks of dirt embedded my forehead.

I collapsed into a pitiful pile right in the middle of the intersection of River Street and Sachem Drive, screaming and crying for help. Of course, no one came to my aid as I bled all over myself and the poor street, probably 'cuz everybody was over at the high school field watching the Ram's big rivalry game today. Just my luck....

Despite not seeing anyone around, I *hoped* that nobody sat staring out his or her window in stitches over my mishap. I quickly got to my shaky feet and dusted myself off. My head pounded and spun in agony. As I wiped the trickling blood off of my face and out of my eyes, flicking it off my fingers and onto the road, I felt all the little bumps and indents from where face met gravel. I'm sure it read Braille for 'dumbass.'

I grabbed the collar of my shirt and dried the tears from my face. A faint sound, almost like a hiss, reached my ears and I quizzically glanced around. I saw nothing until I looked down at the bloodied pavement. Like an egg hitting a hot frying pan, my blood sizzled as it filled in the road's cracks. The ground rumbled softly beneath my feet. Birds that had been perched high in the tops of some neighboring trees by the river squawked and cawed as they took quick flight in the opposite direction.

Again, I looked back down, but my blood was gone. My head swiveled, looking for any sign of where it possibly went. It was as if the road had sucked it all up. "Screw this shit," I said, hobbling over to my fallen bicycle.

I lifted the bike to its tires and noticed that the fall bent the front wheel to all hell. My early birthday present already jacked. "Dad's gonna *kill* me!" I hopped on anyways. Whatever was going on started freaking me out and the faster I got home, the better. Pumping and pumping, I pedaled with all my strength up Water Street with the bent front wheel wobbling in protest. The ground rumbled again, this time from behind as if the sound followed me home.

I ditched the bike behind some bushes in the yard. Dad was gonna go mental either way, so I figured I'd hold off as long as possible bringing him the bad news. Everyone's cars were in the driveway, but I heard nothing but a spooky silence as I walked inside through the back door. A weird moaning broke that silence.

Then the screaming started.

Sam, my stepbrother, was home in bed sick with some flu thing, so I immediately thought it was him screaming. I ran down the hallway to his bedroom. Sweat covered and dripped from his whole body as he sat cowering in the corner of his bed, bawling like a little girl and pointing at the wall.

"Get them off the wall, Buxy!" he wailed. "Don't let 'em get me!"

God, I hated that name! I looked up to where he pointed and saw nothing. "Sam! What's wrong? There's nothing there."

"DON'T LET THEM GET ME!"

"Stop freaking out," I said, not knowing how to help. "I'm gonna get Dad." I bolted out of the room, looking in every bedroom and finding no one at all. "Dad?" No answer. I ran to the kitchen and looked out the side window. "His car is still here. Dad!"

I looked out the other window to the back yard. My father and my little sister, Anna, were walking through the neighbor's yard toward the pond in the woods. "Dad!" I shouted one last time, but between the thick window and Sam's yowling, the call went nowhere. "Shit cakes."

Sam's crying subsided, only to return to that strange moaning chant. "Sam, what's going on?" I asked as I headed back to his room. "I can't understand—"

He stepped out into the hallway in nothing but his underwear hiked up over his stomach like a miniature Sumo wrestler. As he moaned, he held out his arms towards me and stomped his feet in a slow beat. Blood trickled out from his eyes and ears, mixing with the sweat covering his pasty skin.

"What the heck, man!" I said. "Get back in bed. You're sick. I'm gonna go get Dad. He went outside."

Sam didn't listen, he just kept stomping his feet and chant-moaning some gibberish. *What's going on? What do I do?* Sam freaked me out. And when his stomping became steps toward me I took off almost stepping right on my younger brother's stupid Tor the Barbarian action figure.

I ran down the hall, through the kitchen, out the back door, and jumped over the deck railing into the backyard. Behind me, I still heard Sam stomping and chanting. I looked over my shoulder back at the house and a chill shook my body. Sam stood at the window, staring out at me, grinning like a lunatic as he rocked back and forth.

I had to find Dad! When in doubt, *find Dad*.

I broke into a sprint across my yard and through my neighbor's to the pond in the woods in the center of our properties. Not a big pond, just enough for skipping stones and practicing our line casting. I would never swim in it or eat anything I caught from there because it's kinda gross, but usually it was just a neat place to hang out. Except today.

I finally reached the pond and stopped short behind an old tree. My lungs burned, screaming at me for more oxygen, but I didn't dare move or make a sound. Standing all around the small body of what used to be murky green water, a bunch of people from my street held hands. They all swayed in unison to some rhythm I couldn't hear. The dirty pond water, now a gross shade of red, bubbled from the center outwards to the shore. The faster it bubbled, the faster they all rocked.

I spotted my father and sister next to each other at the far end of the pond. Something was wrong. Their eyes and ears bled and their hair stood on end as their skin began to molt like a bug. I tried to look away but my brain wouldn't let me. Something moved behind me and instinctively I turned. Sam was stomping down the dirt path in his tighty-whities ready to join the morbid circle. Thankfully, he didn't spot me hiding behind the tree trunk.

What was I supposed to do now? It seemed like the whole town went crazy. First my blood soaking into the ground and the quakes, then my stepbrother freaking out, and now this?

With my breathing settled down, I realized that my head still spun from my earlier hard luck. I reached up and felt the craters and bumps under all the dried blood. Through all the craziness happening, I completely forgot to—

Snap!

I must have shifted or moved and stepped on a branch. The sound echoed across the water. The swaying stopped. I cringed. "Oh, shit!" I looked up at the crowd. Even though their moving stopped, they didn't seem to notice.

Something started rising out of the middle of the pond, something puke green and covered in bumps. The reddish water cascaded off it as it broke the surface. It reminded me of a toad, but only about a thousand times bigger. In the center of the thing, folds of skin squirmed and parted, revealing a huge, glossy black eyeball.

As it continued to rise, with its boil-like bumps and rotten-looking skin, I saw these long tongue-like things slither across the surface towards my motionless neighbors on the shoreline. They started swaying again with mouths wide open, holding hands and gazing up to the sky. A foul stink wafted off the pond up to me, creating a thick fog. My nose crinkled at the smell and my eyes started watering.

The tongue-things made their way to land wrapped around everyone's legs. I scanned the scene, still unable to make my brain compute what it saw. I spotted my father on the far side of the pond. His own eyes were completely white like they had rolled back into his head. I strained my neck around the tree for a better look, mesmerized by the whole thing. In my curiosity, I slipped and fell forward into a bush. I shot my dad a look to see if he noticed.

Yup.

He was staring right at me like some psycho with his bottom jaw gyrating, grinding so hard into his upper teeth I thought it would dislocate from his skull. I hopped to my feet, aware of my deadly mistake. He nodded at me, pointing with his eyes, still grinding his teeth until a harsh, penetrating crunching sound echoed out of his head.

The water-tongues released their hold. Everyone else turned to me with their grinding jaws and pointing eyes, releasing the same horrible sound. In the center of it all, the bumpy frog-thing's big black eye rolled lazily in my direction, staring me down… or sizing me up.

I started running, pretty sure that my life *did* depend on it. Through the woods and brush, I plowed, forging my own path. *Just run! Run as fast as you can!* I heard the screeching getting closer as they gave chase.

I ran. Ran faster than I did when Toby Gillis and his band of goons chased me across Ram's Field to steal my paper route money. Faster than I did when my father chased me through the house for ruining his work papers with my crayons. This time if he caught me, I bet I'd be getting more than a size ten to the tailbone.

In an effort to gain as much distance as possible, I shot a beeline through my next-door neighbor's yard, through my backyard, and right into my stepmom's nice clean sheets drying on the clothesline. Looking like a cheap Halloween ghost, I flailed wildly to free myself from their tendrils of crisp, spring freshness.

Their bizarre shrieks echoed behind me, closing the gap. I skidded to a stop in my driveway and scooped up my bike. "Damn!" Busted tires wouldn't get me anywhere. I spied little Cara's two-wheel ride sitting over in my other neighbor's yard. Without a second thought, I grabbed it and hopped on, not caring the slightest that it was a hot pink girls' bike. At least she had already moved on from training wheels. "Sorry, Cara."

I pedaled my legs off, so happy not to be on the ten-speed. I ripped down my street, creating a generous amount of space between me and the horde. No sooner than I'd turned onto Texas Heights Road did everybody bust open their front doors. On both sides of the street, people popped out of their houses, all grinding jaws set to ludicrous speed and eyes bulging. The ground started rumbling again. "Oh, great!"

Something in my head told me—*begged* me—not to turn around and look behind me, but I couldn't resist. The horrible, bumpy pond-thing rose above the treetops, its disgusting eye searching the streets. I switched back into speed mode and pumped the pedals just as the townspeople started coming forward to join the chase.

The ground quaked as the thing skulked, making it hard to keep my balance. I glanced over my shoulder to see that it, too, followed me now. As it crept along like a legless slab of amphibian meat, pushed along by its hundreds of slimy tongues, it rolled right over my neighbors, violently crushing and absorbing them into its body. The sick sound of pulverized and devoured skin and bones tortured my ears.

Once I got to the top of Water Street, my heart sank as much as the river had risen. Murky, bloody, dirt-colored water flooded the streets below and raged against the bridge that separated me from the rest of town. I psyched myself up; I needed to cross that bridge. While sucking in a deep breath, I dropped all my weight on to the flimsy pedals, hoping that they wouldn't fail me as I tried to hit warp speed down the small hill.

Something ignited within the welding shop on the far side of the bridge. Shooting sparks lit up the inside, setting the building ablaze. Fire and smoke licked the air as the windows of the welding shop exploded. Sheets of fiery metal careened down the rapids that failed to extinguish them. As I sped towards the chaos, I plotted my course through the burning rubble and wild flooding like a killer game of Zaxxon. You only get one chance at this, my brain yelled.

The river hadn't completely submerged the bridge as the wheels of my stolen, pink bicycle sloshed through the blood red water. I gave myself a well-deserved victory shout and fist pump once safely on the other side. With that out of the way, I looked back at the ever-growing and slimy monstrosity cruising through Central Village. It pulled its hulking mass along the ground with its tongue-things, using them like tentacles to latch on to trees and utility poles. My neighbors didn't seem to care in the slightest as it gobbled them up. They looked as though they welcomed their painful deaths as, one after another, the thing abruptly snuffed out their moans and chanting.

I finally made it to the top of Water Street. With each thrust of my legs, I felt my lungs hating me more than I hated Brussels sprouts, but I couldn't stop or slow down. If that thing had possessed (or killed and eaten for that matter) my family and everyone else I knew, I had nowhere to go... except out of this loony bin that Central Village had become.

I scanned left and right, back and forth. Streets looked empty in both directions, but I knew better. *Pick one!* With that nightmare hustling down the street towards me, staying still was not an option. To the right, I saw movement coming across Main Street and that made my decision for me. *Okay, School Street, don't kill me.* Maybe there were some "normal folks" down at the field watching the game that could help me; in the least, I'd be able to warn them of what was coming.

The ground shook again.

I lost my balance on the bike and almost revisited the face plant scenario. The quake didn't stop; the rumbling and grinding of stone and earth rattled my bones worse than some Twisted Sister blasting through dad's new hi-fi speakers. Help. I had to find help. As the road beneath me jiggled like jelly, I pushed onward to the football field, hoping with all my might that things hadn't gone completely crazy there yet. *Not too much farther! Just past the playground and around the bend.*

From behind the trees that circled the field, came an explosion, not like the one at the welding shop, but more like the one the time my dad put some dynamite he had "laying around" between some rocks and concrete blocks. I skidded to a stop on the shaking ground when chunks of dirt and grass erupted high into the air. One massive clump of end zone flew across the sky, casting a shadow over the playground. *Hey look! A flying cartoon ram wearing a helmet.*

Under the weight of heaved earth, the playground equipment exploded into pieces of colorful shrapnel. Mangled and uprooted trees now gave me view to the field beyond. All around the hole that used to be the end zone, a crater billowed red smoke; it puffed out in waves in rhythm with the rumbling ground. People gathered in a circled around the hole, just as they had at the pond, holding hands and staring up into the sky. Between ground trembles, their moaning, or chanting—or whatever the hell they were doing—persisted. My brain felt like it was on fire from all the craziness.

Oh shit!

In the confusion, I had forgotten about the gigantic Weeble Wobble from the pond hot on my tail. I spun around, hoping that the path to some other, any other, street was clear. I no longer saw the pond creature, but I could hear it sloshing around in the flooded river near the burning welding shop. In its place, another mob of local lunatics had marched up Main Street and now followed me. *I guess they made the choice for me.*

The ground shifted once more. An earsplitting crack toppled lampposts and shattered windows. I fell off the bike again and onto my blood-crusted knee. The weirdoes chasing me also tumbled over like sacks of bricks. Underneath me, the road broke open, releasing a hiss of foul steam. I jumped for safety, but the crevice made my neighbor's bicycle its first victim.

As the ground lurched about, I felt my balance slipping and my good sense wriggling free from the already feeble grasp I had on it. My heart and mind raced as I began to panic. Through labored gasps for air, I felt on the verge of another bout of hyperventilation.

A gas main exploded and part of it rocketed out of the ground and into a two family house, setting it on fire. Trees creaked and groaned as they swayed like a troupe of used car lot inflatable dancers. More steam shot up through the cracks; manhole covers blew sky high from the pressure building underground.

I turned to the football field, fighting to regulate my breathing. Vile, molten sludge, indescribable in color, bubbled up from the end zone crater. The people that were circled around had that same twisted, painful expression on their faces as the pond people. They stood frozen, like statues, as they slowly melted into the ooze.

As soon as they vanished beneath the mire, the earthquakes stopped. I nervously scoped the streets—unable to see another person. The sudden quiet hurt my ears as the cloud-covered sky overhead turned a terrible reddish gray.

I slowly walked toward the field, stepping over the cracked and uneven ground with care. The disappearance of everything, except the bubbling sludge, frightened me worse than anything else had so far today. Not a bird flew across the sky. Not a squirrel ran across the grass. Nothing but the silence and the evil stench rising from the pit... and then came the voices.

As if every soul that had inhabited Central Village started talking at once, the voices chased all my thoughts away. They called out to me, chanting my name amidst indecipherable murmurs. I finally broke and fell on my ass. I began to cry, holding my hands over my ears in a pointless attempt to block out the voices. What had happened here remained far beyond my understanding. Did I do something to cause this or was it inevitable, waiting for the perfect time to sock it to us?

The lake of slime drew closer. Its revolting stench almost corroded my nostrils. I shuffled backwards on my butt, trying to escape its reach. In the center of the pool, a huge bubble from deep within the pit surfaced followed by one after another, popping and spitting up more stink, turning into a sudsy foam. I moved back farther until I bumped into the boulder that held the Ram's memorial placard given to them by the Kiwanis Club for their undefeated season a few years ago.

Too scared, too petrified, my body refused to move anywhere else, so I just pulled my trembling knees up to my chest and continued to cry against the monument. The ground vibrated and the foamy flood of slop receded back into the massive pit, leaving nothing but scorched earth in its wake.

Was it over? Am I dead? Dare I even move? Curiosity (and borderline bat-shit craziness) overpowered rational thought and common sense. I had to see—no, *needed* to see—what lay over the edge of the crater, what further madness awaited below.

I peered over an outcropping of jagged rock into the blackness. My hobbled brain had lost all ability to find words to describe, to classify, the kind of darkness swirling in the depths. The pit seemed to go on forever, swallowing every bit of light in an unforgiving binge. I saw movement, different from the tricks the dark played on my eyes. Something moved, rising back up to the surface—something big.

I lost control, wetting myself. Warm streams of piss streamed down my leg into a puddle under my feet. I began to shake as sweat poured out of my skin.

It continued rising, getting closer and closer. I heard a deep, wet-sounding groan or growl coming up with it. To my accosted senses, it sounded like the bellow of a buffalo played full blast at half-speed. Unnatural and hungry... very, very hungry.

I stepped back until my legs gave out and I collapsed.

As whatever hideous atrocity now funneled up from the bowels of what I could only assume was Hell, it squeezed its hulking mass through the ruptured earth. In slow motion, a monstrous column of unidentifiable flesh grew out of the pit. Its staggering size matched the width of the football field and climbed to dizzying heights. Opaque eyes, the size of truck tires, blinked in and out of focus under putrid, undulating skin. Its alien surface texture, covered in slime, rippled and stretched, making sickening pops and squishing sounds.

I didn't realize screams had erupted out of my mouth until my throat went raw and sore. My hands gripped my hair as they squeezed my skull like a powerful vise.

One of the milky, off-white eyes, roughly about my height, stared at me. Baseball sized irises of varying shades of the worst kind of green ever seen floated around the vitreous gel within. It blinked; a gooey, flaccid flap of skin unrolled from within misshapen rolls of rotten looking meat. The smell of the thing, far worse than the sludge that preceded it, made me woozy to the point of almost passing out.

My brain couldn't handle anymore, wouldn't square what it saw before it. I felt it throbbing, pressing on my skull. I shut my eyes tight and plopped down on my back, ready for either this nightmare to kill me or for my body to shut down from shock.

I squinted through my half-shut lids for just one more peek at it, one last look at its grotesque enormity. I thought that I had witnessed all the horrendous things one should ever be unfortunate enough to see, but what I saw looming before me, more than likely preparing to devour me whole, was a horror beyond all other horrors, beyond understanding and description.

In my acceptance of the end, I heard the pillar of roiling and dripping flesh tearing and shredding. From top down, it began to separate, to peel like a banana, each new slice of it squirming like a tentacle. The horrid appendages moved independently from each other as they spread out like roots and caressed the demolished field. They fanned out like leaves of a flower while, from the center, a single eye, like a hellish nucleus, rose to the surface.

One of the tentacles slithered towards me and attached itself to my leg like a leech. I laid there and let it happen. I just wanted this to be all over, so I clenched my eyes tightly and let it do its thing. Up my leg the tendril crept. Its slimy coldness nauseated me, but I held still, ready to let go. Vomit filled my esophagus, its bitterness burning and stinging the back of my throat as I choked it back down.

All my memories rushed back to me in that final second: recollections of my dad failing miserably to teach me about the *birds and the bees*, my little sister's first dance recital, winning the Pinewood Derby, and my first kiss with my secret crush, Maryanne, as we walked along the river. My tears faded and I forced a smile one last time.

I'm ready... Just get it over with.
"But it had *other* plans for me...."

BEQUEATHED

His footfalls crunched with the weight of each step. The crusty, snow-covered ground revealed no other footprints besides his, not even those of the little girl he swore he'd seen running into the two-story Dutch Colonial which now stood menacing and silent in front of him. Still, Tim felt confident about what he had seen, despite the fog of windblown snow rising off the street.

He glanced down at the antique book of fairy tales cradled in his arm, the only remaining evidence—besides the contents of the urn—that his mother had ever existed.

When he'd received the call from an attorney, he expected that nothing of value, if anything, had been left to him. Not that it really mattered; even if he did remember her, or harbored memories of any special moments normally shared between mother and son, he would never have *truly* known her.

She'd passed away, lonely, in an assisted living home; the maternal bond had been severed when she'd vanished decades earlier. Yet, once the attorney had handed over her remains and the solitary book she had bequeathed to Tim, he couldn't in good conscience deny granting her this one last wish of scattering her ashes around her childhood home.

Wherever that was.

As far as he had been able to uncover, his mother had been remanded years ago, living *and* dying in that same state-run facility. For reasons Tim couldn't fathom, her attorney knew nothing else. This lack of information had only piqued his curiosity more, tantalizing his core with nervous energy.

That night, thumbing through the old pages, wishing that a memory—any memory—of his mother would return, he'd found an address. Scribbled and faded on a scrap of paper, it was buried in the middle of the book and clipped to a ribbon of 35mm film negatives. He'd spent the rest of that night looking at them, losing himself in an unfamiliar sea of monochromatic images.

Replaying the memory of the discovery had kept him lost in deep thought, but he grumbled the whole long, miserable journey. Though he hated driving far for anything, he made good on his promise, hoping he might find some answers—or perhaps at least some closure. Now he had arrived—at last—in this desolate, abandoned town in the cold of December, winter's bitterness biting the back of his neck, he fought the urge to jump back in his car and speed away, forgetting the whole ordeal inside a bottle of whiskey.

But what about that little girl?

He read the address again before looking up at the faded numbers painted on the door. *This was it*. Through the snow he trudged, up the steps and across the porch. The front door stood ajar, hanging off kilter on its old, rusted hinges.

"Hello?" he called, suspiciously eyeing the interior. "Little girl? I saw you come in here. Are you okay?" Tim crept inside, leaving faint footprints on the snowdrift that had blown in through the opening. He shut the door against the cold and carefully placed the urn on a shelf. The pressing silence deafened him, and his eardrums popped.

He heard a faint sob.

A short blur of color raced past the threshold to another room.

"Don't be scared. I won't hurt you." Silence. "It's okay. This is my mom's old house." He tiptoed towards the next room. "Do you live around here?"

In the blanket of murkiness oppressing the room, Tim bumped hard into some sheet-covered furniture littering the space. He dropped his book and the resulting boom resonated, echoing off the walls. "Shit! That hurt." He winced, picking the book up from the floor, the negatives slipping from between the pages.

With book and negatives in hand, he turned the corner, staying on the girl's trail. On the wall in the next room, someone had painted a mural of a flowery meadow. Though it was dull and faded with time, he still found it appealing, and somehow *familiar*.

Then he remembered.

Tim stepped to the window and held up the negatives to the failing winter light. In one of the frames, as if looking through a sepia-colored lens, the same mural had been captured.

He heard the whimpering again, catching him by surprise.

Tim spun, filmstrip still in his hand. When he noticed the imprinted scene on the negative moving, matching what he saw before him, he dropped the film, unnerved.

Nearby, tiny footsteps raced up a flight of stairs.

"Hey, don't be scared." He scooped up the film, shifting the heavy book to his other hand, and followed the sound. A wooden staircase led to the second floor as murky darkness overpowered the pale light filtering through the grimy windows. Gut instinct told him to look through the film again. He awkwardly closed one eye and held the film up to the other, catching the last rays of light. Everything before him took on the texture of old newsreel.

As he moved, the scene within that single frame moved with him. He went back and forth—from film to reality— to confirm what he thought he was seeing. At the top of the stairs, a shadow lurked, but vanished the instant he stopped looking through the negative.

He continued upwards, minding his step and listening for any more sounds.

On the landing, a lone table stood, adorned with a tattered and stained doily. Through the film, though, he saw that a lamp had been smashed against the wall, fragments scattered everywhere, and a fresh bloodied handprint soiling the once-delicate white cloth. He tore the negative away, a gasp lodging in his windpipe.

Something moved in another room.

Awash with courage, he put the filmstrip back to his eye. Waves of dizziness claimed him from the strain on his eyes. But he kept moving. Determined. The grainy tones and quality covered everything as he edged along down the hallway. Yet, he couldn't mistake the wet streaks on the walls for anything else.

A woman's maddening scream froze his blood. He tore his eyes away from the film and the house fell silent. "Hello! Someone there?" Peering through the negative, the shouting returned. Once more, he looked away to test his theory. More of the unnatural stillness. "Is somebody hurt?"

The shrieking reached a violent climax.

He raced to the room at the end of the bloodied hallway. Through the otherworldly lens, the body of a girl, barely six years old, lay wounded and motionless on the bed. Blood trickled out of her skull, steeping the sheets in red. In the corner, a frenzied woman was standing over a terrified little boy. Younger than the girl, he defensively held up a thick book, struggling to hoist its weight. The woman raged, her face marred by a twisted scowl. She raised a hammer high over her head. Ribbons of blood flew from it, arcing through the air. She shouted obscenity-laced gibberish as she loomed above the crying boy.

"Stop!" Tim shouted, hoping to prevent the woman from hurting another child. He leapt over a pile of toys on the floor. He gripped his mother's book—his only weapon—tightly in his fist. Ready to strike—yet unsure how he could possibly intervene—he dropped the filmstrip. Everything fell back to darkness and cobwebs, his momentum sending him spinning off balance and crashing into the wall.

Panicking, he fumbled around for the film, clumsily groping around in the dim room. His fingertips found the celluloid and he snatched it from the floor, putting it back up to his eye like some enchanted monocle. Through the lens, a man rushed into the room, tackling the woman as she was about to unleash her fury upon the boy. Tim stared, reluctant to believe, unable to reconcile what—and who—he was seeing. "Dad?"

He watched in snuff-colored disbelief as his father held down the thrashing, vulgarity-spewing woman. Another man, face pale with worry and fright, entered the room. Eyes wide, Tim vaguely recognized the man as he yanked the big book from the boy's grasp and scooped him up and away.

"It's all right, Timmy. You're safe, now," Tim heard the man say as he rushed the traumatized boy out of the room.

Tim, dumbstruck, looked down at the boy's book now resting on the floorboards, then back to his own copy in shattering realization. Finally, the mental barrier that had kept him safe all his life—the truth of what had happened to his older sister and his long-lost mother—crumbled from the weight of his newfound reality. All the energy drained from his body and he went limp while the film reel of residual energy continued to play in the background.

On recovering, he studied the two books. One version was rooted in the present and the other in the past, but both were part of his reality. Tim opened the front cover to an inscription found only in his bequeathed copy. Frustrated that he hadn't noticed it sooner, it read: *"To my beautiful son, Timothy! I'm so sorry for everything. Love, Mommy."*

Then he cried for the first time in years.

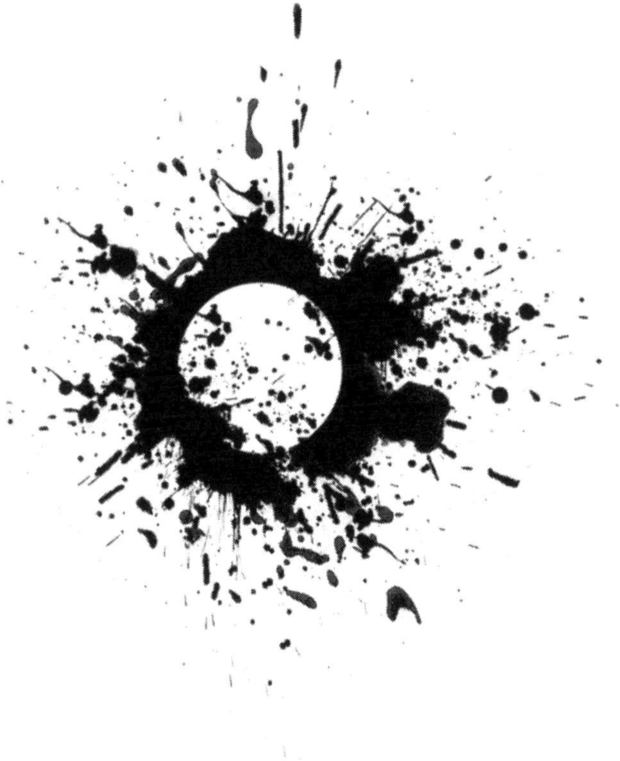

ALCHEMY OF FAITH

The clergyman toiled away in the makeshift laboratory he had constructed in his modest quarters. Without a clue as to whether the experiment would work, all he had was the knowledge the pale blue angel had imparted upon him that night in the marsh. Why he had come to discover her there remained a mystery, but the mere thought of the consequences her mission here would bring to the Church—and the world at large—confounded his mind. He only knew he had to try, even if it meant breaking his vows.

If he were to believe the wounded angel's dying words, and if he were to succeed with the experiment, the outcome would bestow amazing wonders upon him and humankind. He was immediately wrapped up in her; when she had reached into her own abdomen and extracted two small glowing orbs, he was caught in her divine thrall.

"What am I to do with these?"

Her mouth did not move, yet he heard her words. "You must complete this undertaking or else all will be lost for both of our kind. These are remnants of me. All that's left of my dying race. A new beginning that will need your help to thrive and perpetuate life. Time is of the essence."

He prayed for forgiveness as he followed the angel's strict instructions to combine the orbs with his own seed. As he struggled to steady his hand, he injected his semen into the orbs with a crude syringe. Waves of guilt and disgust washed over him. He knew the wrongness of it, not only in the eyes of the parish, but also in those of the god he chose to serve. Though, as sinful as it felt, he trusted that the messenger from above wouldn't have tasked him with something against his calling if it weren't of dire importance.

Immediately, fusion began in the copper bowl, pulling him from his concerns about religious treason. The orbs rotated counter clockwise, bathing the room in pulsating blue light. He cowered, awestruck by the light as it shot up like a beacon. A low rumbling accompanied the beam, vibrating his table while his seed mingled with the orbs.

The glowing persisted, but the orbs slowed, conjoining in the bowl's center. In no time, two orbs became four; four became eight, continuing until the vessel split apart, unable to contain the growth. In the congealed mass, cohesion: visible structures started taking shape before his eyes—and he wept.

Bishop Crane, about to end his nightly stroll, spotted bright blue light emanating from beneath Father Tennor's door. As he approached, a soft vibration spread across the wooden walkway. A rumble shook the air. He knocked, but the rap on the door failed to overpower the incessant humming. Cautiously, he entered the priest's quarters.

Radiance flooded out of the room, and he was stunned. Inside, he saw his colleague standing over a table, weeping. The pulsating miracle continued to organize, now resembling the faceless, shining form of a small blue child. Atop the amalgamation, a single eye was developing from the churning tissue. A tongue-shaped appendage darted in and out of a breach next to the eye. Arms and legs sprouted out at unusual angles. An abrupt cry poured out of the thing and the bishop reeled backwards, gasping in repulsion.

"Father! What in God's holy name is happening here?" The bishop steadied himself against the doorframe, terrified by the abomination growing before his eyes.

Tennor ignored the bishop, unable to rationalize what he had set into motion. The thing grew, morphing and twisting into form. As its terrible cries echoed through the quarters, pulling on his heartstrings, he reached out to it, gently taking hold of one of its hands as little stumps budded into fingers.

"Father Tennor, I forbid you to move any closer to that abhorrent creation!" The bishop retreated from the room, running down the walkway to the security bell as fast as his rickety old legs would go. He frantically rang it as he shouted for help. Rectory doors creaked open as fellow clergymen lumbered out. Panic and confusion crossed their sleep-ridden faces as the bishop continued his warning call.

"Your Grace, what's the matter?" asked Brother Charles. "Are we in danger?"

The clan of holy men surrounded the bishop and listened intently. Crane turned and pointed a gnarled finger towards Tennor's quarters. Blue light still bathed the entryway, spilling out into the courtyard. "The Devil is upon us. He has taken up residence in our rectory and has corrupted our poor brother!"

The clergymen choked back their shock as they watched the shimmering light dance, whispering nervously about the terrible intrusion of evil defiling their sanctuary. "Can Father Tennor be saved, your Grace?" someone asked. "How shall we purge this evil from here?" questioned another.

"An unearthly abomination now dwells and grows within your brother's chambers, taking control of his mind," Crane explained. "We must purge this evil with fire. We must fight the Devil's invasion with flame blessed by our Almighty Lord!"

Each servant shouted in agreement as their bishop riled them into a frenzy. They split off to gather torches and weapons to keep the evil at bay. In the commotion, another priest gestured towards Father Tennor's room.

The priest ran out the door with the glowing bundle before disappearing into the darkness of the forest beyond the rectory. With the newborn swaddled in his arms, its radiating warmth seeped through the blanket that separated it from the elements. Father Tennor, fleet of foot, vanished into the trees. He tried to put as much distance as possible between them and his brothers, unable to prevent the incessant wailing coming from the infant's newly-formed mouth.

Tennor knew the child must be terrified—as he shared that sentiment. He sensed its pain, but he needed to make sure their escape proved successful before he could tend to its needs.

It. He had no idea what *it* was or how the miracle had even happened. All he knew now was the promise he'd made. This child, whatever kind of being it was or would become, was his responsibility.

Behind him, he could hear his brothers' shouts getting louder as Bishop Crane continued to whip them into a holy rage. He chanced a glance over his shoulder in his retreat. Torchlight danced off the canopy of leaves as they gained ground. The newborn shifted and squirmed within his grasp, desperate for the freedom to wail in the throes of growth.

He knew he wasn't equipped to contain or ease its pain. He just needed a place to hide, to secure the child away from his brothers' ears and formulate a plan. "Please be silent, child," he whispered, not knowing if it could understand his plea. Up ahead, he spotted the hollowed-out trunk of an oak. He gently placed the child inside, making sure to secure it in the blanket before camouflaging the opening with branches and bits of brush. "I'm not leaving you," he promised. "I will return."

The priest felt the pain of conflict as he ran down the path in the opposite direction. Unconcerned about the noise he was making, he hoped his commotion would rouse the search party and launch them in the wrong direction, away from the child. He stopped atop a boulder and scanned the forest below. In a small clearing, he saw his brothers, led by Bishop Crane, gathered with their torches. Across the distance, one of them met his gaze and alerted the rest of the party.

Tennor leapt from his rocky perch and darted into the trees, praying the ruse would lead them away from the child. Upon hearing the shouts and rustling of underbrush approaching, he knew it would be safe, at least for the time being. How he would lose his brothers and then circle back to collect the child, he hadn't a plan. But as long as he kept it safe—despite the weight of its burden—he felt more confident living up to his promise.

As he evaded the mob, he heard them shouting his name. They called for him to surrender the abomination unto the law of God— an order with which he could not comply. It was far too late for that now. The miracle of life he had witnessed made him question everything he'd ever known, a feat that shook him to his foundation.

Their continuous roars became first-hand reminders of his greatest, lifelong fear. His faith's inability to tolerate any form of wonder that Heaven's holy umbrella didn't eclipse. Yet, he still felt a twinge of guilt; his brothers were good men: honest and forthright. Even Bishop Crane, despite his antiquated, old-world beliefs, was a decent man and teacher. Nevertheless, Father Tennor's failing grasp on his faith severely buckled under the strain of the magic he had helped create.

The shouting grew closer as the men approached.

In the dark of night, not even the twinkling of the moon and stars could safely light his path. He could feel blazing torches at his back, ready to burn the *evil* he'd brought into this world back to the Underworld.

Tennor overstepped. His foot slipped on a slick patch of moss, sending him tumbling to the hard ground. He thought he was holding a greater lead, but even before he could roll over and get to his feet, he felt the heat of flames.

"Where is it?" Brother Thomas asked, as another prevented Tennor from getting up. "Where is the unholy atrocity?"

He stared coolly back at the men, meeting one rage-filled stare after the next. The bishop had certainly raised his flock's ire, feeding their fear with threats of God's wrath. These men, his friends, his family, did not deserve this betrayal. And that tore at his soul. Yet he trusted in his new mission, his magically granted gift of much greater importance than hurt feelings and disobedience. Regardless, he knew they would never understand.

"I'm sorry, brothers," he started. "I swear I am, but I cannot tell you."

"You must! The Holy Father demands it. He demands obedience and that—that thing violates his very laws," Brother Charles ranted.

Bishop Crane parted the group with his walking stick. As he forged a path toward him, Tennor inwardly trembled at the staunch look of hatred in the man's eyes. The old bishop loomed over him and as he went to stand, Crane shoved him back to the dirt. "Where is the foul creature, Father?"

"It escaped when I tripped over a rock and fell."

"Deceit will not help matters!" shouted Brother Thomas.

Bishop Crane stooped to one knee, meeting Tennor's gaze. "Father Tennor, it is just as much a mortal sin to break God's law as it is to lie about it."

"It's all in the Lord's Good Book, brother," Brother Charles reminded.

"What does the Good Book say about murder?" Tennor challenged, glaring into the man's nervous eyes before turning back to the bishop. "What does it say about the sanctity of life?"

"Sanctity of life only applies to God's creations, not some horrid unearthly... experiment," Crane rebutted. "You are fully aware of the implications of your actions here. Wordplay and feeble semantics will not help you. Now... before this situation turns down an unfortunate path for you, Father Tennor, where is the fiend?"

"Who's to say what is or is not a creation of God? Who are we to quickly judge and attack things that we fear or don't understand?" Tennor questioned the surrounding group. "Am I not one of His creations? Does that not make that which I create--?"

"Enough!" Crane erupted, rising to his feet. "My fellow men of the cloth, it appears Father Tennor is now in league with Satan and is beyond our saving. He must be punished and cleansed of his sins." He raised his walking stick high above his head and proclaimed, "God will see and know the righteousness of our actions this day." He then struck the priest with a mighty blow.

One after another, the clergymen pummeled Tennor with fists and sticks, feet and rocks. Sandaled feet nearly broke his nose as he curled up into a ball, absorbing the punishment that he knew wouldn't end until they had killed him. Beaten and bloodied on the forest floor, he prayed for help, and begged for forgiveness. Whether or not he deserved God's mercy, he knew the choice was not up to him. He cried into his hands and arms as they protected his face from the onslaught.

Had the blue angel had led him astray, betraying him as he had betrayed his faith? But he couldn't condemn himself for the miracle he'd helped create. Even nearing death, he still held fast to that notion.

He felt himself drifting away. The pain became almost a memory and the hate-filled shouts faded into distant murmurs. The ground began to rumble and the air became thick with energy. The men stopped their attack as startled birds took flight from the trees. A brilliant light permeated the forest, casting everything in an azure mist. Through his haze, Tennor could still sense it, even through his closed eyes. He could feel its heat as it surged through the trees and growth.

He finally opened his eyes.

A pained howl sliced through the air and the men covered their ears. The shriek resonated. Throughout the forest, the bushes and trees swayed and bent as something rushed towards the clearing.

The blue light grew brighter and hotter, its nucleus pushing forward. The air all around it crackled and hummed. Tennor clambered to his feet, the pain of his thrashing an afterthought now. In the center of the ball of light, a young, misshapen child—blue of skin and hair—wept crystalline tears.

Tennor's heart ached for the child, who, despite having been a tiny bundle mere moments ago, had now tripled in size. He saw all the telltale human features: two eyes, a nose, a mouth. Yet, he saw no ears or discernible reproductive organs. The alien child continued to cry, its abnormally long arms stretching out as it glided towards the mob.

On the outskirts of the clearing, some of the men attempted to flee but were met by a blue bolt of electricity that set them afire. In seconds, the being's light cocooned the whole area, trapping the crowd within its blazing fury. The unbearable heat overwhelmed the cowering throng and sweat drenched their bodies in an instant.

From inside the bubble of light, the child's cries intensified. Tennor's vision blurred and head spun, but he forced himself to look up at it. In awe, he managed to smile, now knowing the truth of what the blue angel had said. A miracle borne, a beautiful combination of two species forming new life—this being, his new savior.

Its huge sapphire eyes, with tears full of pain and fear still cascading down its face, glared at the mob. One of the braver men, Brother Samuel, raced toward it, wildly swinging a broken tree branch like a club. Through the thin membrane, where the light burned hottest, the child reached for him. It laced its stem-like fingers around Samuel's throat before a scream could even escape his lips. His skin bubbled and popped as it sizzled off his body into a syrupy mess onto the dirt.

From behind it, Brother Charles heaved a stone over his head. Father Tennor moved to intervene, but the bigger Charles shook him off like fleas on a dog. The stone smashed onto its mark and the child buckled under the blow. Its light flickered as it dropped to its knees. More of the clergymen rushed in and piled on top of it now that its heat had subsided. The priest felt powerless as he watched, distressed and full of guilt with his inability to save his child.

The group's sheer force and hatred almost extinguished the being's light, save for random rays that broke through gaps where their bodies separated. Tennor begged them to stop. He dropped to his knees with tears in his eyes and beseeched his lord to take away his pain and anguish, to save his creation.

The being's light vanished as the men wrestled with it. Among the tangle of limbs, the priest saw his creation's terrified eyes desperate for help and safety. It writhed and squirmed, unleashing heart wrenching cries that broke his heart.

Bishop Crane smiled as his brethren held the vile creature down. "See, Father Tennor? Nothing can match the might of our Lord and Savior. God and His Almighty Son will always prevail in the presence of evil."

"Bastard!" Tennor yelled, as he launched himself at the bishop. Never in his life had he felt such a deluge of rage and loathing for another human being corrupt his will. They crashed to the dirt, with the priest getting the better position in the melee. He pinned the bishop down and rained blows upon the holy man's face. Strike after strike, Crane's yelps of pain turned to wet gurgles as blood filled his mouth and throat.

The clergymen's preoccupation with the creature was reducing. Every second they turned their attention toward Bishop Crane's plight, they lost more and more focus. In that loss, they loosened their grasp. The being sensed this and thrashed about, shaking off the last of its captors and finally freeing itself from its shackles of muscle and bone.

Its deafening howl rattled the treetops. Opaque blood—almost silver in color—caked its oblong skull from where Brother Charles had struck it; twigs and matted leaves clung to the wetness.

As the thing's screams reached an earsplitting pitch, its brilliant aura retuned, bringing with it a searing, inescapable heat. It awkwardly lumbered around the clearing on wobbling legs, grabbing at anyone within arm's reach. The terror in its eyes now held glints of anger as the heat of its touch blistered the clergymen's skin. Within its capsule of illumination, screams erupted, the stink of melting flesh inescapable and unforgiving.

Tennor's unstoppable creation flailed about in hysteria, burning up everything it could. All around it, smoldering bodies littered the ground. It saved Brother Charles for last. Both Tennor and Crane, no longer fighting, stared agape as the thing stalked Charles until it had him cornered against a rotting stump.

Its long, bony fingers wrapped about the brother's throat, its face mere inches away from his. As it hissed, it squeezed the life from the man's body until his head burst into flames. Impervious to the fire, the being held Brother Charles up and, with a satisfied grin, almost seemed to study him.

Then it noticed the bishop cowering on the ground, bloodied and hurt.

It marched over to the fallen bishop with purpose. As it continued to grow before his eyes, sinewy flesh stretching and shaping over its bones, Crane reached into his robe and brandished a crucifix. Before he could speak a word of prayer in defense, the being swatted the cross from his hands. He started to crawl away, but it snagged him by the hood of his robe and yanked him backwards through the clearing. He tumbled through the air and crashed into a broken log where one of the jagged branches breached his upper back and exited through his chest.

The rage in the being's eyes burned hotter as its tears sizzled on its skin. Surrounding it, plants and leaves began to wilt from the unavoidable heat within its barrier. Steam rose off Bishop Crane's blood as it poured through the hole in his torso. When it finally realized the bishop was dead, it shrieked and howled, swinging its arms and shaking its head.

The whole clearing caught fire in its wrath. Amidst the rising heat waves, Tennor's eyes welled up and blurred from the sound and the smoke. "It's all right," he said, once the being had finally quieted. "You're safe now. He is not going to harm you any longer, my child."

My child.

The words rolled off his tongue with an ease he felt destined to feel. This child, this otherworldly being, crafted and created in part by his own life force, was his ultimate triumph. He had fulfilled his promise to the fallen angel and, despite his sacrilege, did something that not even his lord could have made possible. His belief system shifted as he gazed upon his creation. He now felt like a god amongst men, having wielded a power no other human could ever fathom.

Tennor stood up, avoiding random pockets of burning brush. He slowly approached the dazed alien child who still stood facing the dead bishop. "My child, you are safe n--"

Startled, it spun around, stabbing Tennor in the gut with its misshapen and dagger-sharp fingers. The priest's sweaty face went white. Even as he cringed in pain, his eyes remained locked in disbelief. He glanced down at the mortal wound and the hand of his creation buried inside of it.

The being's eyes, still childlike and full of terror, stared into Tennor's own. It wailed again as it withdrew its hand and pulled Tennor close. All around them, fire burned out of control. Flames licked at the trees and leaves, igniting them in a scorching frenzy.

As it cried, its light barrier began to flicker and fade, allowing the fire to spread beyond its magical boundary. Tennor gripped his creation in a loving embrace, knowing he had ultimately failed—and that the end had arrived for them both in one final, searing irony.

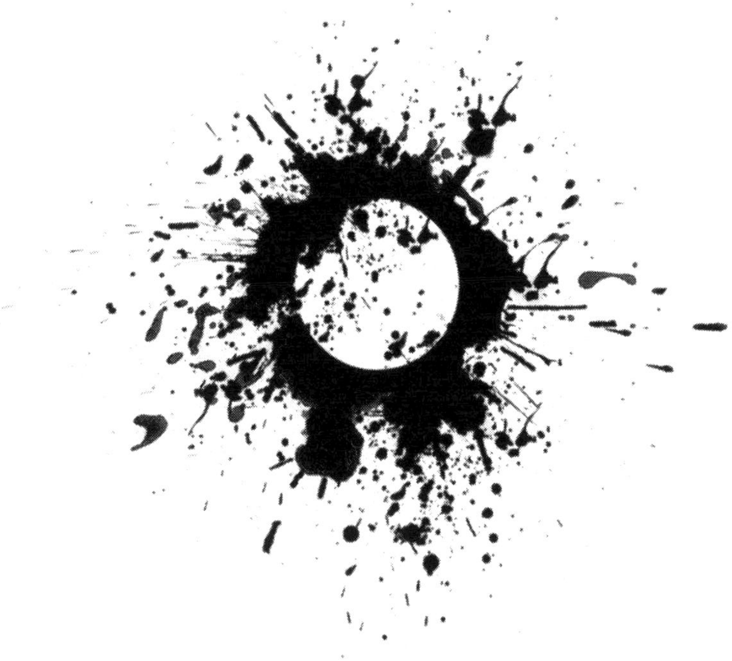

THE YATTERING

What you are about to read is true. As contrived and brash as that opening statement sounds, this story—and the vehicle I'm using to convey it—is as accurate as I can recall and with as much detail as I can muster. I will relay the results of my investigation to you as they unfolded—to the best of my ability, of course.

And, while I fancy myself a creative type, I'm reluctant to admit that proper grammar and syntax is not in my wheelhouse. But my hopes are that the story behind my words overshadow any shortcomings and elicit a response similar to the one I had experiencing it all. But first... some background.

Back in the late nineties, just after returning home from college, I had landed a part-time job at a local independent bookstore in Connecticut. The place was enormous with an impressive horror section. At the time, I needed the cash, so I took the modest salary they'd offered. My nights soon consisted of working as a receiving clerk on the closing shift.

One night, going about my usual routine, I heard my coworker, Tonya, calling me for help. The stockroom—shaped like a backward L—made it impossible for me to see her from my vantage point. So, being the polite and helpful guy I am, I hollered back, "Be right there!"

I put down my scanner and hurried over. When I rounded the corner, almost tripping to my death on some boxes, I expected her to be right there waiting for me. The place was vacant. I thought maybe she was hiding behind a cart in some lame attempt to scare me.

Nope. Empty.

Now, I understand audio matrixing. You know, how it's possible to hear one thing and mistake it for something else entirely. But the fact I had answered back reinforces what I heard. That's how certain I was that Tonya had called my name. I made it all the way to the door and opened it, peeking around the immediate area.

No one there, either.

I ventured out further and found her in the kids' section on the opposite side of the store. With a stack of books cradled in her arm, she was standing on a stepladder and restocking the shelf. Already knowing the answer, I asked her anyway. "Hey? Were you just in the stockroom?"

Negative. As I figured. The probability that she could've gotten that far in the time it had taken me to cross the back room, seemed next to nil. Needless to say, I started tweaking out a bit. I shrugged and reluctantly went back to my duties until the end of my shift.

Incident number two happened about a week later. Working away and earning that pay, I had my back to the rest of the stockroom. Everything was quiet between bouts of shredding cardboard and the annoying ding of the barcode scanner until I heard something unmistakable... a faint giggle.

I spun around: nothing. But as I was turning back, my peripheral vision caught sight of a short figure. I froze, transfixed. A small boy, roughly nine or ten, was standing with his back against the far wall. His skin was ashen, and his clothes were dated enough to be hand-me-downs from my father when he was that age. He stared at me with a deadpan expression through a mop of unruly brown locks that framed his face.

My skin rippled and crawled with gooseflesh. My pulse racing, my heart bouncing inside my ribcage, the fight-or-flight response kicked in as the back of my throat tightened. My feet slid on the dusty concrete floor while I scurried backward, without taking my eyes off the boy.

Panicking, I stumbled over more boxes in my retreat before finally making it to the sales floor. A bit later, after I had calmed down, I pulled Tonya aside. I knew it sounded crazy but I told her what had happened, and it freaked her out too.

Still, to this day, my memory is seared with the image of that sad, ghostly boy.

And as the days turned to weeks and weeks to months, the unexplained phenomena at work persisted: phantom whispers, cold breaths on the back of my neck, shadows without form. Even the automated paper towel dispenser in the restroom randomly spat out sheets unexplainably. I started questioning my sanity.

Yet, I refused to let it get to me—I became determined to solve this mystery. I had to prove to everyone that I wasn't out of my gourd.

Then the business closed, shutting its doors for good. There went my chance—and my job.

Years have passed and my mind still refuses to let it go. I recently learned that the property is still vacant. It's as if the ground it's on has soured, allowing nothing to flourish there. I can't be left to wonder if whatever supernatural force that had tried to make contact with me is still there… waiting.

With no control over my destiny, I have devised a grand scheme to break in and get some answers.

Since no one is willing to join me on this expedition, I alone, will brave the darkness. I'll arm myself with only my wits, a digital camcorder, my trusty voice recorder for catching those creepy laughs, a flashlight, and a pair of night-vision goggles I've "borrowed" from Conspiracy Smitty, the lunatic ex-Navy Seal from the apartment downstairs.

I hope to get to the bottom of this mystery that has haunted me for years. And, once I'm through with this adventure into the unknown, I will do my utmost to recreate the experience for you here, in written form. You'll think you were right alongside me the whole time.

Is it real, or is it Memorex? Or some shit like that...

I didn't want to chance my car getting towed, ticketed, or stolen, so I walked to the abandoned bookstore. Everything I needed, I had packed neatly in my backpack and pockets for easy travel and retrieval. But you know, no matter how much planning you do, you will forget something important. In this case, I had forgotten to figure out how to actually get into the old building. Luckily this was only a minor setback once I saw the broken window ten feet up from the ground. At least I had the dark of night on my side.

After stacking a bunch of old pallets and crates higher than I considered safe—or smart, I carefully climbed the rickety siege tower. It swayed and creaked under my weight as I shifted up it. I could barely reach the window with my hands but with one last kick, I managed to boost myself up and slip in, unmolested by the shards of shattered window glass. The tower outside noisily collapsed in a heap. I lowered myself onto a shelving unit that was once covered in books. As luck would have it, my improvised ladder pulled out of the wall anchors and came crashing down, nearly knocking me over and severing my foot. I wasn't getting out the way I came in.

The resounding boom lifted years of dust and stink into the empty bookstore's already stale atmosphere. Once the mess settled, I found myself in a gloomy cemetery of Retail's Past. Rows and rows of empty bookshelves like nameless headstones stood unkempt and lost to the ravages of time. With what little outside light was breaking through the old, boarded windows, I managed to gain my bearings and dig out my flashlight.

I stood in the center of the space and assessed my surroundings. Aside from the mess left behind, everything looked familiar. Ahead of me: the checkout area and main entrance. To my right and down a short hallway: the restrooms and offices. Sweet memories of secret backrub sessions in the office with my store manager, a spunky blonde with curls that went on for days, wriggled into my head, and I couldn't stop myself from smiling. And behind me: the stockroom—the epicenter of my experience.

Little boy? Are you still here?

Looking around, the place gave me the chills. Seeing it in this condition, all barren and dilapidated and bare bones, it felt… skeletal. With my over-active imagination, I could not dispel my creeping unease. Every sound of scurrying rats, each shadow dancing out of place seemed magnified in the gloom, felt menacing. Despite my apprehension, I felt summoned here… unfinished business and all.

I dropped my bag of goodies on a table in the center of the aisle and dug out my equipment, calling off each as I placed them down. Tools of the trade—well, according to those ghost hunting drama queens on TV, at least. But still, the internet backed up their claims with supporting and substantial information. Evidence of EVP—electronic voice phenomena—and shadow people caught on digital media was compelling stuff and hard to dismiss at times.

A cool breeze tickled the hair on my neck. I knew it wasn't the AC. But doing my due diligence, I flashed my light around and checked for holes in the ceiling tiles or in the high windows of the exterior walls. Locked up tight, save for the window I had climbed in over yonder.

I got that familiar static charge feeling.

Something was about to go down. I rushed to turn on my equipment, hoping I had put in the fresh batteries.

Tee hee…

It began.

The disembodied giggles had always got to me. But this time, in the quiet emptiness of the building, they sounded fuller, like multiple textures laid over each other. Innocent, yet ominous. Echoic. I spun around just as the pitter-patter of little feet raced away.

I hesitated; my mind told me I wasn't prepared for this. But I knew I couldn't live with myself if I turned back now. Digging through my backpack, I prayed I'd remembered the duct tape.

"Yes!" I grunted, as I pulled the roll out of the zippered front pouch. Being a ghost hunting team of one, I would need at least one hand free. So, I carefully taped my digital voice recorder to my camcorder in the flashlight's dim yellow beam, making sure not to cover the recorder's microphone. Satisfied that the devices were fused as one and manageable, I powered them up.

Another giggle... followed by the sound of ruffled paper as if someone whipped past a set of open books. Sweat beaded on my brow from my nervous excitement as I reached for Smitty's goggles. The pièce de résistance. As soon as I put them on, the colors of my whole world reversed into every shade of green.

"Whoa," was all I could say, slightly dizzy. This would take some getting used to. But, I'd be damned if everything I saw wasn't gloriously stark and vibrant in the otherwise dismal blackness that surrounded me. I steadied myself. One final check of the equipment—back to business.

The green turned my world alien, but I found my bearings and my footing. A swallow caught in my throat as I stood in the aisle, staring down the long, shelf-lined corridor that ended at the stockroom door. I held the camcorder out in front of me, making sure to frame everything within the little rectangle on the LCD screen. But without light, I had to fiddle with the camcorder's settings. After a few frustrating seconds, I found night-vision mode. The view in the screen turned negative; everything black now registered as light shades of gray.

Hee hee...

I spun on my heels towards the sound. Nothing there. More pattering of little feet in the next section over. Missed it! They stopped and I jumped in between the shelves—*ah ha!*—hoping I'd catch whatever—whoever—was there, off guard.

Jesse...

I whirled the other way—BAM—and smashed my elbow into a fixture.

Heh heh hehe...

"Laugh it up, you little ghost prick." I rubbed my aching elbow. Ghosts or no ghosts, I hated being toyed with. Yet, regardless of the pain, I hoped I'd at least captured the giggling on tape. Then I remembered. EVP burst sessions! They do them all the time on those shows, so I decided to try it and follow up with a live review. Activity was already kicking up and it appeared to want to interact. What did I have to lose?

I set the devices down on a shelf. "I'm not here to harm you, only to get proof of your existence. Can you show me a sign of your presence?"

Nothing happened. And I felt plain silly talking to myself, but all in, right? In any case, I trusted the microphone would pick up something other than my babbling. "My name is Jesse. I just heard you giggle and say my name. Can you do that again for me, please? You can talk into this device right here." I pointed to the recorder. "If you can see this red light, just walk up to it and speak and it'll hear you."

The giddy nervousness returned. My first EVP session. I clicked the recorder off and fumbled my way through the settings to play the file. All I heard was my own annoying voice spewing back at me.

Something passed through my peripheral vision. The darkness swayed, pulsing before vanishing down an aisle. I grabbed the gear and crept in that direction. "Hello? Someone there?"

The air smelled different the closer I got, the mustiness replaced by something sweeter, almost like Play-Doh. When I reached the spot where the shadow evaporated, I stopped for another attempt at audio documentation. "If you want to make your presence known, please do so now." I paused for effect.

"What is your name?"

I saw this technique used on those shows, sometimes to dramatic effect. I gave it a shot and knocked on the wooden shelf next to me.

Shave-and-a-hair-cut...

...

...two... bits.

I nearly shit myself! An actual response. Knowing something had to be there now, I resumed my questioning.

"Are you the same spirit that showed itself to me twenty years ago?"

No response.

"If so, why are you still here? Are you trapped?"

The air chilled and all the hair on my neck and arms reacted. A puff of my green-tinted breath fogged up my goggles. Something was around me. I felt it as sure as I feel this pen in my hands as I write this. The heaviness of the air pushed down on me like a wet blanket. Such a potent and unfamiliar sensation, my body didn't know how to respond.

A mist formed in the middle of what used to be the Humor section. It took shape, gaining in size slowly, as if collecting energy. The air around me crackled as everything became electrically charged. But with all that circling energy, I expected an orb to form, or perhaps some sort of light anomaly. The fog grew, tendrils of blackness roiling over themselves, getting darker—the shadows feeding shadows.

In the next aisle, I heard more talking, like a crowd of people all whispering over one another. The hushed murmuring was so layered that I couldn't decipher a single word.

My heart thumped, and my shoes felt like concrete blocks. I was so petrified I had to squeeze my eyes shut against the increasing volume of the whispering. My ears popped and my skin crawled. I didn't dare open my eyes for fear that the amassing darkness was right there, ready to devour me. I struggled for a plan, anything to break away from this sensation. Yet, all my mind could come up with was, "Hello?"

One of the remaining fluorescent bulbs flashed overhead.

I felt my skin go slack as the static charge in the air dissipated. And, as I forced my eyes open one at a time, expecting the worse, I found myself alone once more. No hint of the swirling shadow. No unintelligible whispering on the cusp of my hearing. Nothing.

Then I noticed my recording lights were still on.

Excited, I tore off the goggles and cradled the devices in my palm. I fiddled with their buttons, trying my best to sync them up. I hit play. My patience waned as I waited for something interesting to happen on the recordings. I'd only screw it up if I tried to fast forward.

What at first sounded like a field of crickets chirping evolved into language, a constant back and forth of glottal tones and consonants. Again, the voices overlapped, streams of whispers competing with one another. The murmurs alternated between the recorders' microphones, giving off a strobing, stereo-like effect.

I stared at the little screen and watched the shadow figure manifest on the footage. But what had appeared dark and wispy in real-time coalesced into a syrupy mass. It undulated and rolled into itself, boiling in slow motion. The whispering grew louder, its highs and lows working in time with the churning form.

I didn't realize I was shaking until my hand started hurting from its death-grip on the camera. Still, I couldn't pry my eyes from the video. "What the hell is going on?" The puddle of darkness bubbled, and little nodules rose from its surface, taking no apparent form. More bumps broke through, differing in size and shape. Then those bumps cascaded into greater shapes—like heads—as the viscous form melted into shoulders and torsos—all the height of...children?

help...

us...

I finally started making sense of their words.

save...

us...

Hundreds of soft voices and tones poured from the recorder's tiny speaker, now ever so clear and discernable.

Help us...

Save us...

"How?" I shouted at the camcorder. "Please, tell me how!" A flash of light briefly distorted the images on the screen.

It's here...

Tee hee!

The congealing form expanded, before imploding into a hole unimaginably dark. "No! Don't go yet."

Please...

Again, I was alone, but the lingering sense of despair clung to everything. My nerves were shot. I took a moment to reflect. Clear as day, I heard the plea for help. *It's here?*

What's here?

So many new questions arose that my reason for this experiment now seemed pointless. If all those shapes trapped in that miasma were the spirits of dead children, I was dangerously out of my league.

Something crashed—the boom of something hefty hitting the ground—and it tore me from my contemplation. I knew exactly where it had come from: the stockroom. After taking a moment to restart my equipment, I put the goggles back on and hesitantly headed for my old workspace.

At every turn, as I trekked across that abandoned retail wasteland, around every still standing shelf, I envisioned something reaching out to grab ahold of me. Every sinister creak I heard became another shadow about to snatch my soul. What—or who—was it? And where the hell was here?

The closer I got to the stockroom door, the more certain I was that I'd uncover the answers on the other side. The unknown waited for me beyond that door, dark and foreboding, devoid of everything that had once been ordinary and familiar to me. Yet, through the thin window above the handle, the intermittent flashing of light slicing through the gloom told me I'd find my first answer.

The yattering returned the closer I got, with whispers and hisses and hums. I double-checked the status of my equipment and did a quick survey of the area. Even with this evidence, I knew people would still call me crazy—or a fraud. But I knew it was true.

The murmurs persisted. I wanted to scream for them to tell me what they wanted me to do. *Needed* me to do. The flashing of the stockroom light mimicked the whispers' cadence.

The voices grew louder.

I reached out for the door handle with my free hand.

Louder and louder still.

Help us...

Words upon words rolling over and over like a landslide of syllables.

Louder and louder. No longer hushed.

Save us...

I touched the dirty metal handle and turned it until the tumbler clicked.

The strobing of the light sped up. Faster and faster.

help us save us help us save us

I winced as the disharmonic chorus raged.

The peal of the old door on its rusted hinges blended with the ghostly caterwauling as I pushed it open. At the back of the room, I saw the overhead flashing light—right where I'd first seen the little boy. I stepped into the stockroom, barely able to hear my own footsteps over the ghostly cacophony.

The door clicked shut.

Tee hee...

And, just like that... silence.

I paused, the now-solid beam of stockroom light shining on what appeared to be a solitary book discarded and laying open on the floor. Next to it, the source of the crash, a library cart that had somehow tipped over.

I didn't want to get any closer, but I had to—needed to. The spotlight on the book, that cart toppling over... they had to be signs. Benevolent, malignant, or otherwise.

From behind me... *Jesse*. Succinct and terrifying.

Properly motivated, I headed toward my quarry unaware of what I was about to discover. The flashing of the light resumed, the blinking getting more intense the closer I got to the book. I felt like it was summoning me, demanding my attention like a parent to a child. Get over here right this instant!

The book, an oversized tome of fairy tales, was opened to a black-and-white drawing of a little boy kissing a little girl on the cheek. Under that read, "Georgie Porgie."

"That's an oldie but goodie," I mumbled, as I removed the goggles to make sure I'd captured the discovery on video. I felt another cold breath and I shivered. They were back. "Hello, again?"

A charge raced from my head and out through my fingertips, and my camcorder's battery icon blinked before it died, completely drained. Another beam from the overhead light cut through the dust and onto the book. With uncanny precision, it shone directly on the name "Georgie" in the nursery rhyme's title.

I gasped. "Is that you, the little boy I saw? Georgie? Is that your name?"

The light blinked! Was that a direct response? Was it answering me? I had to make sure. "Please blink the light once for yes and twice for no." My pulse was racing. "Is your name Georgie?"

One blink.

"Are you the same little boy I've seen before?"

Another single blink. My brain was now chugging along at the same pace as my pulse. Theory has it that spirits absorb the energy around them and use it to interact. But there was no electricity in the building, nothing to give off that kind of energy. Something stronger than my camcorder battery had to be feeding them enough power to pull off this kind of activity.

Questions threatened to pour from my mouth, a deluge of nonsense. The last thing I wanted to do was make this an interrogation. Then again, I was talking to a light bulb. "Are you alone?"

Two blinks this time.

"There are others there, too? Like you?"

It flashed, paused, and then flashed again.

More than one entity occupied that space, somehow trapped there in limbo. A purgatory. I was pissed that the camcorder had died, and hoped the voice recorder had at least captured the excitement in my voice from this one-sided conversation. I may have sounded like a lunatic, but I knew my ravings must sound authentic.

Another giggle flitted through the air. Only this time, it gave me pause. It had a thicker quality to it—darkly playful and menacing—like a schoolyard bully. Again, gooseflesh rippled over my body. A plume of breath escaped my lips.

The light beam turned erratic. The pages of the book flipped on their own until the book slammed shut.

"Georgie? What's wrong? Are you in danger?"

One blink. Then everything went black.

Tee hee...

The density of this new darkness pressed down on me and made my eyeballs hurt. It brought with it a coldness that made my bones feel brittle. What was happening? Somehow my connection to Georgie cut off. He and the "others" either abandoned communicating and went into hiding or were forced away. But forced away by what? What was there on the other side with them—among them—that frightened them so?

With no time for rumination, I groped in the dark for the goggles. My ears popped and started ringing. I sensed eyes boring into me. I was no longer alone... something was behind me.

I turned, hoping not to fall over any of the junk littering the floor. But with darkness as my enemy, I lost my balance and crashed into some metal racking. Though I managed to stay upright, my eyes refused to adjust to the coal blackness that had descended upon the space. Yet, I knew—no, I felt—that something had crossed some barrier, had stepped through a veil and into my realm.

"Who's there?" I scanned the area for the source of my unease. The darkness pulsed. Pockets of inky blackness, impossibly darker than anything I was already experiencing, moved about, as if stepping in and out of reality. I couldn't wrap my mind around the notion of something so densely black, so harshly unforgiving. My eyes watered.

I pulled on the goggles and then tried to steady my outstretched arm from shaking as my digital recorder continued to work. My voice trembled. "Wh-who is here with me now? P-p-please, give me a sign of your presence."

Nothing.

"Georgie? You still there?" I knew he wasn't, but still hoped he could hear me. "I will help you out of there. I promise." I had no idea how I would fulfill such a promise and I cursed myself for my brazen ineptitude. Somehow, I had allowed myself to get attached to this entity, this possible figment of my imagination.

What was I hoping to accomplish? Was it because this little ghost boy shared the same name as my late grandfather? Or did my subconscious just assign it that name because I missed the man so? Amateur night at the Haunted Bookstore, for sure.

My vision became garbled for a second, a wavy distortion zipping through the goggles. Every shade of green darkened, each gradient rounding down to pitch until only fuzzy, indistinct outlines remained. I had no doubt the ectoplasm was about to hit the fan.

The murmuring returned, harsher than before.

Mournful voices whispered for help. Deep snarls barked out from the nether.

Heavy footsteps approached from all sides. I squinted through the goggles and fought for focus. The darker shades of blackness hovered near me, blocking any path of retreat. Whether I could've walked right through them or not, I was too terrified to try. So, I cowered against the shelving, pushing hard against it, just wishing to become one with it and out of this phantom's crosshairs.

The footsteps stopped. All the moaning and growling ceased. As my goggles cleared up, details returned to the scene, all converging on the growing nightmare trapped in my sight. The shadow absorbed any and all light, greedily collecting it within its mass. It churned into shape, forming what I took as a head and two shoulders. Its torso filled out with a breadth that surpassed my own husky frame. Two obsidian tornadoes swirled and flanked both sides of the wraithlike behemoth, forming arms.

It reached out for me.

I could neither scream nor move. I stood paralyzed, gazing into the smoldering orbs of light that were the phantasm's eyes. My skin prickled as it came closer. Its unremitting blackness engulfed my entire field of green-tinged vision. A pressure built inside my head as my Eustachian tubes struggled to equalize. All I could hear was my thumping heart. Then, with a piercing squeal, everything went silent. I thought I had gone deaf until the murmurs returned. The incessant ghostly blabbering now filled my head from the inside.

The shadow's eye-orbs flickered as if it were blinking, and I felt my bladder almost give out. I started talking again, pleading with the phantom shadow for mercy, to leave me be, but absolute silence was its only response. I closed my eyes to the insanity hovering over me, but it didn't matter. What I saw behind my eyelids was just as terrible, equally as unfathomable.

Before I knew what was happening, I heard the distant clang of Smitty's night-vision goggles crashing in the distance, having been ripped off my face by some unseen force. Orbs that were once tinted a brilliant white through the goggles now burned a fiery red. Mere inches from my face, I could feel their heat, could see into them like a portal to a darker, more hopeless dimension of pain and sadness. I started to cry, a waterfall of tears streaming from my eyes.

The whispers turned violent, a deluge of curses and insane laughter mocking me... calling to me. Louder and louder. Why were they so mad? I didn't realize I was screaming until my throat burned raw and the salty taste of my tears coated my tongue. My body felt heavy with an enormous pressure building on my bones. I panicked. The searing pain of hyperventilation racked my chest and lungs. All the while, its eyes burned into me.

The laughing!

Oh my God, the laughing!

I screamed and I cried, but I was frozen and defenseless. The darkness consumed me as my world went black.

While the weeks have stretched on since I've returned from my adventure, I'm at a loss as to what had truly happened in there. What I thought was only a four or five-hour excursion into madness for me was actually longer—a lot longer. Turns out, I've been missing for a few months. I've lost my job and my apartment; they even repossessed my car! Despite waking up in the stockroom, I have no idea why I was gone for so long. Any and every plausible explanation eludes me. So much missing time.

Thankfully, Smitty, from downstairs, was kind enough to offer me his couch to crash on despite still being sore with me for taking—and losing—his night-vision goggles. I figure, as long as I routinely entertain his conspiracy rants and other assorted nonsense, I should have a roof over my head until I'm back on my feet.

Back on my feet… Such an odd notion these days. Since my return, standing up straight is growing harder to do. Every day, my body feels more and more locked into this uncomfortable slouch. There's this pressure on my upper back and shoulders as if I'm carrying a backpack full of cement that seems to get heavier every day. The constant headaches aren't helping much either.

Exhaustion keeps me supine on Smitty's couch most days, but the days I force myself to sit at the kitchen table to finish the epilogue to this dreadful and draining experience are the worst. At this rate, Smitty and I will end up roommates forever, or until he kills me, which would be upsetting, considering he's the only person who still acknowledges me.

The only thing that'd make telling this easier would be the evidence I'd collected. So why don't I get to the point—and the good stuff—and show the world the proof of the afterlife? Again, as miserable luck would have it, I discovered all the files corrupted. Every single shred of watch-this-I'm-not-crazy is gone, lost in some dreadful limbo, probably just like the entities I had recorded. All I have left are the haunting memories and these words.

Anyway, here I sit again, at the table, hunched over like Quasimodo and getting worse each day. But I'm determined to reach the end of this… with you. If you're still reading. I hope so, because it's all about attachments—and, as silly as it sounds, I feel attached to you all.

Death has weight. I'm not talking about the heft of the corporeal jigsaw of body parts we leave behind when we die. I mean our *spirits*. They have substance. Our souls contain mass collected as energy. And that energy is eternal. Where it goes when we die is anyone's guess. But sometimes… sometimes it latches on to something, casting its oppressive shadow over it, smothering it with its inertia.

And this time, that something—that *it*—is me.

I thought I could help, but what I had brought home with me this time is far beyond my understanding or my ability to dispel it. To this day, I don't know if Georgie was a demon in disguise or a desperate spirit. Either way, it screwed me over for good. But I'm now consciously aware that this supernatural weight bearing down on my body—on my very soul—is collectively older than time itself… and is not going anywhere. I am its vessel—its new home—and it will end up crushing me. It's already hollowed out my spirit, and, if its persistent yattering in my ear of horrors beyond all comprehension doesn't drive me mad first, soon its miserable burden will subjugate me entirely.

These murmurs are maddening!

They say demons can appear in many forms, as a ghost, or more specifically, the ghost of a child. And if you let your guard down, let your fear subside long enough to offer comfort to that presumed poor and helplessly trapped child, you become fodder for the beast. For demons never existed in human form and are pure evil. Was Georgie just a demon pulling at my heartstrings, trying to hitch a ride into my realm of existence? Or was he truly a little boy trapped among a throng of other trapped little children cowering in fear from that thing in the bookstore?

On the other hand, not all spirits may be evil or cruel, but they can be bloody tricksters in their own way. Users and manipulators. Spirits can be assholes. After all, they want what they can no longer have. Life.

I prove my case in point as I glance sidelong into the full-length mirror mounted on the back of Smitty's open bedroom door. In my reflection, I can see it almost as clearly as I feel it: the deadness of its eyes, the ghostly outline of its mass breaking me down and forcing me to bear its weight. Soon, I sense we'll become one and it'll be too late. It has kept me too tired and weak and eventually it will assimilate this husk I once called my body.

Yet, as it continues to phase into this new reality of mine, becoming whole on an earthly level, I see its cold stare through its mop of brown hair and wonder... you've gotten what you wanted. Why are you still so sad?

EGREGORE

Click click... bleep... click

"I don't know... what the... okay. There we go." The camcorder whirred, sputtering to life in Sonya's hand. She spotted the lightbulb symbol and pressed it, illuminating the opening of the sewer tunnel in artificial camera light.

"Hey, cuz, you mind?" Jason covered his face as the mini spotlight stung his eyes.

"Sorry. My bad." She lowered the camcorder, scanning the filthy ground at the mouth of the tunnel. "When *exactly* did I sign up for this job? And why, might I ask, can't I be on film? Between the two of us, I am definitely the prettier one."

Jason almost belly-laughed at his younger cousin's proclamation before saying, "I told you, this is my pre-initiation. The fraternity needs to *see* me on camera finding and taking some sorta statue from the hobo's stash inside the sewer. That's the only way to get my foot in the door. They make only the most promising of the pledges attempt it." He beamed with youthful pride.

"Yeah, fine. Still sounds insanely stupid no matter how much you try to fancy it up. Whatever happened to simply stalking a sorority girl and stealing her vibrator?"

"First off, that's kinda gross. And B, you have no sense of adventure." Jason smiled at her. "Plus, you love me."

She smiled back. "Right. Actually, I love that bag of weed you promised to steal from your stepdad a wee bit more." She continued to swing the camcorder over the ground and the overhead trees trying to get a feel for the device.

"A deal's a deal."

"Damn straight!"

"Okay. How do I look?"

"Sexy," Sonya blurted. "Can we just get this over with? This isn't the safest job I could be doing right now. If you smell what I'm cookin'."

"Really, So-So?" asked Jason. "You know what? I don't even wanna know."

Sonya giggled.

"So gross." Jason shook his head in faux dismay. "Just flip on the night vision and we'll get the show on the road."

"Flip on the night-what?"

Jason grumbled. "How are we even related?" He stepped over and pressed a button on the top of the camcorder. Everything on the screen switched to varying shades of green and white.

"Whoa! That's cool," Sonya said, mesmerized. "Just like those ghost hunting shows, huh?"

"Yeah, just like 'em." Jason rolled his eyes. "Please be careful. And keep me in the shot at all times. Okay?"

"Got it. I'm not completely stupid."

"Hello?"

"Daniel," the man's authoritative voice boomed over the telephone. "Where are we with the acquisition of the Godhead Simulacrum?"

"Oh, hi, Dad. It's going down as we speak."

"Good. Has The Collective's anonymity in the participation of its collection been protected?"

"Christ, Dad! You ask me this every freakin' time. We're not a bunch of fraternity knuckleheads. As usual, we have everything under—"

"Shut up!" roared the man's voice. "I suggest you remember to whom you are talking and know your place. Need I remind you of the seriousness of The Collective's business?"

"Apologies, father. I completely understand."

"Good," said the man. "Now, again, where are we with the plan? If I'm not mistaken, we have made ten previous attempts to procure this item, all of which have failed."

"That's correct. We're using one of our high potential pledges under the guise of an initiation. He appears to be very ambitious and shrewd, unlike our other efforts. So I expect success this time."

"Well, I would hold off patting ourselves on the back until the item is in The Collective's possession. The guardian is formidable"

"If this is such a high priority target, why won't The Collective just use their resources to just take it?"

There was momentary silence. "I believe you know that answer to that asinine question, Daniel."

"Yes. Anonymity. I got it."

"Just be aware, the board members are getting impatient with our lack of success in this matter. Unless you want their funding for your other activities and obligations to end, I would suggest you make sure the plan doesn't fail again."

"Understood, father. I will contact you once it's done."

"This place has too much of a rapey vibe for my tastes. An almost *murder-y* feeling. Reminds me of Uncle Phil's place," Sonya joked.

"Good thing I'm not the prettier one then, huh?"

"Well, it's not an *exact* science."

With his flashlight, Jason led the way as the natural light vanished the deeper down the tunnel they walked. Sonya reverted to switching back and forth between views only to lose her footing several times. The inside of the dank tunnel revolted her, and the stench of sewage burned her nostrils.

"Jesus Christ, it fucking stinks."

"No shit. Pun intended."

The walls, where filth and trash didn't cling, were covered in graffiti. Wet moss and weeds hung overhead. Every step they took through the muck of the sewer made a sick squishing sound.

"So nasty."

"Just remember the paycheck you have coming to ya," said Jason.

"You got that right. Should be getting hazard pay, too."

Jason ignored her whining, just as he always had. "I remember hearing about this guy while growing up. Even my dad has heard about him. Weird old hobo has to be at least a hundred by now. Wears this goofy suit made out of aluminum trash cans."

"A metal hobo suit? That's stupi—"

"Shut up for a sec! You see that?" Faint light flickered from around a bend in the tunnel. "We're almost there."

"Jay, I don't like this. What if he's down there? You really think this is safe, messing with a homeless person? In a sewer? At night, on top of all that?"

"Relax. He's just a harmless old bum, if he's still even alive. In, out, and we're done. I promise," he assured. "Okay?"

"Alright, fine," Sonya conceded. "Still doesn't explain why there is light up ahead, though, if he's dead."

"Just c'mon, will ya? And make sure to get it all on film."

"Relax. I heard you the first ten times."

They couldn't hear it from the mouth of the tunnel or over their own footfalls and hushed conversation, but sounds of moaning, almost like whimpering, grew louder as they approached the bend.

The dim yellowish light continued to sputter as if caught in the tunnel's natural breeze.

"Is that candlelight?" whispered Jason.

"I don't know, but what the fuck is that smell?" Sonya covered her nose with her sleeve as the stink brought a tear to her eye.

"I told ya, we're in a sewer. What'd you expect? Axe body spray?"

"Nah, it's worse than that. Don't you smell it?"

"Nope. I swabbed some cologne around my nostrils before we got here." He turned and smiled, taking the moment to admire his ingenuity.

"Smells like someone's boiling rotten meat. Dude, I don't like this at all."

The groaning increased. Several distinct moans like a bunch of people in pain. Jason crept closer, trying his hardest not to slosh around or step directly in the sewage.

Sonya whispered harshly. "No, really, let's get out of here. GTFO. I mean it."

Jason glanced back over his shoulder at Sonya. "So-So, what if someone's hurt and needs our help? Stop being selfish."

"Then stop being stupid, Super Jason. Always gotta be the hero." Worry caught in her throat, but she submitted to her cousin anyway. The glimmering yellow light danced a foggy white in the night vision only to brighten as she caught up with her cousin. "I *don't* wanna do this. I *don't* wanna do this. Don't make me do this." Sonya clenched her eyelids tight.

"Shut up!"

They rounded the corner.

Sonya yelped. "What the holy fuck?"

Jason waved his hand for her to stay quiet as he stepped closer to the source of light and moaning. His flashlight reflected off something wet on a slab of concrete. "What the hell? Looks like some kind of altar." It was massive and covered in dark candles that had melted onto its surface by mounds of spent wax; something completely unexpected and out of place, here in the sewer tunnel. As the candles shimmered, they, too, reflected the wetness that covered its rough surface. "Holy shit, So-So! Look! That must be the statue."

In the center of the altar stood an unusual figurine, sculpted from red quartz. It had been raised even higher by a battered wooden box. It looked to be about a foot-and-a-half tall with vague humanoid features, but the odd and jagged angles cut in the lucent rock were devoid of any artistic logic. The area where a head would be was nothing but a single, disproportionate eye carved right into the stump that was the top of the idol's torso—no neck or shoulders, just the solitary eyeball with a cored-out pupil.

"What's going on in here? Looks like some satanic bullshit or something," Terror trembled in Sonya's voice.

Something clawed at Jason's leg as he stood transfixed on the idol, catching him off guard. He stumbled, but caught himself. His flashlight caught something—a glint, the sparkle of an eye.

Out of nowhere, a woman, crawling towards him. She reached out. Pained cries escaped through a gap in her melted, bloated lips. Jason dodged her sewage-logged hand and hopped up onto the concrete block, his hand slipping in the sliminess.

Blood. The beam of light confirmed it.

He rapidly scanned the rest of the chamber—red fluid was everywhere, puddled in random smears of coagulation. Writhing bodies, in different stages of trauma and distress, littered the foul sewer floor in a half-circle pattern around the makeshift altar. Scarlet scrawl covered the walls, with bizarre shapes and symbols foreign to both cousins.

Sonya jumped as another dirty and mangled arm stretched towards her. Jason, out of reach, focused the beam on them but couldn't grasp what was wrong—or what he was seeing.

"There's so much blood," he said. "Look at all the... cuts. W-we need to help them."

Sonya, almost at the point of hyperventilation, forgot she was still recording when something on the screen caught her eye. She gagged, choking back the bile. "Fuck their cuts! What's that shit crawling all over them?" Blisters and sores bubbled across their skin, under their bleeding wounds, rippling over them in clusters with an apparent hive mind intellect, just as determined to reach Jason and Sonya as the victims' hands were. Inside the boils, writhing, thread-like worms swam through the ochre pus.

"Oh my god. I'm gonna puke." As disgusted as she was, she couldn't make herself stop looking—or filming. She went from body to body with the camcorder, zooming in and out on the nomadic colonies of blisters, mumbling about the wounds and lesions on each person. "Jay! It looks like someone carved symbols into them, into their skin for fuck's sake! Like the ones on the walls."

"Sonya, don't get too close. We don't know what this is."

"I do! It's sick fucking devil worshiping shit!"

"Stop with that bullshit," scolded Jason. "Turn on the video light."

"No way!"

"I can't see, and we gotta call for help!" Jason dug in his pocket for his phone. "Hit the light and keep shooting!" As he punched in 9-1-1, a hand gripped his leg and tried pulling him down into the muck, launching his phone into the deeper darkness of the tunnel. He instinctively reached out for a handhold and latched onto the misshapen red statue. Its opaque surface singed his skin and he yowled in pain. With his balance compromised, his momentum carried him to the ground, fast. The sculpture wobbled before smashing into the altar's hard stone surface.

"Jason! Don't touch it!" Sonya called out, contemplating hurrying over to help her cousin, but it was too late. In the green glow of the camcorder screen, she watched as the swarming pustules bubbled through Jason, overtaking him the moment his hand made purchase with the crystalline abomination. They merged over his face and lips, a migrating conglomeration of pulsating sores, stifling his screams.

Something shuffled beyond the altar, moving closer. Sonya bolted from the slab, slipping on blood. "No..."

Everywhere she turned, even without the benefit of night vision, she could sense the sickly bodies writhing all around her—thousands of disgusting blisters ready to pop and unleash their squirming load. As she stumbled in the dark, more infected hands tried to snatch her, to make her sick, to make her dead. She avoided their touch, running through this pestilent obstacle course, all while the shaking camera continued to film everything—the bloody symbols, the bodies, and the worming decay around her.

Something followed her, whatever it was she had heard hiding beyond the altar. She pushed harder, crying in hysterics now. "What do you want from me?" she bawled through her ragged sobbing, still unsure of what shambled through the dark of the tunnel. "Leave me alone—please…"

Footsteps splashed behind her, their heavy force stunting the moans of those dying people laying in the waste in their wake.

Sonya called out for help but her voice's ragged echo pinged off the walls, going nowhere. She rounded the bend too fast, tripping into the sludge. The camcorder flew from her grip and hit the ground, bouncing onto some flattened sheet metal. On impact, the video light popped on and the device slowly spun like a top on the discarded metal surface.

"Get away from me!" she begged.

As she lay there, swallowed by the intermittent light and shadow, she heard her pursuer approach. In the murky tunnel, all she could see was the twirling camcorder light as it cast grotesque silhouettes over the mossy walls. In those flashes, he appeared, imposing and completely wrapped in rubber with a symbol-covered outfit made of old battered aluminum over that, skulking towards her, getting closer and closer with each revolution of the light.

THE SICKENING

Everything went back to dirt.

For all that he had learned, he believed this lesson to be most true. Alone and helpless, he watched all that he had known turn back to dirt. All chances for hope and salvation fell to the same fate as the crumbling hollow and empty bodies around him. Whatever the method, the means by which all things perish, this finality was unmistakable and inescapable.

And he now believed this to be true.

The gaping chasm, the deep terrible hole, yawned as he crossed the bridge.

Its fetid and ancient breath abused his nose and lungs. He dared not look down into the mouth of nothingness as he breathed shallow breaths. Carefully he trod, stepping over piles of corpses and bones.

Nothingness.

No soul, living or dead, knew what lay hidden at the bottom of the abyss. The thick dense fog blurred the depths in coal blackness, permitting no one to see its secrets. Razor sharp edges of rock jutted out, lining the walls until they blended into obscurity.

The wind's icy tendrils blew from below. Waves of malevolent, acoustic murmurs followed the primeval smell of rotting earth riding with the currents. A shiver claimed his body, raising the flesh of his nape. He wrapped his arms around himself in a futile attempt to rub some warmth into his extremities. He struggled to breathe, sucking in ragged gulps of air the higher he climbed into the mountains.

Gray clouds hung threateningly low from the sky like a rebellious child testing the limits of his mother's patience. At times, the howling laughter of the gorge grew to mind-numbing volumes, blurring his vision. The bridge, swaying and dancing to the volatile rhythm, felt ready to collapse. Sure-footed, he continued across the centuries-old span of bridge masterly constructed by some long-forgotten tribe. Over the trail of frozen dead he went, as the bodies thinned out in number the farther he traveled.

He was formerly known as Torhan Ulk.

Once the leader of the proud Ullsburth tribe—the richest and most prosperous in the land— he knew no name now. Without a soul to speak it, to call on him, he soon chose to forget. His name... nothing but a haunting whisper on the wind, a nagging recollection in the back of his mind.

Everyone had perished, and why the Gods had spared him, he didn't know. As time passed, that grew to be his quest—a search for answers. Whether they were answers based on truths or masked by lies, he cared not. If he was indeed the last, he just needed closure. The simple notion of comprehension, the tangible evidence in which his mind could grasp, spurred him on. He needed to satisfy the deluge of questions hollowing out his soul. However long that took, it didn't matter. Alone, all that he had left was the thirst for comprehension—and that thirst fueled his will.

The peoples of his land called it The Sickening.

One by one, they had fallen victim to the plague. Like an outbreak, but considerably worse, it spread throughout the populace, not just of his clan but throughout the entire known world. This wildfire of affliction was passed on by mere touch, causing violent fits of rage and uninhibited hatred in its victims. Nothing could stop it, for they knew of no cure. Unbiased, it had infected without prejudice.

Day after day, The Sickening claimed more and more people with its deadly chain reaction. Panic ran rampant, arm-in-arm with sorrow and death. Brothers killed brothers in cold blood; children murdered their mothers; and strangers showed no remorse while slitting each other's throats. Having witnessed his own father rape and kill his beloved sister, Samantha, he knew first-hand the damage caused by the blood hungry sickness. It happened right before his eyes—and the only thing he could do was to put his father down like a rabid dog.

Those that had escaped, barely lived long enough for a sigh of relief. Among the uninfected ones he encountered on his quest were those bent on surviving by any means necessary. By his side, snugly fit into its scabbard, his sword, bloodstained and dull, attested to that will to live. However, as time went on, fewer and fewer people did he pass until near certainty ruled that he was, in fact, the *last*.

Throughout his travels from one corner of his world to the other, countrysides lay ravaged. Broken and scattered bodies covered the hills as bloody water, vermilion in its muddiness, washed and rinsed over everything. Animals, filthy scavengers that fed upon the remains, sized him up with snarls and growls. Cities and towns billowed smoke from their buildings, dulling what sunlight seeped through the clouds. Just like his own village, the affected and unaffected alike had pillaged and destroyed in the vicious melees The Sickening had purveyed. All that was left behind—the ruination and death—was a burning skeleton of what once was. History continued writing itself but there was no one left to pass it on. All that was left was the dirt—the bloodied dirt.

As he stepped over the last body, the sky rumbled like a bad omen.

He felt more alone than ever. The last corpse, a man in tattered and worn leather mail, lay stuck to the ground at the end of the bridge, the last vestiges of his face frozen in a twisted display of fright. *Or perhaps rage,* he thought. Dead fingers clenched tightly around his sword.

Something about the corpse struck him as familiar—the engraving on the hilt, the stitch on the leather mail. *Could it be a fellow tribesman?* Yet, the skin on the dead man's face had succumbed to frostbite and decay, revealing nothing of the familiarity he was feeling.

The sky threatened to open up and cover the diseased world in a white ritual cleansing. The cackling birds circling overhead offered their prayers. The time had come to wash away all the bad, infected dirt and pave the way for a fresh start. However, decades might pass before anything would possibly resemble its former self. After all the decay, nothing would ever be the same again.

The cliffs of the high peaks sung the wind's song, lifting white powder from their faces. Snow covered the tops of the mountains, painting them white against the somber backdrop of the sky. A light crusting of snow crunched under the weight of his step as he walked toward an opening in the side of the cliff face.

The trail ended right where the last body had fallen.

He squinted to see through the squall of windblown snow. Up ahead, he saw the entrance to the mountain, a jagged hole cut into the side of the behemoth of stony majesty. His face burned as the cold grew bitter and the wind threw needles of snow. He buried his face into his hands and peeked out between his fingers, despite his appendages harboring on the brink of frostbite.

In what felt like slow motion, he carried on toward the entrance that was beckoning him. Useless resistance urged him to learn the secrets it might hold—the answers it might reveal. With death as the only alternative, he had nothing left to lose.

The dark of the cave embraced him with a welcoming escape from the biting cold and for a moment it soothed his mind. From his leather satchel, the same satchel that contained all his worldly goods, he pulled out one of three small torches and the flint he kept. As he struck the stones together, the darkness swallowed the sparks until finally the torch ignited.

Outside, the wind raged, piercing his ears as it funneled into the cave. The torch's flame offered only a weak glow, illuminating the space with pitiful yellow and orange flickering. Strange symbols decorated the wall and the farther he walked, the more carvings he saw as his footsteps echoed down the solid corridor. Beyond his offering of light, he could not see; the torch's power faded into the universal blackness.

He traced the symbols with his fingers. The rock wall felt smooth and cold. If the glyphs had a meaning, if they were in fact a language, he didn't understand. A gust of wind blew down the tunnel chilling him, a constant reminder of nature's hostility outside.

Minutes crept by. The staggering depth of the corridor seemed never ending. Yet, he knew all things had to end sometime. Soon his torch would burn out and he'd have to light another one or wander blindly in this alien darkness, an idea he didn't relish. He knew this forsaken path had to eventually lead to somewhere of consequence. Just as the thought floated through his mind, the rocky trail ended.

What had been a slope turned into makeshift steps. Crudely cut and projecting out at random angles, they continued deeper down into the earth. The symbols disappeared, replaced now only by stone handrails carved with roughly-etched lines. Paranoia crept under his skin. His echoing footfalls haunted the eerie quiet.

Down, down, down he went. Step after step, his torch desperately struggled to cling to the oxygen in the air, but was failing fast.

As he minded the uneven steps and his footing, he noticed sconces lining the wall further ahead. A sense of momentary relief flooded over him. One by one, he lit the row of torches until his own finally gave up. In a magic moment, the blaze set the stairwell aglow. Macabre shadows flowed and danced on the cold stone wall, forming grotesque silhouettes.

The corridor stretched farther than he had imagined.

At the base of the steps, he stood silent and listened to the sounds of the stone vault. In the distance, he heard moving water. Overhead, the chamber grew massive; high rock walls stretched up to a cathedral-like ceiling laced with stalactites. He could only see an expanse of darkness in front of him; it spread out past the torchlight, engulfing everything beyond.

With each cautious step, he made his way down the tunnel. More of the strange symbols, the foreign writing carved there by an unknown hand, lined the walls. He just then realized that he hadn't stumbled across any more bodies, not even a solitary bone.

Why weren't there any more bodies? What had the last person to leave this place come in contact with that had destroyed Torhan's race in a handful of weeks? So many questions. This place had to be the source of The Sickening. Without a doubt, he knew this to be true.

The clack of his boots reverberated throughout the hallway. Beads of sweat broke out on his brow despite the cold. Anxiety consumed him, but he couldn't turn back. *What was there to turn back to?*

The palpable silence unnerved him the most, until, in a lightning quick moment, it evaporated like water on a hot stone. A horrible shriek vibrated the air, so loud that he had to cover his ears. His vision shook, and gooseflesh rose on his skin.

Up ahead, the shadows moved as the screaming stopped. He halted, but the sound of footfalls continued. The numbing realization hit him; he was *not* alone. He thought about calling out but held his tongue. *Were they footsteps?* Their repetition made him think so, but the shuffling, almost dragging quality left him pondering the question.

Now, as he stood in an antechamber, the rows of sconces depleted into randomly-placed beacons in the dark. He still needed to reach the rest to light them; however, they were farther ahead and out of his reach—and right from where he'd heard the footsteps. In one fluid motion, he lifted his sword from its sheath. A metal-on-metal *ting* split the air.

A single figure shambled forward out of the blackness. Hunched over, it dragged its leg behind, as if hobbling. In the dimness, he couldn't make out much detail, for the figure's silhouette blended in with the background. As it approached with its crippled gait, he stood fast, his heart pounding, and assessed the situation.

A pathetic moan gripped his ears. He wrapped his fingers tightly around the hilt, his knuckles burning as he waited for the thing to lumber closer. Then the smell hit him, the rottenness. Just like all the piles of corpses in the many towns and cities he had traveled through, the stench was the same—the stench of the damned. He covered his mouth and nose with his free hand. The closer the figure came, the worse the stink grew.

Then it came into the light.

Torhan gulped as he investigated the empty voids where its eyes should've been. Empty or not, they bore into his soul. Its flesh had peeled away from its bones and its muscles sagged like wet strips of meat.

Bile roiled in his gut and his teeth clenched shut at the sight.

Maggots and bugs crawled over and under its skin. Its skin: pale green and masticated, it revolted him more than the fetor. Loose rotten teeth hung from blackened gums. The thing's tongue swam about its grin like a blood-filled leech. It moved as if in a trance; its arms outstretched, blindly reaching for Torhan, as it stumbled over its own feet. The suit of leather mail and tunic it was wearing drooped from its frame, almost falling off its slouched shoulders. It slogged closer.

It.

He had no other word to describe the creature, no other classification for future reference. He just stood watching it draw closer before raising his sword. As shivers of fright and cold wracked his frame, Torhan aligned his cold blade with the walking corpse. It hissed foul breath right before he struck the thing with swift brutality. Like an over-ripe piece of fruit, the head exploded upon impact. The long sword glided through the pulpous tissue and bone with unanticipated ease. Its hollow eye sockets stared back at him as they separated from one another, the weapon continuing its trajectory of wrath until the one piece became two.

Dark, viscous fluid spilled from the dead body. Was it dead? Could it possibly have been living mere seconds earlier?

The dead liquid seeped into the ground, pooling amongst the cracks and crevices in the cavern floor. Inside the vicious wound he had created in the beast, Torhan recognized nothing; all its organs had decayed and mottled into one congealed mess.

He lit another torch and stepped around the pile of dead flesh and bone. The blackness swelled around him as sconces became less accessible. What torches he could light cast only a hazy glow about the cave. Just as his pulse had finally regulated itself, he heard the ear-shattering wail again.

It all happened so fast.

More of the dead beings melted out from the chamber's shadowy corners. Their desperate moans of hunger filled his ears. Without a doubt, he knew these creatures to be evil and that they would stop at nothing to sink their decaying teeth into his hide. Even more alert now, he scanned the cave for safety, searching for an escape but realizing he was outnumbered.

Breathing through his mouth did little to stop the stench from turning his stomach and watering his eyes. He ran deeper into the stony cathedral. At each turn, more of the living dead greeted him with snarls and claws, but they stood little chance of grabbing hold of him as he rushed by. He could tell just by looking at them that they were frail and clumsy. Yet, in their growing numbers, he wouldn't stand a chance. He swung his sword, clearing the way as he passed.

In the distance, a deep purplish light glowed. As he ran toward it, he felt the hollow-eyed stares of his hunters on his back. The swirling light beckoned him. He had no choice; there was no other direction to turn. From inside the base of what he took to be a stone well of sorts, the light spun, shooting high into the air where it filtered into another well-like structure built into the roof of the cavern. The shimmering column of beautiful purple light rotated and swelled.

He stopped in front of it and gazed up at its colossal size. In the swirling mix, vague shadows and images swam. Somewhere within the column of purple twilight, power hummed. He peered over the edge of the well but saw no bottom, just the same indistinguishable fleeting images.

The dead!

He spun around on his heels, sword raised. Nothing. He was alone again. Even the rotten stink of the horde became a memory as he turned and stared at the spinning column of light.

"Torhan...."

Someone called out. He turned once more with a swing of his sword, half expecting the army of ghouls to be right behind him yet again.

"Torhan Ulk...."

Had he heard his name called in his mind?

Were his ears deaf to the sound of another voice? The name repeated, and he finally recognized it as his own. The pillar of light pulsated.

"Where are you?" he demanded. "Show yourself!" His knuckles ached from his unyielding grip on the hilt of his weapon.

"Silence! How dare you demand of me with that tone after all I have done for you!"

Torhan's anger boiled inside of him. His mind raced in countless directions. "How dare *I* be reprimanded by a coward who won't show his face!"

"Mind your words, boy, or else you'll be right at home reliving the death of your family. Your sister," the voice boomed, disturbing the air. The purple light spun faster.

Reason eluded him the moment he realized the voice was coming from inside the well. Understanding seemed foreign. If losing everything to The Sickening hadn't already driven him insane, this magical cylinder of talking light might.

"Torhan, where are you? I can't see you, brother." The voice of his dead sister echoed in his head.

"Samantha?"

A form rose from the shimmering pool of spinning radiance. Long blonde hair glistened, and a shiny white robe flowed behind her as she stepped from the well.

He repeated himself. "Samantha? Is that you?"

It looked like her, sounded like her. He stood aghast—his dead sister stood in front of him, looking very much alive. *Perhaps she isn't truly dead*, his ravaged mind wondered.

"Oh, Torhan. I miss you so. Please come with me. I'm so lonely now," she whimpered. Her emerald eyes sparkled with life.

He missed her as well.

"Is it really you?" he asked. He moved to touch her hair but stopped short. Dread's icy fingers gripped the base of his spine.

"Daddy misses you, too," she offered, smiling. She moved closer to him, trails of glittering purple light rippling behind her as she left the confines of the well.

"What?"

"Everyone misses their magnificent leader." Her smile fell to a subtle hint as she softly batted her eyes. She stood so close to him now that he could smell her; the scent shooting arrows of memories back into his mind. *"I love you, brother,"* she said, taking his hand and placing it on her breast. *"And I know you'll love me, always."* Her hand slid down his torso and over his pelvic bone, rubbing ever so softly.

Repulsion tingled through his nerves; as his body reacted to her touch, he'd never felt more unclean. Through his clothing, he could feel the cold deadness of her hand. He breathed a saddened sigh as his tearing eyes searched the cavernous ceiling for comprehension. His mind screamed—*this* can't *be happening*.

"It is happening, brother."

Samantha moved to kiss him. He finally mustered up the courage to push her away. She began to cry, needing the comfort of her eldest brother just as she always had. His heart wept with her, for her, though he dared not touch her again.

"Why don't you love me?" she asked.

"I do," he answered, trying hard not to meet her gaze.

"No you don't, brother," she spat. "Or else you wouldn't have let me die."

"I tried to save—" he began.

"You let me die. You let our father rape me... to *death*. Why didn't you protect me?" Her anger rose with each word.

"There was nothing I could do," he cried. "Why are you saying these things?"

"Liar. He raped me, and you watched. Loving every bit of it," she yelled. The pillar of light spun faster—pulsated quicker as she ranted.

"No!"

"Yes, you did brother. You wished to do it yourself, but father beat you to the task. So you killed him for it." Samantha hissed a vile breath. Her teeth rotted and flesh decayed instantly, turning a vile color right before his eyes. Her contemptuous, staring eyes became dark empty pits.

"NO!" In a swift, calculated moment, rage overcame him. With an exacting slice, Torhan's blade soared through the air, connecting with her neck.

Yet his sword never touched her flesh.

The thing that was Samantha exploded into shards of amethyst light before crashing to the ground as liquid. Tiny rivulets moved and formed a puddle. Samantha was gone again, and as the shimmering puddle flowed back into the spinning column of illumination, he wept for the first time since this nightmare had started.

"Oh, such a sight to see," the voice started, its words laced with ridicule and wickedness.

"What do you want from me?" yelled Torhan.

He turned to leave, not knowing if he'd be able to survive the army of the dead he knew hid in the shadows let alone endure the harsh elements outside. The voice called to him again. He turned back.

"And where might you be going?" The purple column throbbed with energy as myriads of formless shadows swam through it, weaving in and out of each thread and stream of light.

"I'd rather die alone than be subjected to this," he spat.

"You cannot leave. This is your providence. Your fate."

"Why can't I leave?"

"Turn around."

Torhan gazed up to the staggering heights. "Please, Gods from above, help me." He knew the terror waiting behind him as he prayed for aid.

He whirled around, a bellow catching in his throat. A throng of the snarling, stinking beasts stood no more than five paces behind him. Empty, dead sockets stared back at him with a yearning, a craving, as they had clearly succumbed to the control of some mystical force. Their limbs hung loosely from their gnarled frames; their vile, twisted grins hissed and moaned their unearthly need. He again fought the torrent of nausea crawling up his insides.

A booming laugh echoed throughout the ancient stone chamber.

"What are you?"

"I am everything. I am nothing. The beginning and *the end."* As each sentence boomed and echoed, the column of luminescence flashed as if to punctuate its sincerity.

"No more riddles... please," he sighed. If this was the end, the source of the Sickening, he didn't know how it could be possible. "This cannot be." Delirium caressed his mind as the horde stood transfixed mere feet away.

"It is," the voice assured. "And you are here to bear final witness to the ultimate end... the answer to the questions that burn you hollow. Whether you believe what I say or not, it doesn't matter. It is true. Everything goes back to the dirt."

"Perhaps. But I still refuse to believe the words of some cowardly magician hiding behind some spell."

"Magician?" the voice responded. "Hardly. I am far beyond your feeble comprehension, but I will forgive your ignorance, boy, just this once."

"I am no boy!" Enraged, Torhan lashed out with his sword, striking the spongy head of a dead walker. As it crumpled to the ground, none of the others moved; they just continued their soulless-eyed staring. "What do you want from me? Why am I here? No more of your petty tricks!"

"Petty tricks?"

The ground below Torhan's feet violently shook and he lost balance, falling onto his back. All around him, the ghouls shrieked, their hideous cries stinging his ears.

From within the well, the purple beacon of brilliance evaporated, leaving nothing but a bottomless pit upon its departure. He backed up against the outer wall of the well as the quake thrashed the deadspawn about.

Just as quickly as the light vanished, it returned, erupting out of the mouth and eyes of every vile creature that surrounded him. The beams shot high into the cavern, illuminating the dagger-sharp protrusions of the ancient ceiling. As the horde stood motionless, still screeching through the shafts of light, their putrefied flesh began to sizzle and bubble, devoured from the inside out by an immense heat.

He felt a new shaking, a rumbling even more deafening than the screams, coming from above his head. All at once, the creatures ceased to exist as the swirling light beams burnt them into nothing but a recent nightmare.

"Stop this!" shouted Torhan. "Stop this madness now!"

"My poor Torhan." The voice returned, filling the cavern and even drowning out the cracking and rumbling above. *"So reluctant to believe, yet so close to the truth."*

"I want to believe. I want to understand."

"You've come here once before, looking for an answer. Do you not remember? Have you yet to put the pieces of this puzzle together?"

Torhan froze as if all reality came crashing down upon him in one fell swoop.

Vivid images flooded his mind, visions he had locked away, hidden for whatever reason. He saw the column of light, pulsating, and welcoming. All around him, his men stood at uneasy attention, eying the beacon with confusion and distrust. They had been on a mission to find their lost elder, but their path had led them here, to this primeval cave. Torhan recalled hearing faint whispers beckoning him to approach the light, to bathe in its warmth. His men called out, begging him to stay away, but he was lost to its siren's call.

The purple radiance twirled and danced around his hand as he penetrated its barrier. Something grabbed hold of his arm, a frigid sting despite the heat of the light. Broken from his trance, he called out to his men, but the spiraling vortex had sucked him in before they could come to his aid.

Moments had passed before the column spat Torhan back out onto the cold stone floor. Boils and blisters covered his now yellowing skin. He screamed out in agony as the onset of disease ravaged his body. Someone grabbed his arm, pulling him away from the light. Instantly, the infliction overcame the guard and *his* skin began to molt and pop. In his death throes, Torhan reached out to another, clasping tightly onto his leg. A chain reaction began as the infection spread to each man, each succumbing to the same hellish fate.

As Torhan pulled himself along the hard ground, the fallen bodies of his men littered the cavern in heaps of rotting flesh. For whatever reason, the sickness spared him the same immediate fate. He crawled along, slowly making his way back through the stony corridor and up the chiseled steps to the entrance in the mountainside. Standing by the bridge that spanned the chasm, more of his men stood guard, waiting for the rest of their band to return from the cave.

The frigid air engulfed Torhan's sick body as one of the guards pulled him to the bridge. Just as before, the disease transferred. On down the line like a sentient being unto itself, it jumped from host to host, determined to spread, determined to stay alive. At the foot of the bridge, cold and dying, Torhan Ulk took his final breath.

Everything went back to dirt. It had told him this and he believed it as true.

AND THE HITS JUST KEEP ON COMIN'

The old man set down the sun-dried bones on the small stone altar. He pounded the worn and battered mallet down upon them in a controlled rage and didn't stop until nothing but dust remained. *"With these bones, I now do crush!"*

With his craggy hand, he swept the mound of bone dust into a small burlap bag and turned back to the ancient symbol he had scrawled in chalk on the cold wooden floor. In the four corners surrounding the sigil, the ceremonial black wax melted and dripped, hardening into a pile around the candlestick bases, securing them in place. The man drew another circle in the center of the symbol. Reaching into the satchel, he pulled out a dusty photograph, and began to chant.

"There has been unfairness done to me... I summon the elements... I invoke them... I conjure them to do my bidding!" He chanted in his native tongue as he placed the photo of a man in the

center of the bone dust circle. Then, from the satchel again, he retrieved a bound locket of hair. *"I call upon the Ancient Ones from the great abyss to do my bidding!"* On top of the photograph, he placed the hair, before grabbing one of the candles, letting the wax drip to seal the pieces into one effigy.

Behind him, a young boy rang a bell three times.

The old man pulled a crude blade from the floor beside him and sliced his left palm open. With the blood dripping from his wound, he extinguished the four flames around the sigil while chanting. *"The four watchtowers shall lay their eyes and minds... there shall be guilt and fear and bad blood... there shall be submission and no pity."* Each candle sizzled, releasing their final plume after he read each line.

"Bones of anger, bones to dust, full of fury, revenge is just... I scatter these bones, these bones of rage... take thine enemy, bring him pain... I see thine enemy before me now... I bind him, crush him, bring him down," the old man recited while dumping the remains of the dust onto the effigy. "With these bones I have crushed, make thine enemy turn to dust... torment, fire, out of control... With this hex I curse your soul."

He raised his bleeding hand over the pile, letting the blood flow freely, mixing with the dust to create a ruddy sludge. In a sudden blaze, the candles reignited, casting dancing shadows over the room. *"I point the threefold law against thee... against thee it shall be... threefold, a hundredfold, is the cost for my anger and pain. Thou shalt be blinded by the fear, blinded by the pain, blinded by me... bound by me... cursed by me... So mote it be!"*

The candles flickered out and the room fell completely silent and still.

"What the hell are you talking about? I'm the epitome of perfect health!"

"Are you absolutely sure about that, Mr. Wright?"

"Of course, I'm sure. Healthy mind, healthy body. And please don't call me Mr. Wright. Every time you do that, I think my father's in the room."

"Very well, Jacob. You've always been our best asset, yet ... you seem ... *off*, lately."

"Bull! I'm on the top of my game," Jacob blurted out, before taking a sip of his drink.

"Tell that to our Haitian clients. They are none too pleased with us at the moment."

"Screw them. The job got done, didn't it? So what if it lacked some of my usual finesse. They were gonna kill that other guy anyways. I did them a favor. Was just a matter of time." Jacob poured the rest of the bitter liquor into his mouth. "Shit happens."

"Yes, you are probably right. Apparently, shit does happen. Please realize that your actions, whether just or not, have deadly repercussions in our industry. The quality of your work is the unseen face of this organization. Your *finesse*, as you put it, is an equally important part of our business model."

"With all due respect, spare me the lecture, alright? Do you have another job for me or not?"

"Of course we do. It's a two-for-one for a new client. It's yours, as long as you don't plan on mucking this one up as well."

"Like I said, chief. Top of my game."

The "buy-one-get-one-free" gimmick didn't usually pay well in this line of work.

In an effort to bring in more prospective clients, the bigwigs upstairs at The Collective sometimes rolled out these bargain hits. Jacob hated when they screwed with his paydays, but in light of his screw-up down in Haiti, he sucked it up and took the job with a smile. Being the consummate professional, he always talked a big game but never downright disrespected or challenged the bosses. Just wasn't good for business, or breathing.

Nestled in his meager safe house in town, he laid out all the files from the dossier on his kitchen table. He slowly sipped away at his three fingers of scotch, the good stuff, aged three times longer than he'd been alive, given to him years ago for a job well done, a job that put The Collective in the murder-for-hire arena.

The clients had printed out vague notes, explaining how each hit should go down. The first needed to be from a distance, preferably in public with plenty of witnesses. The second needed to feel personal, no witnesses, just a brutal mess that would send a precise message.

The client left the details up to him. As long as he met those two non-negotiable terms, he had free rein. Explosion or sniper shot, garrote or blade, he had ultimate say in his victims' demise. And he liked it that way.

He studied the information, the photos, and the files. He didn't care who they were or what they had done to be put on his list; they remained faceless, and he remained detached. That's how he did the job and, to be successful, objectification was key. His brain worked over the details, building the schematics of the kills in his mind. After he had set everything to memory, he tossed the dossier into the sink and doused it all with the remainder of scotch from his glass. He lit a match and tossed it in, setting the file aflame.

As he watched the paper smolder, he felt half-guilty for wasting such expensive hooch. *Fuck it*, he conceded, *I hate scotch anyway.*

Jacob had decided that killing the first mark in public would be a solid way to start the day. It had been months since he'd had a chance to play with his Dragunov SVD. Lightweight and durable, the sniper rifle was a Russian masterpiece. His plan went off flawlessly, as he knew it would. Lunchtime in the city would give you some goddamn witnesses—witnesses covered in brains, but witnesses nonetheless.

He knew the second half of the job would be a little trickier—up close and personal. With timing and opportunity being essential, he chose the only logical option to make sure he met his client's strict demand—a hammer.

So, in the hallway closet he waited, hammer in hand, for the next poor soul on his list to arrive home. As much as killing didn't bother him, he never really liked the messy ones. Just the mere thought of ruining his clothes and shoes on some chump's blood and guts gave him anxiety, never mind the chance of it getting into his mouth. Thankfully, he always had a set of scrubs and booties at the ready, along with his gloves and face mask.

Keys jingled in the lock.

The doorknob turned and the hinges squealed.

Time to work.

The mark entered his home, mail and a bag of groceries in his hands. He walked right by Jacob's hiding spot; shadows momentarily blocked the light shining through the breaks in the door. Jacob slowed his breathing, timing it with the creaks of the man's footfalls on the hardwood floor. He gripped the weapon tightly in one hand and slowly turned the doorknob with the other.

Out in the open now, Jacob stalked the man who stood at his kitchen counter, thumbing through his mail. Poor guy had no idea what was about to happen. As much as Jacob disliked getting this close to his kills for pure sanitary reasons, he still enjoyed seeing that final look of disbelief in his victims' eyes right before the strike. And that almost made ruining some clothes worth it ... almost.

"Psst."

Jacob slept soundly on his twin-size mattress with his head squished against the soft pillow. The deeds of the day behind him, he rested without a care in the world, satisfied with a job well done.

A noise roused him—a bell chiming. He sat up and wiped the sleep from his eyes. In the dark of the bedroom, he saw nothing. The bell chimed again. This time he could tell it came from nearby, but he still couldn't pinpoint exactly where.

He reached for the lamp on the nightstand, grabbing nothing but air. Confused, he swung his legs off the side of the bed to get up. When his feet touched carpet, he grew concerned. Not only could he not find his lamp, his hardwood floor had somehow grown a rug during the night. Knowing full well, at this point, that his gun would not be where he kept it, he felt for it anyway. "What in the hell?"

A bell rang again, the third time.

Jacob didn't scare easily; still, uneasiness crept across the back of his neck. He got up and started walking slowly in the direction he thought the sound was coming from. As he bumped into the doorframe, inhaling sharply from the sudden pain, he found the light switch and flicked it on. Incandescence chased the darkness away and Jacob stood frozen.

He wasn't in his apartment.

Someone started pounding against the front door so hard he thought the banging was in his head. He steadied himself to gather his senses. He looked out into the hallway. At one end he saw the front door that someone was mercilessly beating upon, and at the other he saw the familiar kitchen that he had used as his office earlier in the day when he'd bludgeoned a man to death with a hammer.

"What the—"

He crept to the front door, feeling naked without a weapon. In the center of the cheap board door, he saw a peephole just below his eye level. Thankful that the pounding had seemed to stop for at least a moment, he put his eye up to the cold, fish-eye lens. Standing on the other side was a man in a bloody three-piece suit, with a head that looked like an M-80 had gone off in it. The man reeled back and slammed both fists violently into the door.

Over and over, banging and pounding.

Jacob's head snapped back into his pillow as if someone had just cold-cocked him; his eyes jolted open from the incessant pounding on his front door. The fright sweats broke out, exuding cool perspiration all over his body. His eyes watered as he reached for his gun under his pillow. With the weapon gripped tightly, he stared up at the ceiling, confused as hell.

The banging persisted.

Someone's at the door, asshole. Snap out of it!

He sat there and collected himself. When his feet touched the familiar coolness of his hardwood floor, he knew that he had been dreaming. *A nightmare was more like it.*

The knocking tested his patience. "Hold on, for Christ's sake!" he yelled. "I'm coming." Still in a bit of a daze, he kept the gun primed as he opened the door—as far as the chain would allow.

"Hello, Mr. Wright."

Jacob sighed in relief and undid the chain lock. "Jesus Christ, man! You scared the crappola out of me. I was having--" He paused, details of the dream flooding back into his memory, the man with coleslaw for a head and the American flag pin on his lapel that he now remembered seeing through his scope the day before. "—the weirdest dream. "Do you have any idea what time it is?" Jacob asked, gesturing the man to enter.

"I know, Mr. Wright," the man started. "It's very ear—"

"No, really. What time is it? My brain is still in a fog."

"It's five o'clock in the morning, Mr. Wright."

"Ugh. That's too early to be alive," Jacob said between yawns. "And what did I say about that mister crap?"

"Apologies," the man said. "But it couldn't wait until a more reasonable hour. We have an issue to discuss."

"Okay, great. But I'm gonna need some coffee first. Want some?"

"No thank you, Jacob."

"Suit yourself," he said with a shrug.

"I'll just begin, if you don't mind," the man insisted. "I have a very busy day ahead of me in light of this new situation brought to my attention."

"Alright, no problem." Jacob fiddled with his fancy coffee machine before turning around. "Go ahead. Shoot."

The man groaned before he began, not once moving from his spot on Jacob's floor. "It appears that you left a job unfinished, Mr. Wright."

"Bullshit!" Jacob blurted. "That guy's face looked like a bowl of Spaghetti-O's after I shot it."

"Not him," the man started. "The other job. The one in the Village that needed to look personal."

"With all due respect, that's impossible, sir."

"Yet, the fact remains. He was seen late last night walking down the main strip. A little worse for wear, but alive and walking, nonetheless."

Jacob, caught off guard at the revelation, put his palms to his face and slowly shook his head. He stretched and opened his eyes wide as if to retune himself. "There's gotta be a mistake. He was deader than ... dead ... when I left him on his kitchen floor with about ten extra holes in his head. Are you pos—"

The man unceremoniously pulled out a high-resolution photo of the target and handed it to Jacob, who studied it in dismay. "Yep. That's him," Jacob admitted, almost embarrassed. "He looks like some bad hamburger helper, but that is him."

"As if I would come all the way over here at this ridiculous hour if I were wrong," the man spat. "The Top Floor is not very impressed with you at the moment, and I mirror their sentiments."

"I guess that's understandable."

"This needs to be addressed immediately, Jacob," the man said. "That is, if you enjoy your current position and the livelihood afforded you by The Collective."

"Yes, sir. I do. And I'll get right on it."

"Final chance to win back their trust," explained the man. "Don't make me regret sticking my neck out for you."

He stood at the counter, sipping on his third cup of coffee and contemplating his predicament. Yet, the prior night's dream gnawed at his guts. Jacob didn't dream much, if at all, let alone about work or his targets.

"I need to get my shit together," he announced, as he stared ahead in a daze. With a big sigh to calm himself, he dropped the mug into the sink and headed to his bedroom to get ready for the long day ahead. At the mirror over his dresser, he looked at his reflection, studying it for any signs of coming apart at the seams. "This is the last thing I need," he said, through another round of yawns and stretches, still exhausted from his troubled sleep.

He had upset the bosses; not something you do—bad for business. Getting back into their good graces was paramount. "Snap out of it, buddy," he grunted, as he slapped his face a couple of times to psych himself up.

Not only an expert marksman, Jacob also excelled at tracking people, a talent he'd honed after many years of black-ops work overseas in "The Sandbox." Therefore, he figured tracking a man whose face looked like someone took a brick to a cantaloupe should be like a jaunt through a meadow.

He started with the hospitals and struck out. Not one person reported a case even remotely resembling the target. Outside the man's apartment building, Jacob watched from a safe distance as police cordoned off the area and stood at attention by the entrance. Detectives shuffled in and out of the complex, obviously confused by the grisly scene with a missing dead body.

His patience waned. He had until the end of the day to rectify the situation or else he'd end up a free agent with a target on his own back.

Think, think, *think!*

He decided to backtrack to where witnesses had last seen the mark. The main strip of town was a big area and had its good and not-so-good sections. A guy as banged up as that might stand a chance of hiding out in the shadier parts of town. Up and down each filthy alleyway, Jacob looked for any signs that his target had been around. Witnesses. Bloodstains. His *body*.

Still no dice. "Where would I go if I was a half-dead, bloodied mess in a shirt and tie?"

As daylight began to fade between the tall buildings, the town's more unique and unsavory residents seemed to ooze from the cracks in the pavement. Jacob continued his search, determined to finish the job he thought he'd finished once already. Up ahead, a woman strutted forward along the sidewalk. Definitely out of place around these parts, her uptown fashion sense and sparkly jewelry immediately caught the attention of the neighborhood dregs. She met Jacob's gaze and kept it there. From a distance, she seemed well put-together and ready for action, but as she got closer, he noticed dirt stains on her arms and legs. Her hair that he thought she had pulled back into a bun was actually matted to her head, her outfit disheveled on her frame.

She smiled at Jacob as she approached, her smirk nothing more than a mouthful of rotting teeth and gums. Jacob tried not to maintain eye contact, but couldn't help himself—she looked like a damned walking corpse. He grimaced as she licked her dry, cracked lips, her tongue darting out like a bloated slug.

Then he noticed the deep gash around her neck, from when he'd garroted her about two months earlier. Worms and maggots weaved through the breach in her throat, squirming between the desiccated folds of the laceration.

This is impossible!

Jacob never sugarcoated it to anyone. He was a monster and he never denied it, not even to himself. It was his detachment from his fellow humans, the desensitization he carried with him his whole life that made him such an asset to The Collective. Since the beginning, it was what had helped him carve out a lucrative career in the murder-for-hire field, even before he hitched his star to the Machiavellian corporation. He had also seen some shit in his lifetime. Whether here in the States or across the ocean in the sandstorm of enemy territory, he had seen *and* done more than his fair share of primal evil.

But... this business before him was just absolutely ridiculous.

People on the street pointed at her, gawking as if she were a sideshow attraction, but they sure got out of her way in a hurry, not wanting anything she might be selling. Oblivious to the spectators, she reached out toward Jacob, who, still staring in disbelief, reached for his gun. She hissed at him through her putrid scowl and then lunged.

"Fuck this!" Jacob blurted out, just before firing three rounds, center mass, into the woman's chest. The street cleared of all witnesses as if the sound of gunfire made them evaporate back into whatever hole they called home. The woman dropped to the sidewalk with a meaty thud. No blood spilled out of the wounds, just a fetid stink that made his eyes water.

He saw something on the back of her neck, a small flower tattoo that he recalled from their previous encounter. *Yup, that's her, alright.* He slid his gun back into its holster, looking around nervously before booking it down an alley.

Jacob paced in front of his building, trying to release his anxious energy. He did his best to keep his voice to a whisper as he talked into his phone. "I don't care what you say. This is impossible! She was like a walking friggin' corpse and she had the smell to prove it."

"Let's not get carried away, Jacob," said the man on the other end. "Discussions about the reanimated corpses of the people that you've already received payment for killing is not going to help your case any."

"Listen to me, asshole," he spat into the receiver, immediately regretting his choice of words. "I know how this sounds, but I know what I saw." He left out the part about the maggots writhing around her opened throat. "I don't know how or why, but someone is seriously fucking with me."

"Mr. Wright, do I have to remind you that you're on a timetable here? Time is running out and you still have a job to finish. All this nonsense you're spouting is making me regret my decision to continue soliciting your services."

"You don't understand," Jacob said, almost pleaded. "Something is wrong. I just need some time to—"

"No!" the man boomed. "Finish the job now and maybe you'll still have a life to retire to. Is that understood, Mr. Wright?"

"Unquestionably."

"Good." *Click.*

All Jacob wanted to do was take a long, hot bath and let the insanity of the day disappear. He tried to remind himself that none of it was real. *Couldn't be.* If someone wanted him dead, had gone to such lengths as to make him think dead people were after him, he most certainly was going to make their success as difficult as possible.

He slid his key into the lock and shuffled right down the hall to his secret room behind the wall in his bedroom. "Now where did I leave my vest?" he asked himself, as he rummaged through totes and shelves of all sorts of tactical gear. "I seriously need to clean this place. Looks like a goddamn Army & Navy store threw up in … ah, there you are." He lifted the Kevlar up to the light, admiring the craftsmanship that had saved his butt multiple times, as demonstrated by the dents left by some not-so-stray bullets.

With his determination renewed, he slipped on the vest and grabbed a new gun strap lined with reserve clips, just in case things spun even more toward the absurd. Jacob backed out of the handmade doorway in the wall and slid the fake panel back into place. Something tickled his sixth sense, the same reliable sense that had saved him on many a prior occasion. It rarely belied him.

Someone whispered.

Jacob whirled around and pulled his gun out in one fluid motion. He saw no one, yet he didn't relax his aim as he surveyed the empty bedroom over the barrel's sight. Seconds passed as he stood on alert. Finally satisfied by the silence, he lowered his aim and holstered his piece.

He checked his alarm clock as he walked by the nightstand. "Christ! Running out of time."

A faint metallic, sickly sweet smell crinkled his nose as he neared the door to the hallway, giving him pause. His cell phone burst to life in his pocket and startled him dizzy. After a couple of rings, he grabbed it. "Restricted number?" Against better judgment, he answered the call. "Hello?"

"Hello, Mr. Wright." A man's voice, thick with a Creole accent. "I hope this evening finds you well and that I'm not," he started, only pausing to chuckle, "interrupting anything."

"Who is this?" Jacob asked. "How'd you get this number?"

"Relax, Mr. Wright. No reason to get excited. I take it you received my message?"

"What message? What are you talking about?"

"Oh, I am sure you know." His voice brimmed with confidence. "Have any bad dreams lately?"

Jacob's aggravation grew to exponential heights. "How did you know about … who are you?" Incredulous, he stared at the phone before placing it back to his ear. "Listen, fella, I have no frickin' idea who you are or what you want, but you are fucking with the wrong son-of-a-bitch!"

"The dream was the first of many things I have planned for you, as I'm sure you are intently aware." He chuckled again. Jacob could feel the man's twisted coolness emanate through his phone. "Things are going to get much more interesting for you this night, Mr. Wright. Soon you will understand and feel my wrath, my pain."

"Eat me!" Jacob shouted. "You got some brass balls, buddy. I don't have time for this!"

As he was about to hang up, Jacob heard the man laugh, clearly amused. "Farewell, Mr. Wright. My son, Nicolas, wishes you safe travels on your journey. You remember Nicolas, don't you?"

Jacob's face dropped; color drained from his complexion. His head spun, whipping up ghosts of the recent past.

"He wants you to know that he will be there to greet you in the Afterlife!" The man continued to snicker.

"Then I guess I'll see him in Hell!" Jacob pitched his phone across the bedroom. It smashed into a mirror and exploded, raining fragments everywhere.

Images flashed through his mind: the nightmare with no head in his dream, the woman he had strangled to death in her office late one night, the face of Nicolas when the bullet had ricocheted and sliced through his carotid.

That *wasn't* my fault, his inner voice screamed. He was gonna be as good as dead soon anyway!

For the first time in years, Jacob began to panic. He was well aware that he no longer had time on his side, regardless of the job's outcome. "Calm down," he told himself. "Screw that voodoo horseshit." He pulled his gun, reflexively checking the clip, and headed out of the bedroom. "Let's get this show on the road."

At the threshold that separated his safe haven from the lunacy befalling the world outside, Jacob took a deep breath and caught another whiff of that same metallic scent that had bombarded him earlier. He yanked the door open.

Two hands reached for Jacob's face and throat, intent on inflicting maximum damage. The nail of a crooked finger raked across his face, digging out a hunk of cheek with it. Jacob stumbled backward, losing his gun before slamming into the wall. The force of the blow knocked him into a coat rack and the hanging picture on the wall behind it. He fought to remain conscious after his brain collided with the inside of his skull from his abrupt impact with the laminate floor.

Everything started crashing down around Jacob. Sanity no longer spun out of control; instead, it quickly rose to the surface like the dirtied water of a clogged latrine, threatening to overwhelm him. And here he was—without his plunger.

With a cursed glint in his one good eye, Mr. Hammer-Smashed-Face lunged again. Jacob, with the determined—albeit sudden—wherewithal of a man in mortal danger, snatched a broken arm of the fallen coat rack and thrust it between the third and fourth rib, puncturing the half-faceless man's lung before imbedding it with a sickeningly wet *squish* into his heart. That seemed to halt his forward momentum and he fell flat on top of Jacob like a sack of beef innards.

Jacob gagged at the awful stench that oozed out of the wound. "Get the fuck off me!" he yelled, as he shoved the man's motionless corpse away with a mighty heave. "That's the second time I've killed you. You asshole!" Whether the reanimated cretin had been breathing prior to having his lung ventilated, he didn't know.

Jacob could only stare as black sludge poured from the breach—*glub, glub, glub, glub*—its wretched, oily appearance matched only by its revolting stink.

He gave the corpse one last, solid kick for prosperity before scooping up his firearm. "Piece of shit."

"Hey. Is everything o—?"

BANG!

Jacob realized his adrenaline pump was on overload. His nerves were tighter than razor wires. His neighbor from down the hall must've heard the commotion and, in her infinite nosiness, decided to check out the situation. Now, her elderly brains streaked across Jacob's front door, sliding down with the consistency of raspberry jam.

"Why'd you make me do that? You stupid, nosy old bitch," yelled Jacob as he holstered his gun and leapt over the reservoir of blackened sludge pooling on his floor. He already knew that Mrs. Fitzgibbons was gone, but he felt for a pulse, regardless. While she was an annoying little snooper, she didn't need to have her skull aerated in such a manner. Soon, all the noise and gunfire would rouse the other inhabitants of the apartment complex. *Shit's getting even deeper!*

As Jacob knelt before Mrs. Fitzgibbons' corpse, he heard the distinct sounds of locks disengaging and door chains sliding off their guards. *Fuck!* He bolted down the hallway as all the doors opened in unison. He would have to forsake his abode and all his possessions, knowing that he could never step foot back inside this building. He was through ... done. No more jobs with The Collective and no more freedom if the police caught up with him.

All the opening doors were a blur as Jacob made his hasty escape. He didn't recall this hallway to the elevator being so long. Every time he turned a corner, he found nothing but more opening doors and the deadpan faces of his neighbors. In chilling unison, they all opened their mouths and spoke, their collective voice saying the same thing, "*Feel my wrath ... feel my pain.*"

Right away, Jacob recognized the voice as the father of the man he'd accidently killed while on the job in Haiti. Nicolas.

In time, all the doors of the ever-expanding hallway opened and filled with the gaping and whitewashed eyes of his neighbors as they repeated Jacob's tormentor's mantra like a broken record.

The hallway branched off to the right and Jacob picked his pace up a notch, hoping the exit to his current metric fuck-ton of problems would be around the corner. He did his best to ignore the thunderous voice that filled the hall and vibrated inside his skull. All they did as he raced by them was glower while repeating the same thing. As he zoomed by one open door, he launched a right hook into one fellow citizen's pale face to no reaction whatsoever, despite the resounding crack of the man's head smashing into the doorjamb.

Yet, he had the corner in his sights. *Almost there—!*

No sooner than the thought popped into Jacob's head did the ragged, moldy corpse of Nicolas turn the corner before him—all the way from Haiti. Everything switched to half-speed as Jacob's face contorted into a grimace with a side order of what-the-fuck.

Feel my wrath… feel my pain… feel my wrath… feel my pain…

To Jacob's utter dismay, the undead behemoth of a man lurched forward, looming like a mountain, his shadow engulfing the hitman's puny form. Nicolas opened his mouth, "*Feel my wrath… feel my pain.*"

Jacob's eyes watered, and his vision wavered. "Oh my Christ! Stop saying that!" He scrambled backward, the treads of his shoes gaining traction in the cheap carpeting, clambering to his feet. Now that he faced the opposite direction, he noticed that Mr. Bullet-To-The-Head and Miss Garroted-Zombified-Bitch had joined the soirée. Behind them was the mindless throng of his neighbors, their cold eyes now blackened and dead.

Feel my wrath… feel my pain… feel my wrath… feel my pain…

The chant was getting too much to bear. Each one of them repeated the words in the Haitian man's voice—all except the guy he'd shot in the face. He sounded like a quasi-catatonic slurping soup from a spoon.

Nicolas shuffled closer. Jacob could still see the mortal wound on the young Haitian's neck amid the rancid decay and vermin crawling all over his mottled flesh. "I'm sorry," shouted Jacob. "It was just a goddamn accident!" Nicolas kept coming. Jacob pressed up against the wall in between the incoming gang of walking nightmares. "I didn't... mean it... I was..." he stammered, unable to piece together a full sentence.

What Jacob knew as reality had evaporated. All that it left in its wake was this numbing sense of defeat and lunacy. He began to sob as he slid down the length of the wall into a broken pile of a man— once strong, logical, and capable, now just a quivering heap of jelly.

They advanced on Jacob, crowding around him like gawkers at a crime scene. With a sharp inhalation, he threw his head skyward, eyes clenched tight and beseeching the heavens. "I'm so sorry," he screamed over the droning of the mob, apologetic for the first time in his life. As his returning victims hovered over him—including Nicolas, his ultimate mistake—Jacob yanked his gun from his holster and pressed the cold barrel against his temple. With a vice grip on the weapon, he forced himself to look up at Nicolas.

"With these bones I have crushed, make thine enemy turn to dust... torment, fire, out of control... With this hex I curse your soul," chanted Nicolas, in his father's voice.

"Fuck it!" Jacob responded, hoping, in the end, for a sweet release as he pulled the trigger.

Click.

Empty.

Nicolas smiled, maggots swimming through his gaping grin, as the horde converged upon Jacob, piling on to his screaming form with teeth and fingers ripe for rendering his flesh into dust. Nicolas's reawakened corpse stood over the bloody maelstrom of ripping skin, pleased.

Feel my wrath... feel my pain.

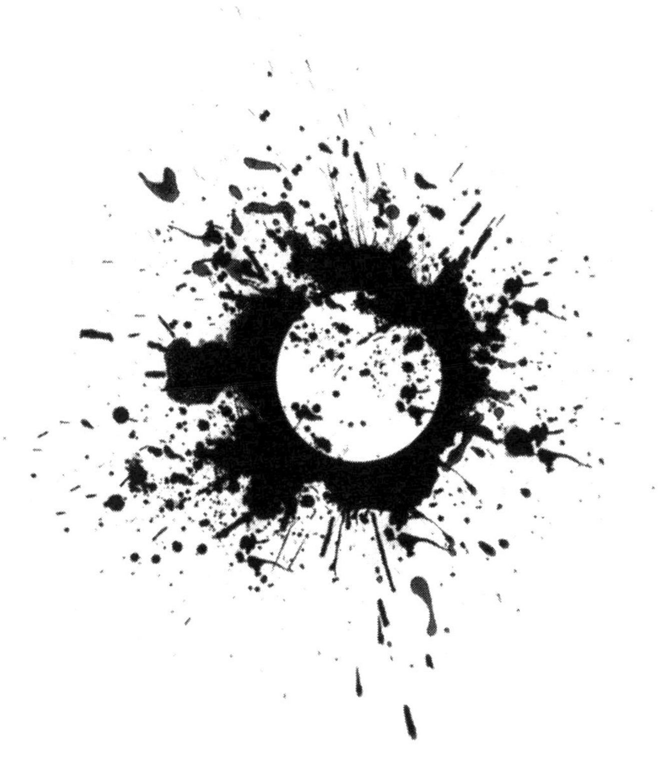

LOTUS PETALS: LIMINAL PERSONAE

The darkness was terrible. The kind of darkness that ripped you right from the here and now and thrust you back in time, trapping you in its womb-like blackness. An obsidian amnion fraught with the emotions of endless childhood fears, and the consequences of every conceivable sin you'd ever committed, leaving you caught and fearful in its webby mire.

Her vision refused to adjust to the blank slate of night pushing on her eyeballs. Was she floating and freefalling at the same time, devoid of any sense of direction in the miasmic vacuum? The air clicked with a distant static. Though she breathed, the stale scent of nothingness muddled her thoughts.

If she was just dreaming or reliving everything in real-time through a blackened lens, she did not know. She tried to move her arms and legs, to swim against some invisible current, with no success. Her nerves were on fire, but she couldn't see her limbs, couldn't feel them colliding with each other as she fought to find stable ground in the amorphous quicksand of night. Her body felt myriad sensations both familiar and alien. All she wanted to do was wake up if she was dreaming or die if this was her reality. Then, she started tumbling through the nether, falling through her cherished memories like falling out of a tall tree and hitting every branch on the way down.

She had told him that she loved him.

Not only did she say it in passing, a quick admittance under duress, she'd said it without being completely sure. The fact, she later realized, was that she didn't want to risk losing his affection—or even, his attention—by not returning the sentiment. How many more times was she going to be able to see him, let alone bask in his warmth or the feeling of being wanted? She struggled with these emotions constantly, as she was hopeful that he did as well—and in his own way, he did, she supposed. Just knowing that he did fall for her first made all seem right with her world at times. Even if he couldn't convey with words or wasn't entirely sure what to do with those feelings, she knew it was true.

He made her drunk with passion, his scent, his skin, his eyes as they looked at her. They created magic in their union. She never wanted it to end. But, as most good things do, the finality of events to come weighed heavily on her mind. Yet, she still battled with the notion of loving him. Did she love the physical connections they shared, the attention he gave her, the sense of not being alone? Her head continually spun from the magnitude of her racing emotions.

One fated day, groggy and sick from the previous night's poor life decisions, she sat alone at home, missing him. The two of them talked sporadically throughout the day, mostly via text. He was out and about and couldn't commit to coming over to spend time. She thought their dedication had reached a new level, an attempt at real-world romance and not just words on a screen or a disembodied voice over the airwaves. Defeated and dejected, she continued lounging the day away and recuperating. Hours later, still in the exact same spot she had fallen asleep on the couch, the doorbell rang.

He stood at her door, his eyes as gorgeous as ever.

She smiled wide. She had missed him and—she assumed—he felt the same, despite declining her invitation to come inside. He said he had his reasons, even as the glint of malicious excitement sparkled in his dark eyes. So, they stood in the doorway making awkward and meaningless small talk, looking at each other, holding hands. He noticed she didn't look well and he grabbed her, pulling her close when she admitted to feeling worn down and tired.

Their embrace alone held more fire and passion than either of them had ever felt with anyone else. It was instantaneous—she fell in love holding him. The way they just seemed to mesh seamlessly together, the way her head fit perfectly in the crook of his neck caused little moans to erupt and escape her lips as he squeezed.

At that moment, it all clicked. Her heart and mind aligned as one. All the confusion, all the doubt, vanished without a trace. It made her ache with sadness that she had to let go, ever, because she had finally realized that not only had she fallen in love with him, but in fact, truly loved him. Madly and unquestionably. She held him tightly, savoring and memorizing every nuance of the moment. Everything felt perfect, he felt perfect. And she hoped it would never end, but as most good things sometimes do...

David held his homemade garrote over the blowtorch's flame, heating the metal wire to a white-hot hue. This was step one, his preferred method of slicing through muscle before he brought out the big guns to finish the job and cut through the bone. Sure, he had a guy for that kind of work, but sometimes he just wanted to see if he still had it in him, still had the stomach for getting his *own* hands dirty. As he fumbled with the tool's wooden handles, failing to secure a tight grip on them, he cursed his most recent abomination of body modification.

Enhancement meant *better*!

He genuinely thought that having fewer fingers per hand, as long as they were longer and wider, would make most types of handiwork easier, make him better—more efficient. The more knuckles, the better articulation; the thicker the two fused main fingers, the better the grip. With both pinky fingers removed right at the metacarpals (they were useless appendages anyway and he always wondered why humans had yet to lose the dead weight) and all the webbing cut and resewn for more flexibility, he struggled more than ever to complete his tasks. Not-so-deep down, he worried his choice of additions was based more on aesthetics than functionality, hoping that he just needed to grow accustomed to them as they healed... words of wisdom from his psychosis—the only voice he truly trusted anymore.

Weeks passed, turning to months as their love bloomed. They shared everything; her life became his and his became hers. Their deepest, darkest secrets were no longer drenched in the curse of shame their environment and circumstances placed on them. The sense of autonomy was exquisite, the unabashed freedom to reveal wants and needs and the comfort that came with that ability.

He told her about his abuse at the hands—and strap—of his mother. The stigma of her words of his uselessness and her disappointment in him was finally replaced by a sense of fulfillment—and almost adoration in who he had become after her passing. He told her of his dreams of wanting to fly, to free himself from the chaos of home life and his mother's spite and anger, to fly high into the sky and feel the non-judgmental warmth of the sun on his skin. How he wished to fly to a faraway place where people like him, those trapped in unfamiliar bodies, could escape their torturous husks and truly be who they are.

They spent many late nights on the roof of Pace Woodworks where David worked. After being expelled from medical school for certain infractions, his father had talked him into running the family business. He loved working with his hands, but cabinetry and carpentry were a far cry from surgery. After his shift, though, he cherished the time spent with Darla up there, drinking and laughing—

but mostly talking. They loved telling stories and secrets and listening to one another. All her hopes and dreams were slowly being realized the longer she was with him.

Months had passed, and even though he never pressured her or made a point to mention it, she still hadn't allowed him to make love to her. The reason was the one thing she didn't think he'd understand despite all he had trusted in her about himself and his unconventional life choices.

She sat with her back to him, cradled in his lap, his arms wrapped tightly around her. Her hands traced a path through the field of subdermal implants and scars decorating his arms. The shooting star streaming overhead was all the sign she needed, and she rolled over to face him. He looked at her, soaking her in with his deep gray eyes. And he smiled. As if bottled inside her for an eternity, her words poured from her lips. And he just listened.

Darla opened her eyes. Though still in the dark, the blackness was nowhere near comparable to that of her drug-induced dream world. The narcotic cocktail David referred to as Twilight Sleep locked her psyche in a cycle of waking dreams. Part morphine and part scopolamine. All diabolical. And it was wearing off.

Recognizance sluggishly returned and the piercing silence in her room—her cage—exacerbated her pain. She felt every sting, every stitch holding her together, heard her organs working to keep her calm—to keep her alive.

thump-thump-thump-thump thump-thump

Her heart bounced inside her ribcage and her weak, emaciated frame jolted in time to the unhealthy rhythm. A stray hair tickled her cheek, but as she went to brush it away, her arm felt heavy. Not as though it was bound by straps to the bed frame—that was a separate feeling altogether—but as if it was asleep. She reached up, electrified pins and needles racing up her arm to her hand. But when her hand never reached her face and the burning pain grew unbearable she realized why...

He had taken her other arm.

"You're a fucking lunatic!"

David glanced over at the man shackled to the floor as he returned to his work area. Even through the clean room curtain, he could read the man's fear. "Okay, doc," he said, "time to get a new line." He gently placed the severed arm down on his table and peered through the break in the curtains. "Really, I'm not a bad person. And you've been very helpful so far. As much as I appreciate it, I'd hate to think you've outlived that usefulness."

The doctor growled and yanked on his tethers. The metal links clanked on the sterile green linoleum. "Where's my daughter? I fucking want to see my daughter... Now!"

"Doctor, please. Aren't you tired of the same song and dance, day after day after day? I know I am."

"You can't keep me here. You can't keep doing this to yourself or to tha- that woman."

David banged the table with his fist. He stepped to the curtain and flung it open. Halogen brilliance flooded into his workspace and cast stark shadows across his face. His long beard—scraggly strands of competing and complimenting colors—curled down to the middle of his chest and pointed to Gustave Doré's *Depiction of Satan* tattooed in blacks and grays across his torso. The light hitting his head obscured his features, making the two subdermal implants above his skull's frontal bone rise up like horns. "I can and *will* keep you here. Until I've completed what I've set out to do." Though he smiled at the doctor, his sullen and sunken eyes looked more sinister than tired in the harsh glare of the homemade operating theater. "And only *then* will you get to see your daughter."

"You son of a bitch!" The doctor launched himself as far as the chains would take him, creating a racket of metal on metal.

Caught off guard, David bounced backward and bumped into a metal basin full of ice, and bins of assorted limbs and appendages at random stages of decay—failed experiments and works in progress. The writhing, quivering mounds of maggots that were feeding on the dead flesh, cleaning the wounds of detritus, crumbled from the sudden blow. David composed himself and checked the table's stability. "You almost got me there, doc. Thanks for reminding me I need more ice, though."

Both men stopped and looked up at the rectangular opening in the ceiling. Moans and mumbles echoed down through the sheet metal chute. David smiled. "Aw... She's talking in her sleep again." The sentiment seemed to warm his heart and he glowed for a second.

"Fuck me." The doctor glowered at him. "I swear to Christ I will let you and your *plaything* upstairs die if you do anything to my Lauren."

"Hmm." David stepped forward. "If I remember correctly..." He tapped his finger against his upper lip as if contemplating his next words. "Oh yeah. 'Into whatsoever houses I enter, I will enter to help the sick, and I will abstain from all intentional wrong-doing and harm, especially from abusing the bodies of man or woman, bond or free.'"

The doctor scoffed. "You gotta be kidding me! Pulling out the Oath like you have a clue what it stands for."

David stroked his beard—an artifact of anxiety from his younger years when he would nervously rub his head in times of trouble or confrontation. "You swore it. Not me." He paused for a moment to savor the unique sensation of his elongated fingers caressing the hair, titillated as the nerves fired impulses to his brain. "I'm starting to really feel my new fingertips, Doc. I think my body finally accepted the nerves and they're healing."

"I don't care, you fucking psychopath," the doctor spat. "We'll continue playing it your way. Just understand... I give less than two shits about that antiquated, Greek horseshit. I just want my daughter unharmed and set free."

"Like I said. I'm not a bad pers—" David noticed the doctor grimace, a wash of concern and disgust covering his face. "What's your problem now?"

"Your ribs... what happened to them?" He nodded to the line of eggplant colored bruises and sutures sealing up the amateurish incision under his diaphragm. "You know what you're making me do is insanely foolish and unhealthy, but doing that shit to yourself is suicidal."

David touched the tender areas under his tattoo where he had his four floating ribs removed to make ready the next stage of his plan. "What are you talking about? I didn't know you cared, but you know *exactly* what I'm doing whether you admit it or not."

The doctor snickered. "Well, for all I know or care, you broke your ribs so you could suck your own dick."

David snarled, looking for something to throw at him, but found nothing in reach. He collected himself and smiled. "I'll admit I've been a little impatient and took it upon myself to start without the maestro." The bruises lightened when he pressed on them and he savored the burning pain. "You're not the only professional I have at my disposal. Well... actually, you *are* at the moment. Unfortunately, Doctor Savartin managed to sneak something sharp past me. A shame, really. She's sleeping pretty on a nice dose of Devil's Breath so she won't be bothering me until we need her again."

"Sick bastard."

"But you, my good man..." David leaned in, giving the doctor a better look at his subdermal horns and the shimmer in his eyes of a man on some unholy mission. "Listen, I didn't just *choose* you straight outta the blue or because you have such an outstanding rating on plasticsurgeon.com—you *do* by the way. Good job." He stood up straight and twirled the tip of his beard between his thumb and fused index/middle finger combination. "I did my homework."

"What the hell are you talking about?" asked the doctor. "You aiming to make me just as friggin' crazy as you?"

"Does Doctor Samuel Rosen ring any bells?"

The doctor's face dropped.

"I know you were one of his... disciples. Before his fall from grace, that is. You know, radical theories on reconstructive surgery. Modifying the human body. Advancing evolution through neural remapping."

"You're even *more* fucked in the head than I thought," the doctor said. Another wave of anxiety rushed through him as he trembled. "Rosen was a quack! We all realized that. Eventually."

"The science was sound. And you know it!"

The doctor clambered to his knees, stretching as far as the chains would allow, genuflecting before his captor. "Don't make me do this. Please. Anything but this. I'm begging you. I can't apply his theories on human subjects. It's not ethical, not even practical to attempt to do so by myself."

David shook his horned head. "I think we're beyond begging, I'm afraid. We both have missions, and this is yours. You have sweet Lauren to think about."

The doctor's face burned red with rage. "But even if the body doesn't reject the procedure and everything attaches anatomically, having wings with no arms will never work!"

"Who said anything about having no arms?" David glanced over at the two arms with missing fifth digits chilling in their ice bath. They were the perfect size for his needs, delicate enough not to succumb to gravity, and gifted to him by the only person to ever understand his dream. This allowed him to retain his own arms and, after some final modifications, enabled him to maximize his potential and attain the image of near-angelic perfection he'd sought after all his life.

Apotemnophilia.

She could never say the word correctly, always devolving into gibberish like, "aponomanoma-feel ya," and such. They had many laughs over it. He admired her innocence in the face of such adversity and didn't take her plight lightly. He still just listened. Listened as she explained the horrors of feeling like she was in the wrong body, how her flesh and bones felt foreign to her, and that the only solution was to amputate. Her parents didn't agree or understand, refusing her needs at every turn—to keep their little girl safe and whole in spite of the ugliness she felt.

Eventually, she learned to keep the urges a secret, settling for the release she attained through cutting—all while dreaming away, fantasizing of finally feeling at peace in her body. Body Integrity Identity Disorder aside, she knew it was a symptom of her mind, but the feeling—the knowing—that biology had it all wrong, kept her crippled with anxiety. Even if she couldn't convince her parents or a doctor to help her, she still preferred the idea of cutting off the bad parts, leaving her without proper replacements, than living with them forever.

David stroked her soft hair while she stared up into the heavens and continued. She finally felt safe enough with him to share the history of her missing pinky fingers, which were too long and unsightly to continue to be a part of her. The desire had grown too strong, the meds and constant scrutiny of her parents becoming inadequate for her condition. The fingers had to go; they weren't hers, they didn't belong. With the help of her mother's pinking shears, she ended up in the ER, followed by months in the psychiatric facility next door. But, at twenty years old, it was the first time she had ever experienced an orgasm. And it changed her world. The intoxication of release was addictive.

They spent the next few months discovering each other's bodies. David took care to respect her limits, wanting nothing more at that point than for her to feel safe and wanted, to revel in their newfound art of seduction while still quenching her need for anatomical subtraction. She found his love and tenderness supportive and fascinating as they experimented with levels of intensity. Perversity in the eyes of most, but magical to their hearts and minds.

It wasn't so much the pain; *that* she could handle. Ever since she first discovered the reward for the agony she put herself through, first alone, then with help from David, she relished the waves of white-hot torture and the orgasmic release that always followed. But in her current state, she was more a prisoner than a willing participant, suffering through the aftermath of his brand of haphazard surgery.

Every now and then, David told her he still loved her—always and forever—but he had grown dark in his transformation, his journey to ultimate satisfaction. Yet, Darla knew nothing would quench his need. His search for ways to achieve a newer vision of self, that superior manipulation of the carcass God had originally cursed him with, would never end. Just like her quest for the perfect sensation, an adequate fulfillment of her physical being, she knew it was a fool's errand.

As she lay there alone and tethered to the bed, bags of IV medication pumping through her body, she knew she'd never reach that enlightened state again. And neither would David... she was running out of body parts to offer him. A tear rolled down her face onto the pillow. She selfishly wished—more than anything at this point—that he would just inject her with enough Twilight Sleep to keep her lost in that dark place forever, trapped inside her own mind, and free from her heart that kept breaking more and more for him.

David loved carving animals out of wood. Little, whittled totems of nature's wonder and grace. Yet, he gave each of these creations wings—a side-effect, Darla had grown to learn, of his fascination with his ultimate plan, his deep-seated desire to alter himself in homage to those wonders in the sky. Once, she'd asked for a carving of a lion complete with a full mane of feline majesty.

That was the first and only time she asked...

So in love, Darla could not see his spiral into chaos until it was too late. Nor could she anticipate becoming his captive, bound and cursed by that same swell of affection free-flowing through her ventricles and atriums, coursing through her arteries and veins, unprotected from his smothering, his danger. His obsession.

If only she had heeded the signs and let emotions take the backseat for once...

Again, living as a prisoner in her own mind and lost in the fog of the drug, Darla had no idea how long she'd been unconscious. With all the meds David was pumping into her, he could have easily forgotten she existed, all alone and desperate for his attention in this small room, somewhere. Set it and forget it... until he came calling for something else he needed from her, of course.

From the condition of her wounds and the color of her skin, Darla guessed that she was at one with the dreaming void for about ten to twelve days. How her brain wasn't fried by now, she couldn't fathom. Now awake with her full remaining senses coming alive, she agreed with her estimate the instant she smelled the condition David had left her in. Immediately, she grew self-conscious and embarrassed. She wondered what he would think of her now, in *this* state. Was this what he wanted from her? Was this how little he thought of her now?

She got angry.

A flood of charged emotions rippled over her skin, boiling in her belly up to her tear-stung eyes. This *is* what David wanted! She is *exactly* where he wanted her to be! Had his love always been a lie? Had he been full of shit all this time?

Or had *she*?

The blinding light of the overhead surgical lamp caused sweat to dampen the doctor's brow. Trepidation and doubt threatened to overwhelm him. His brain fought to work all the angles, yet he still wondered how in holy hell he was going to perform this radical operation. With barely any planning, he'd only have the assistance of Doctor Savartin, who was pretty much a zombie slave to David's mind-fuck drugs. Even if this type of surgery wasn't completely unethical and experimental, it would take an expert team weeks—if not longer—to map out how it all would work. The success rate would be minimal—best case scenario.

This was *not* a best-case scenario, even in the mildest of terms.

Lauren... If I do this, I get my Lauren back.

That notion was the only thing keeping him alive with a modicum of sanity remaining. If it wasn't for her, he would've found a reason for David to end his life long ago. But he still didn't have a positive outlook. How could he? He was bruised and scraped and in constant fear for his life *on top* of the malnutrition and mind-altering exhaustion. That was his biggest fear, being so tired that he'd royally fuck up and, perhaps, kill David in the process. While that wasn't an altogether bad plan, David was the sole keeper of his daughter's fate.

The exhaustion kept him docile; the fear over his daughter kept him obedient and, unlike Savartin, free of the drugs. If he just held on a little longer, let the memories of his Lauren stroll through his mind to keep him honest *and* vigilant, everything would work out. And this nightmare would end.

He stared at David laying prone on the operating table. Every conceivable tool and device was present on the surrounding metal carts, all laid out in specific order. Where he had acquired all that equipment was a mystery in and of itself—another conundrum to add to the enigma that was David Pace. He even, at some point, had to have conned someone to take X-Rays and run blood work to make all of this happen. If he hadn't been in mortal terror for the better part of a month, stuck God knows where as a prisoner, he'd be impressed.

Wires linked David's body to monitoring devices, while Savartin busied herself with intubating the patient. In the corner of the counter, Darla's two arms, already modified into wings, waited on ice for the doctor to attach them to their new body. Everything seemed in order. Savartin appeared attentive enough—no doubt due to a system full of scopolamine, which allowed the doctor control over her actions. "Let's get this train wreck started."

"Yes, Doctor."

"Scalpel." Savartin placed it in his waiting hand. He leaned forward to begin, catching sight of David's pulsing jugular underneath the surgical drape. *It would be so easy...*

About ten days had passed since the surgery, and David was up and about, walking through his home—against doctor's orders and without sterile bandages covering any of the traumatized areas. Despite the doctor's rousing success—given the limited planning and equipment available—bedrest had grown tedious and David couldn't lay on his stomach and stare at the walls any longer. Boredom made him restless and being restless made him anxious. He had to move around, had to feel better on his own terms. His mind governed his body, not the other way around. Confidence was key, and he'd just will himself to mend quicker if need be, regardless of his impressive rate of healing already apparent.

Definitely mind over matter.

With the new figurine he'd carved in his down time just for her, he entered Darla's room. Positive that she thought he'd forgotten all about her request, his extended fingers caressed the wooden—wingless—lion, complete with a full mane. He hovered over her as she lay in half-consciousness, caught in the waking dream-world he left her in for days at a time to keep her safe.

Her eyelids fluttered, sometimes getting stuck half open, making her appear awake. But David knew she couldn't wake up—not with the amount of Twilight Sleep he'd pumped into her.

He stepped back and placed the sculpture on her nightstand, facing her. Immortalizing and idolizing the moment, he watched her eyeballs rolled back and forth. "Bet you thought I forgot all about it, huh?" he said, and smiled. "I wonder what you're dreaming about." She had been there for him through it all. The fact he was lucky to have found her was never lost on him; he appreciated her love, tenderness, and understanding, as well as her willingness and devotion. All necessary things to complete his transformation. All things he felt for her in return.

That was why he needed to end it… to release her from her mortal coil.

With a deep sigh, he resisted the urge to cry as he removed Darla's straps and IV. Instead, he focused on the bigger picture—the exquisite pain and weight of his healing wings. He leaned over her again, this time with a syringe filled with a fatal dose of Twilight Sleep. David stroked her cheek. "Thank you for everything, Baby."

Darla groaned, her eyelids fluttering and her head twitching. She was waking up.

"Shit!" Panicking, David jabbed the needle into her jugular vein.

A crash came from downstairs, a solid thud followed by a clang of metal hitting the floor. David spun around towards the door. The sudden commotion pulled him from his task and he failed to press the plunger, leaving the syringe buried up to its barrel in Darla's neck. "What the fuck?"

He ignored the pain in his back, yet his new appendages fluttered as if in reaction to his requirement to leave Darla's room to investigate. With Savartin no longer in the picture, it could only be the doctor. David still hadn't revealed where he was keeping the doctor's daughter, and since he'd forced the man to wear the shock collar to move about freely during David's recovery, he'd definitely become more submissive. Having played a game of show-and-tell with the collar, the brain-fried Savartin, and a hidden electric perimeter set to unleash a crippling charge to the neck if crossed, David was positive the doctor got the picture.

Nothing appeared out of place as he traveled through his keep, searching all the rooms and corners along the way. The only place left to check was his work area in the basement which housed a separate room with the operating theater and the good doctor. He wondered what the man had gotten himself into; perhaps he was trying to pry off his collar with one of the surgical tools. Unless the doctor's head shrunk, or he was somehow able to cut through the metal or padlock, he wasn't getting it off.

"Doc?" David called. "I hope you're not doing anything stupid down there." He slunk down the stairs, cursing for not having armed himself for protection in his still vulnerable state of recovery. "If you thought the shocks hurt, just imagine what'll happen next if you fuck with me."

No response save for the static hum of the fluorescent lights.

David reached the bottom step and turned the corner, taking care not to hit his wings against the doorframe. He found an unconscious and bleeding doctor sprawled out on the floor. Scattered all around him were the sources of the noise; the doctor had crashed into a cart loaded with stainless steel containers on his way down to the hard floor. Flooded with random, conflicting emotions—relief, concern, amusement—David watched blood pool around the doctor's head from a deep gash in the back of his skull.

A plume of smoke wafted from the shock collar, bringing with it the smell of electrical discharge. The powerful device had proved reliably tamperproof. The shock must have zapped the shit out of the doctor, sending him collapsing into the metal cart and to where David now found him.

Startled awake, Darla bolted upright. Every remaining nerve she had roared to life, sending lightning streaks of pain through her body. The full syringe, now starting to bend from its weight, bounced in her peripheral vision. She drew in a deep, sharp breath and tried to scream. But all that came out was a raspy whine. She was so dehydrated she thought she could drink the ocean. If this was what it felt like to be on the brink of death, she welcomed the imminent numbness of finality.

As she sat there, wondering why her straps were off, she scanned the room for David. Her eyes were stinging from disuse, and she was so dry and withered it amazed her that she held enough moisture to supply the tears that brimmed in them. At least her hearing was fine. Even in her fleeting stupor, she'd heard David softly speaking—and the loud metallic crash. Now she heard nothing, but knew he was lurking somewhere. She strained to listen, the silence's pressure building in her ears.

Compared to the rest of the pain she was feeling, the syringe poking out of her neck was merely an annoyance, bouncing in and out of view as she assessed her situation. She knew without question what it contained. Yet, why David hadn't finished the job, she couldn't answer.

Sudden noise from elsewhere gave her a start. Her mind scrambled for a way out, a plan to gain safety and distance, any distance from David. She rolled on her back then to her side, wincing as she pushed herself up with her left arm nub, and swung her leg off the side of the bed. Her foot touched the grimy Berber rug that lay on the floor under the bed—and it felt amazing, as if her skin had never touched anything so soft.

She had no idea where she was, let alone where to go or how to get out of this place. For all she knew, he was keeping her underground or on an isolated farm somewhere.

David's voice drifted upstairs sounding angry and purposeful, followed by more metallic banging. If she ever had a chance to escape, it was now. Damn her mutilated body... she had to try!

Across the room, she spotted a small rectangular hatch in the middle of the wall and her heart leaped. *A laundry chute! A way out!* Then doubt crashed around her. Even if she could manage to open the door without arms, she might as well be in Siberia. Not having been out of bed for God knows how long, she knew she couldn't trust her nonexistent sense of balance. Still groggy, she tested her limits and stood up on her leg and immediately dropped to the carpet.

Darla seized up in pain, hoping she didn't alert David in the process. Anger built inside of her and eclipsed the pain. Planting her foot into the texture of the Berber beneath her, she pushed, locking her heel and extending her knee until she wiggled along closer to the door and the chute behind it. A sad little inch worm struggling toward safety.

Bend, push, bend, push. Over and over until she bumped her head against the wall. Above her was the hatch to the laundry chute. What was beyond that, she couldn't think about. Over-thinking caused doubt. Doubt caused panic. Panic caused fight, flight, or freeze, and all she could do in her condition was freeze. Freezing would allow David to find her.

No. She needed to get the fuck up off the floor, pry that goddamned door open—with her face if she needed to—and take her chances at the bottom. With her back now pressed up against the wall, Darla shimmied and wriggled up its length. She pushed the bounds of the strength in her remaining leg until she was flush with the wall.

The chute door was waist high on her. She contorted her torso while maintaining feeble balance, praying she didn't fall over, until the stub of her right arm scraped against the lip of the hatch. Rivers of sweat stung her wide eyes. She worked her nub back and forth, grimacing, hoping not to undo her stitches. Just as she almost relented, she pried it open and fell into the gap up to her shoulder, the corner of the door gouging her soft underarm tissue.

But she got it open!

Using her shoulder and chin, she pushed herself further inside the chute. The darkness within unnerved her; she had no way of knowing how deep or steep the chute was, let alone where it ended.

Made it this far. Can't give up now. If I just... lodge... myself against the walls... and take it a little bit at a time, I will make it. I have to make it.

Inside the laundry chute she went, her cold, naked skin rubbing against dust-covered sheet metal. With all her might, she pressed herself against the chute to prevent the thin metal from pushing outward and popping. Running out of strength, she wondered how long she could keep up this pace. The metal rivets cut into her skin. Burrs of old welds took their share of flesh, as well.

But she persisted... determined to escape this torment, or die trying. This laundry chute would not be her tomb.

Around a curve in the chute, pale light fought through the darkness of her steep free climb. She could hear David somewhere in the distance grumbling and groaning still, moving stuff around. After all her progress, after all the effort and willpower she summoned, she was bringing herself right to him. Without a backup plan, she froze, unable to will her muscles to obey her commands any longer. Her back and leg seized from overexertion and she went limp, sliding down the rest of the chute into the light. Into the fire of her keeper's will.

Something large tumbled down the laundry chute in the ceiling of David's operating theater. As he finished picking up the doctor's mess, he watched Darla fall out of the ceiling and hit the floor with a hard rebound. If it wasn't for all the noise of her bouncing around against the sides of the chute, he would've thought she'd just passed through a membrane in the ether and into his reality. It took all he had not to laugh, but on the flip side, it took all he had not to march right over and crush her skull for ruining his well-crafted plan for her.

Darla groaned and fought for focus as the room spun around her at Mach speed. She had no idea where in the house she was, but she knew David was near. With a surge of fear-charged adrenaline, she rolled over onto her back and scanned the room for a place to hide. She heard movement coming from the next room. Coming closer.

David stood on the other side of the curtain, his features obscured by the heavy plastic. But even half-conscious, Darla knew it was him. She had always remarked on his imposing stature and, and with the ceramic horn implants, his shadowy form looked like the devil himself cast against vinyl. Yet, she saw something else helping to paint the newest picture of the man she loved, something that seemed out of place and natural at once.

"Darla..." He called out for her. The lovelessness in his voice hurt her more than the syringe he'd stabbed into her neck. "That wasn't the smartest thing to do." His subdued outline grew longer across the curtain; his footsteps echoing closer.

She forced her tired and bleeding foot to push her along the floor and closer to the wall, out of sight, out of reach. Through all that had happened and what they had shared, after every blissful, sexual odyssey that made them who they were, all she wanted at that point were her arms back... if not for anything more than to cover herself, to wail uncontrollably into her palms, to ball up her fists and beat them against her skull. She'd give back every moment of ecstasy they'd shared, every quiver of passion from the blade of their knife, to feel safe again. Like he used to make her feel. Safe when his mind was whole.

"I only want to help ease your pain. End your suffering."

Cowering, she pulled her knee up, protectively, to her chest. "I'm only suffering because of you. You call this *love*? *This*?" She looked down over what remained of her body—all stitches and bruises remnants of her extremities. Covered in filth, her frail body glistened with sweat. "I trusted you and all you did was take and take. You've just about killed me." She wept, the pain in her heart unbearable. "Just finish the fucking job then!"

The doctor had no idea how long he'd been unconscious. His eyes rolled open. Just the weight of his shifting eyelids brought rivers of agony across his head. He thought he was in the dark, and heard distant voices murmuring, then realized he was face down on the floor of David's work area. His head felt heavy and damp. A painful check revealed the back of his skull had been busted open. Even for a spot with very little muscle and blood flow, it still bled like a son of a bitch. The distant murmurs persisted—two voices—one sounded weak, the other confrontational.

Had to be David.

He forced his eyes wide and everything blurred as if staring at television static through cheese cloth. Staying still until the wave of nausea rolled over him and away, he dreaded what he might see once his eyes and mind were able to refocus. The not-so-distant bantering continued, and he assumed the female voice belonged to Darla. Even though he had yet to meet her awake and coherent during this mindfuck of an experience, he gathered it was her from the fragments of phrases that made it through his spinning thoughts.

The overhead lights finally chased the fuzziness away and he fought to sit upright. As he turned his head, the pain from his skull raced up his nerves. He blinked the remaining blurriness from his vision to see David, naked and framed in the threshold to the operating theater, standing over Darla, posturing and talking with his hands. When he saw David's new "wings" protruding from his shoulder blades, rising and falling with every bodily movement, he felt sick to his stomach. Not so much from the sight of it, but for the fleeting sense of shameless pride in what he had managed to accomplish under such duress.

While David's body had yet to accept the nerve endings of the new additions—if they ever would—they still looked majestic. A Cretaceous angel—the flightless, featherless bird of prey. And that summed up the man that was David Pace. A true beast.

The doctor witnessed the result of his obscene work. If only Doctor Rosen could see him now, surpassing his old mentor's wildest dreams and, in a way, his genius.

First, he had created a bird-like carpometacarpus by fusing the outer bones of the wrist and the hand bones. By allowing the thumb to remain free, the appendage resembled the alula, which helps birds in flight. All the other fingers he had fused together. The hardest part had been rearranging David's muscle and skin to allow anatomic cohesion with Darla's upper arms, which would allow potential articulation of the new bone arrangements.

How David was already upright and moving was beyond his comprehension; he should still be in a bed recovering and pumped full of meds for several weeks—at least! Instead, he was up and animated, almost as if high on methamphetamines, ignorant to the pain and trauma his body was in. *How long have I been out of it?*

The doctor had made so many cuts and errors along the way, hoping for the sake of his daughter he didn't kill David in the process. More sutures, staples, and bruises covered David's back as the healing process continued. In spite of himself, he wished he'd had the time and means necessary to build a brace for David, an armature constructed from surgical steel for stability and durability to graft to his body and wings. An external meshing of metal and flesh to protect the final result. Nonetheless, the most important thing left for David's body to do was allow his motor cortex to adapt and create new neural maps for the new appendages—to change his brain into a winged one.

All the blurriness dispersed from the doctor's left eye and he could clearly see the scene before him. David made a grand gesture in his speech to Darla and the wings appeared to unfurl, revealing a thin webbing between the joints not part of the original plans. The webbing looked like skin cut and stretched to suit its purpose. On both wing membranes, he saw markings, like tattoos or brandings.

When the doctor realized what they were, he vomited.

"But, Daddy," Lauren began in her little girl voice with her pleading eyes, "I don't wanna wait until summer break."

"You know I'm on rotations every weekend at the hospital this month. Besides, you're too young for tattoos, Honey."

"That's why I need a parent for the consent paperwork. And it's not like I'm asking you to pay for it. I got my own money."

"Why do you want tattoos, anyways? They're trashy and you'll regret them when you're all old and wrinkled."

"You know why!" she shouted. "They're in memory of Mom."

Her father sighed, knowing he was going to give in anyways, but still not ready to see his baby girl grow up. "But not one tattoo. Two tattoos? Angel wings? On your back, at that?"

Lauren smiled. "Where else would angel wings go? Besides, you always said Mom was an angel. Our angel."

"Angel wings for Mom, huh? You know how much that's going to hurt?"

"Yuh-huh," she said. "I'm perfectly aware. Please, Daddy."

"Okay, but not—"

Lauren jumped up and down and sprinted at her father, squealing with happiness as she embraced him and kissed his cheek. "Thank you, thank you, *thank* you!"

"All right, all right. But you have to wait until next month when I have some time off. And I'm not paying for any of it."

She squeezed him around the neck again. "I love you, Daddy."

"What the fuck did you do to my daughter?" The doctor jumped to his feet and wiped the remnants of bile from his lips and chin. Off balance with a spinning head, he grabbed David's work table to steady himself.

David stopped mid-sentence in his one-sided conversation with Darla, who remained motionless on the floor in the corner with the syringe still jabbed in her neck. His hands were still raised as if some mad preacher delivering a righteous sermon to his flock had infiltrated his soul. He turned his head ever so slightly until only one eye peeked around the side of his new wing. His slick sneer would've certainly driven the doctor further over the edge if he had seen it. "Well, hello there, sleepy-head."

Brought to tears upon seeing his Lauren's wing tattoos, the doctor fought through the sobs to speak. "What did you do? You said we had a deal." He dropped down to his knees.

David turned finally, standing naked and engorged, towering over the collapsed doctor. "As I've just made abundantly clear to my dearest Darla, my vision—my elevation to superiority—trumps any *deal* you thought we had."

"Fucking monster..."

"And, to be honest with ya, I really thought the wings-on-wings aesthetic would be a nice touch," said David.

The doctor licked his lips and spat, sensing another bout of stomach-heaving agony. He snarled and glared up at David with palpable disgust.

"Hmm... So you think they're too much?" David wiggled his shoulders to make his new additions appear to flap and flutter. He nodded his head in the direction of the far corner of the room and the doctor followed his gaze. Savartin's body was propped up against the wall, a plastic bag cinched over her head. The contorted expression of abject fear frozen on her face was evident even through the cloudy plastic. The doctor choked back a whimper.

"Doctor Savartin finished up since you were still passed out from exhaustion, or stress, or whatever it was this time. Her last task before fulfilling her usefulness. Plus, after that zapping demo I gave you, she became unhinged. Besides, I didn't think you'd be up for the job. You know, considering..." David flapped one more time to accentuate his meaning.

"Sorry about the head, though," he said as he feigned pain, grabbing the back of his head in a similar spot. "When you passed out after shocking the fuck outta yourself, you dropped like a sack of shit and clipped your noggin on the corner of the bench." He chuckled. "I'm no doctor, so I just left you there. I'm sure you'll be fine."

The doctor scrambled to his feet and lunged for David. "We had a deal!"

The doctor spanned the distance between them so quickly that David panicked. Surprisingly, despite his head wound and exhaustion, he still had some life left in in that feeble frame of his.

"Why?" the doctor screamed over and over. He rammed his shoulder into David's midsection, carrying him back against the wall and almost crushing his new appendages. Flinging his fists in a whirlwind of hate and anger, not caring where they landed as long as they landed on David, his banshee wails turned to sobbing and slowly his momentum diminished. "You evil mother fucker…"

From the counter that dug into his lower back, David grabbed for anything of substance to ward off the raving doctor.

Even in his state, the doctor's punches still had some sting. "I'm going to kill you," he cried. "… Lauren. Why?"

With a blur of surgical steel, the doctor's ranting stopped. David back-pedaled into the operating room to get away from the arterial spray surging out of the doctor's opened throat. Blood coated his hand and the pair of tying forceps he had used to fend off the doctor's ill-fated attack. In the background, Darla finally saw what David had done to himself.

Breathing heavy and still surging with adrenaline, he watched the doctor—the man who had helped him achieve his vision—gasping for air while clawing at his gushing throat. The moment felt bittersweet for David. He wasn't about to let the doctor—or anyone for that matter—end his dream, but he appreciated the man for his skills and truly respected the extent he'd gone to for the sake of his daughter. And even for the care he'd given Darla in between her surgeries.

As the doctor bled out on his floor, David's thoughts took flight. *What if I need more medical attention? How do I acclimate back into society if I'm not completely healed?* The idea that he'd now need to find a new doctor to assist in his healing angered him. He cursed himself for not anticipating the anger the doctor would feel at the sight of his daughter's excised tattoos. *Why the fuck didn't I lock him back up?*

Darla took this moment, this break in David's awareness as he watched the doctor die, to make a play against him, her captor… her lover. She concentrated all her energy, focusing on the perfect time, readying herself to kick the steel rolling cart that separated them, right into his legs. She knew she was too weak for her plan to be effective, but she needed to try. She needed an end to this nightmare. Not only for her, but for David as well. He had taken this beyond too far—his insanity was evil. Plain and simple.

One.

David snapped his head to the side. His neck cracked. Click. Click. Pop.

Two.

He inhaled sharply and held the breath, his sinewy muscles rippling.

Three!

David turned around just as Darla thrust out her leg. Though weak, she mustered enough strength to send the cart shooting into his turning knee. Still sidetracked executing the doctor, he stumbled forward as his knee twisted at an awkward angle. He plunged his hands in front of him to break his fall—muscle memory taking over. Yet, his modified fingers took the brunt of the fall, bending painfully backward until they snapped askew in all directions.

With a bounce and a grunt, his head hit the cold floor, face first. Blood sprayed from his nose and then from his mouth from that well-placed heel kick. "You bitch," he groaned, spitting blood. "I'm going to put you out of your misery now."

"David, please," Darla said, as tears streamed anew. "You don't have to be like this. You need help, you can change. We can get help together. I love you, please."

He crept closer to her on broken hands.

His bloody grin, chipped teeth and all, ravaged her soul. Darla looked deep into his eyes, knowing they spoke volumes of his dementia, knowing this was the end without his having to say another word. But he did...

"Change? I've already changed," he informed her as he pulled himself up onto her worn and crippled body. "I've become Divine. And you were an integral part of it all. I thought you understood that." He was right on top of her now, crushing what remained of her fleshly prison. "Please, believe me... I've never loved or needed anyone more."

Darla craned her head up to the ceiling and wailed, the syringe in her neck bobbing and swaying with every sob. The grief of the moment overwhelmed her, yet she refused—if this was truly the end—to bring that sadness and fear with her in death.

David pulled her head close to his, cradling it in his left hand. His other hand pressed the plunger and sent the dose of Twilight Sleep into her veins. "I *will* always love you."

"I forgive you, David."

He told her he would never leave her, that their love—their bond—was eternal. No power was strong enough to break what they shared. Yet, she'd believed for too long that everything breaks, every positive has a negative. Though her love bubbled over, her heart expanding to the brink of cracking from joy, she was powerless in his arms. Blind to the warning signs, the what-ifs, the danger of loving someone so completely.

A part of her died that night, the part that loved him and still wanted him. With her head nestled in the crook of his neck, fitting like the missing piece of their unfinished puzzle, she clenched her teeth—the only defense she had left—into his jugular, taking him by surprise. As she gnawed, he struggled, his blood draining from his body until he collapsed upon her. She willed herself not to gag or relent as his life gushed into her throat and out the sides of her mouth. No amount of modification or fleshly improvements would—or could—save him now. With her leg locked behind him, wrapped up in his wings—her arms—she felt him going limp, but prayed he'd die before the overdose locked her in dreamtime forever.

And despite all he had put her through, all the anguish she'd suffered at his hands and his dementia, she could not bring herself to hate—or blame—him for what he was. He would remain the only one to truly ever understand her. She prayed that the memories of his affection wouldn't fade in the afterlife as she held him tightly, savoring and memorizing every nuance of the moment. This was how it was meant to end. Everything felt perfect, he felt perfect. And she hoped that feeling would never end, but as all good things sometimes do....

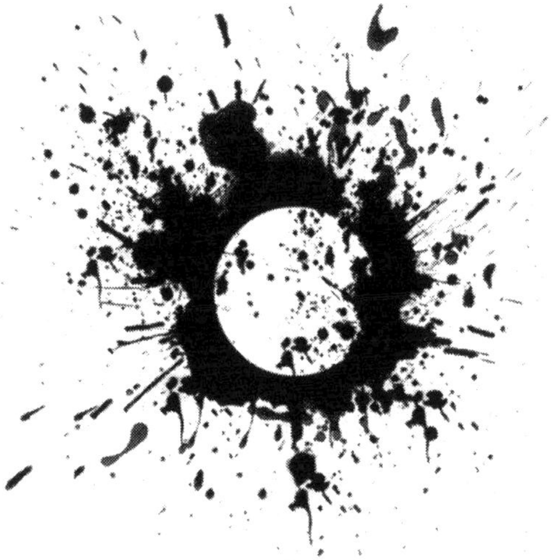

THE JATINGA EFFECT

Swirling shapes in her refrigerator's reflective shine grabbed her attention as she walked by; the woman knew something was wrong. An immediate feeling of loss, a parental phantom limb sensation, made her go limp. She swayed, grabbing the countertop for balance and staring into the remnants of the tiny water splashes in the sink. In those minuscule drops she found more trepidation. Though vague in detail, maternal instinct rarely lied.

Focusing, she plugged the drain and turned the faucet on, full blast. Something horrible had happened, and she needed to know *what*. She stared into the maelstrom where the flowing water met the rising pool, and muttered in her native tongue.

Less skilled at scrying than her other *daayani* abilities, her power of retrocognition was limited by her devotion to other spells and incantations. Gazing into the running water, images moved fast and clear, creating a more cohesive vision. Performing this advanced witchcraft drained her of considerable energy, yet, she knew—no, not knew, *felt*—that the direness of this situation would require all her strength and concentration if it was to work.

As usual, Edson sleepwalked through his day, start to finish. If it wasn't for the trash compactor inside his skull squeezing his bloodshot baby-blues through his sockets, he would've thought he was in a perpetual dream-state. The fringe of his vision blurred as he gazed at his computer screen wondering if he really *needed* to finish this report today.

His thoughts drifted to his newest bad habit—sleep driving. It happened again today, becoming all too frequent for his liking. He recalled his sleep study results. A quality of life disrupting sleep disorder was what the doc had called it. *Figures.* He called it just another reason to eat a bullet. *I'll have another heaping portion of shitty life, please. And a side order of I'll just go fuck myself then, too.*

His phone rang, the sound drilling into his skull. Cursing, he scanned the phone's LCD screen but didn't see any numbers, no extension listed. And all the lines appeared to be ringing at once, the red lights flashing like the warning of a runaway train hurtling toward an intersection.

"Hello?" Nothing but a weird digital silence answered back. "Hello? May I help you?" A shrill spike of noise pierced his brain through the ear piece. He yanked the handset away, cringing and confused. *What the fuck!*

"Hello," a faint voice on the other end replied.

Edson eased the phone back to his ear and listened for a second before speaking. "Hello? Can I help you?"

"It's all *your* fault." A woman with a thick Indian accent spoke. "You *will* pay for what happened to my Anusha." Edson had trouble following, but he found her intonation fluent enough to make her point. "She was my morning star and *you* snuffed her out."

"I'm sorry ma'am...." Edson scrambled for his words. "You must be mistaken or have the wrong number. I don't understand what you're talking a—"

The voice cut him off. "You left her to die. Prepare yourself, Edson Doherty."

"*Excuse* me? How do y--?"

Click.

Edson stared at the phone for a few seconds, cock-eyed and now more confused. "I need a nap," he said, dropping the handset back in the cradle.

His cell phone buzzed, rattling against his keyboard. He snatched it up and flicked open the text app.

ba arlte l! d'dio yhe tho onwd tiviar o'yu t'ra fer?

Edson shook his head, trying to set the sluggish marbles in his skull back into place.

hey dildo! you down for trivia later at the bar?

"That makes much more sense." He grumbled into his hands, rubbing the fuzz from his eyes. "I *really* need a nap."

As if hearing Edson mutter was an invitation to converse, Bogdan poked his head over the shared divider between cubicles. In his thick Russian accent he asked, "You observed Celebrity Dance-Off on the television last night, yes?"

Edson looked up into the fifty-something's brown eyes. "No, Bogdan. I didn't *observed* Celebrity Dance-Off last night." Edson's eyes pleaded for the man to leave him alone.

"That is too bad. It was hash-tag amazing-spheres."

"I think you mean *amaze-balls*?" Edson curtly replied. It wasn't that he disliked the big Russian, he just preferred not to see his face, hear him speak, or smell whatever the hell he microwaved for lunch every day.

Then there was Tim…

Edson heard Tim plodding down the carpeted aisle like an elephant. He grumbled again. *Please… keep walking*. Life wasn't that fair.

"Hey fellas!" Tim, over-caffeinated and preferring to go by 'T-Bone', asked enthusiastically, "You catch last night's—"

Don't say it!

"—Celebrity Dance-Off?"

Fuuuuuckkk...

Bogdan's eyes sparkled at his comrade in commercial bullshit. "Yes! It was awesome cream."

Edson sighed. "It's sauce, Bogdan. Awesome *sauce*." He glowered at Tim. "If you're gonna teach him these obnoxious catch phrases, Tim, can you make sure you teach him right?"

Tim scowled. "Remember, it's T-Bone there, buddy." He tossed Edson a wink and a shot from his finger gun.

"You're literally a special brand of idiot, aren't you, *T-Bone*?"

Tim's face dropped.

"I mean like special order, third-party, mongrel brand idiot you can only find at the Dollar Store."

Insulted, Tim scrunched his forehead. "Well... Your mother!" With that, he stomped away, and Edson smiled, throwing his arms over his head in victory.

Yet, he was still beyond exhaustion, feeling it in every fiber, from the tippy-top of his head to the frizzy straggles of hair on his big toe knuckles.

Bogdan's square head lingered above the partition. His unblinking eyes hovered somewhere between confusion and anger. "Why do you holler at your boy?"

Edson tried rubbing the annoying Russian out of his field of vision with the balls of his fists. "That's... that's not even—w*hy even bother*—what that... means." Bogdan made a hideous face, contorting his lips into some frightening debutante/duck hybrid before slowly dropping behind the divider as if his noggin was on an invisible elevator.

I'm surrounded by dolts.

He returned to his monitor and grimaced at the spreadsheet screaming at him with all its arbitrary colors and numbers, begging him to finish the calculations. He ran his fingertips over the keyboard and then banged ALT-TAB with burning hate. His FriendFace page filled the monitor screen. "Politics. Politics. Racist. Asshole. Racist asshole. Somebody's cat walked across their keyboard." He went down his news feed, sneering as he read the myriad of pointless comments. "So stupid... blockity, blockity, block-blocked."

As he was about to remove the latest digital "friend" from his account, the image of his boss' face, a pale red brick of a head topped with ginger sprigs of hair, popped up in the bottom corner of his screen. *What now...?*

Nothing but scrambled gibberish filled the instant message window. Edson's eyes burned and the pressure behind his sockets swelled. He squeezed them shut and rocked his head around and then opened them once more.

Come to my office... when you get a chance.

"That's just great on two different levels." Because he knew his exhaustion was possibly making him crazy and a 'when you get a chance' from his boss meant, without a doubt, right this damn second. He stood up and stretched. The fatigue dizzies continued to make his head pound and his eyes fill with dancing glitter. When it wore off he marched towards his fate, wondering what he'd done this time.

"Hold down the fort," he said, as he passed Bogdan's desk. "I got called to the principal's office." Out of the corner of his eye, he spotted Bogdan thrusting his fist up in the air in a circular motion. "Thanks, Arsenio." Edson wondered what decade Bogdan lived in inside his bulbous head.

On his travels to the wonder-filled office-wing of middle management, Edson passed Veronica's office. The door was open but it was dim inside save for the natural light of the outside world filtering in through the windows. Veronica stood facing the glass, staring out over the parking area. Edson lingered in the doorway for a second and noticed that his coworker was shivering. He peeked his head in—*not cold or anything... maybe there's a draft.*

"Hey, Ronni," he said expecting a response, a vacant head nod in the least. "You cold or something?" Nothing. "Should probably get away from the window then, late spring and all."

She shivered, facing the window and ignoring him.

"Good talk." Edson huffed and continued on his way to the boss' office—but not before noticing a distant fog rolling in over the tree-lined horizon.

Edson arrived right outside the office of douche-master extraordinaire, boss-man Aaron Hill, and paused. He dreaded any interaction with this bane of his working-class existence, but he sensed an abnormal amount of horror with this summons—no sense in making it any worse. He stood at the semi-closed office door, frowning as he rapped his knuckles on the window.

"You wanted to see me, boss?"

"Ah, yeah. Eddie." Pecking away at his keyboard, Aaron barely looked up at him. "C'mon in and have a seat." He finally hit the ENTER key and perked up, leaning into his high-back, leather executive chair. "Come, come. Sit."

"If this is about my email to Ops about having a working coffeemaker in the break area," Edson began as he sat in the chair, still feeling uneasy. "I apologize. You don't pay me enough to afford Café Beanery every day. I just *really* need my caffeine." He let loose a tiny chuckle, hoping some levity would break the ice. Then he spotted the large Café Beanery cup on Aaron's desk….

Aaron politely half-smiled, his way of saying 'shut it down'. "Actually… I asked you in here today because…"

Edson's jaw dropped, his eyes widening. On the opposite side of the building now, the fog he saw earlier from Veronica's window was creeping towards the office complex from this direction as well. It left him awestruck and he had no idea why—it just felt…off. Ominous.

Seeing Edson's face, Aaron followed his gaze out the window behind him to the low hanging clouds filling up the landscape. "It's just a fog bank, Eddie. You know, the collection of water droplets suspended in the atmosphere near the earth's surface?"

But Edson wasn't listening. His eyes were locked onto the incoming mist which was darkening by the second. He realized he was gripping the armrests too tightly when he swore he felt the building vibrate and the windows shimmy.

Aaron didn't seem to notice and grew annoyed. "Eddie... Back to business. We have important stuff to talk—"

"Boss. Look." Edson gestured to the window. Aaron just glared. "Jesus! Would you just fucking *look*?"

As Aaron turned around, Edson climbed from the chair and backed up to the doorway, half in the office and half in the hallway. "Why are you being so diffic...?" Aaron's words dropped off as he saw the darkening fog thicken. Within the gray haze, organic things moved making the mist look alive. "What the... hell...?"

They weren't the only ones in the office witnessing the event. Everyone was up and looking outside, but what really bothered Edson, what made his blood freeze in his veins, was the that all his female coworkers appeared dazed or entranced, shivering—o*r are they vibrating?*—just like Veronica had been when he walked by her office.

"Boss," Edson called. "I think you need to come out here."

Aaron stood, placing his hands on the glass, mesmerized. "Do you *see* this? What on earth...?"

"Aaron!"

"What?"

"Something's wrong!"

Aaron tore away from the window and walked towards Edson. "No shit. Ya think?"

The floor resonated and for a moment everything seemed to pulsate. Edson's ears popped and his vision blurred in unison with the shallow vibrations passing through his feet and up into his core. Aaron braced himself against his chair as a wave of nausea rolled his stomach. A quick glance into the main office alerted Edson to the same phenomenon affecting all the males. Yet, the women remained in their awkward trance-like state, rippling like rung bells.

"They look like they're phase shifting. Or changing frequencies or some shit," Aaron said, sticking his head through the doorway.

"Just like on *Star Trek*!" Bogdan came around the corner, his eyes glued to the window at the end of the hall.

"What's going on out there?" asked Edson. "What's wrong with them?"

"I don't know, but—how do you say—fans are about to spray out the shit."

Even before Bogdan had nodded to the window for them to look, Edson already knew many shits were about to spray. The sky blackened, casting erratic shadows inside the office and dimming everything despite the overhead fluorescents.

"What *is* that noise?" Aaron had to raise his voice over the incessant droning emanating from the fog bank.

The murkiness in the office deepened. Something pelted the windows and building, pinging off it in sporadic intervals. The sound echoed on all sides, some sounding stronger than the others, little tectonic percussions rattling the structure.

Edson peered out the window in Aaron's office. "Are you fucking *kidding* me?"

Out of the fog, swarms of bugs—mere specks at first—rocketed toward the windows. Splat after splat, bugs of all shapes and sizes flew into the glass like insectoid Kamikaze pilots. Edson almost laughed aloud. *What's the last thing that goes through a bug's mind when it hits a windshield?* "Its asshole," mumbled Edson, his mind floundering.

Within the span of minutes, their suicidal onslaught against the office building smeared the windows in grotesque shades of greens and yellows and purples. Aaron gawked as well, shaking his head and shrugging his shoulders with a complete inability to respond to the situation. Behind the furious swarms, an even darker collection of swirling blackness barreled out of the mist still crawling toward the complex.

From across the office, Bogdan shouted, "Birds!"

Aaron moved closer to the window because he didn't believe his ears *or* his eyes. The birds were flying so fast he couldn't identify them. In an endless frenzy of feathers, they crashed head first into the building on all sides, shaking the inner walls. Beaks smashed into windows, causing the glass to spider-web near the point of shattering. In some spots, their beaks broke through, but the birds were oddly silent until they plummeted to the ground.

"Christ, Aaron! Get away from the window!" Edson shouted.

"Holy shit," Idiot Aaron blurted, his face pressed against the window, straining to see the ground. "C'mere, you gotta see this. If they're not breakin' their necks the first try, they friggin' get up and try again!"

The more birds and bugs that flew out of the fog and into the building, the colder Edson's blood grew. The silent bombardment of the birds was what terrified him the most. Not a squeak or a squawk—just the thuds and the crackling sound of the windows giving way. And the finality of thousands of tiny snapping necks.

Another beak penetrated the window, almost stabbing Aaron in the eye as he gaped at the chaotic world outside. "Whoa, shit!" He jumped back a foot and turned to Edson who was staring at him with disbelief and disgust. "That was clo—"

The window shattered. A shockwave of transparent daggers shot inward, ripping into the side of Aaron's face before he could cover up. As he squealed in pain, birds flooded in—black and brown streaks of avian death-wish—crashing headfirst into the walls, the furniture...and Aaron. He dropped to his knees in futile defense as the birds continuously struck him, gouging and stabbing with their beaks.

Edson stood frozen, his blood finally going full glacial. Before he could snap out of it, a strong arm shoved him from the threshold and slammed Aaron's door shut before any more birds could escape into the office proper. "The birds are very angry today," said Edson's Russian savior.

Angry, possessed, or what have you, it didn't matter; neither could divert their eyes as Mother Nature ran amuck on their boss. Yet, as far as Edson could tell, Aaron wasn't the target of their fury. Even though the birds' pummeled him, shredding his flesh during his vain efforts to wave them off, their trajectory seemed aimed at Edson. Thud after thud, hitting the wall and door at maximum velocity, the birds exploded upon impact, filling up the office with an eruption of feathers like some hellish pillow fight gone wrong.

With the bird tornado situation igniting his nerves near the point of spontaneous combustion, it dawned on Edson that he hadn't heard a peep from his female coworkers. In fact, he didn't hear or see *any* of his colleagues. All that registered was the sickening cacophony of bug and bird versus brick.

"We must hide." Bogdan's abrasive voice bore into Edson's head.

"Hide? Where? Where exactly would you like to go?" Edson didn't mean to take his frustration and fear out on his coworker. After all, the man did just save him from becoming an avian pincushion. "I'm sorry, man. Between this bullshit and my eyes just wanting to close, I've just about had it."

The building was totally engulfed in the thick fog. "I understand, but this is very bad news, my friend." Bogdan paused and listened. "The birds are no more hitting the building."

"That's good news, though. Right?" Edson looked around. "Where the hell is everybody?" He was about to call out when Bogdan slapped a meaty hand over his mouth and swiftly pushed him into an alcove between offices. The Russian gave him the international hand signal for "shut the fuck up" which only confused and angered him more. He peeled Bogdan's hand away. "What the hell, dude? Even if I swung that way—"

"Please, shut up."

He zipped it; the intent in Bogdan's his colleague's eyes drove the point home. Something moved down the hall in the center office space. Bogdan peeked around the corner. "No more angry birds," he whispered. "Angry womans."

Edson recalled the disturbing vibrating thing all the office girls were doing during the bird-storm. "Are they... you know. Still all...?" asked Edson, mimicking their jerky movements.

The Russian snuck another look and bounced right back into the alcove, smushing Edson against the door handle. "Yes. And walking like they have the poop in their pants."

Edson grimaced and clutched his side. "We need to get out of here." He jiggled the supply closet's handle. "Shit! Locked!" The noise echoed through the office, but a weird humming sound was filling the void, getting louder—or closer—every second.

"Oh no!" Bogdan grabbed his arm and dragged him out of the alcove and into the corridor. "We need to go now."

It was easy for the women to organize and zero in on their target; the two men had made few attempts to keep their voices down. Edson had no choice but to follow the Russian, who was dragging him down the hall and away from the twitchy women.

He managed to glance back at them. Each was indistinguishable from the next except for the piercing glow of silver eyes that fixated on him, despite their undulating bodies. As the two turned a corner, trying their damnedest not to step on any of the bird carcasses littering the floor, Edson swore he heard them utter his name.

The boom of the door smashing open mattered little to Bogdan as he pulled his associate into the stairwell. Edson peered over the railing to the lower floors. A strange grayness swirled below them, accompanied by some otherworldly magnetic resonance.

Bogdan took a peek as well. "Going down is not option. We must go up."

"But what if we get trapped up there?"

"Good point." Bogdan eyed the upper floors. "But nothing good will be down there to greet us, I am certain."

"Point. Counterpoint."

The Russian yanked on Edson's arm again. "We must go up and hide. Find a place to collect thoughts and make strategy."

They bolted up the stairs trying every door on every landing until they found one that opened. Once through, Bogdan grabbed a nearby folding chair and braced it against the door handle for whatever security it could offer. Even through the steel door, they could hear the whirring sound funneling up the stairwell.

As they gathered their bearings, they realized they were on the unfinished part of the office building. An outside company had leased the floor but had run out of funds and now the whole space stood in disarray. Through the hanging plastic sheets they found the one finished room, complete with a door that locked. Although it was the most obvious place to hide, it was a tight fit full of building supplies. Regardless, they barricaded themselves in before slumping to the floor, exhausted and terrified.

"What the hell is going on?" said Edson, catching his breath. "I mean, I can't be going any more insane than I already am because you're seeing this shit, too." He was so tired he felt like crying, but being on the verge of hyperventilating kept the tear valves shut. Instead, he balled up his fists and pressed them into his clenched eyelids. "What in the holy fuck?"

"Jatinga," muttered Bogdan.

"G'bless you?"

Bogdan rolled his eyes. "No sneeze. Jatinga."

"Thanks. Cleared that right up."

"In 1971, my Uncle Arcadi was in Soviet Army during India-Pakistan War. His troop was stationed in Indian state of Assam near small village called Jatinga."

"That's great, but this is *the* worst time for war stories, dude."

"I have point to make if you would keep your mouth silent," Bogdan snapped. Edson huffed, but zipped his lips. "He told me of a strange, um…" He struggled for the word. "In Russian we say '*yavleniye*', like something odd you can't explain, like UFO or Bermuda Triangle."

"A phenomenon?"

His eyes lit up. "Da! Exactly." In the weak light from the overhead construction lamp, the Russian looked like a crazed man telling a campfire tale. "One night, he was at his camp inside his tent. It was monsoon season and the troop was frightened of being swept away by floods. When weather cleared, he heard odd sound coming from village. He called it "a magnetic vibration." All of a sudden hundreds of birds started flying straight into the ground and into all the homes and buildings in the village, knocking out lights and hitting people—killing some."

"Sounds familiar," Edson said.

"Uncle Arcadi said scientists blamed it on atmospheric conditions and heavy fog confusing birds, but he said villagers knew better. Evil spirits in sky controlling the birds to do their bidding… an endless battle of witches—*daayans* they call them—and their covens that'd been raging for years and years for control of the villagers' souls. White magic versus black."

Edson rubbed his temples. *Yeah, okay. Witchcraft. Why not?* "Jesus…."

"Exactly. Jatinga."

Bogdan returned to his history lesson, but Edson no longer listened, the words fading to a dull mumbling in his ears. All he could think about was that phone call.

It's all your fault. You ran her down and left her to die. Prepare yourself, Edson Doherty.

He buried his face in his palms.

You snuffed her out.

"No!"

You will pay!

"I didn't do anything wrong!"

Prepare yourself.

Edson smacked himself in the head, desperately trying to rid his mind of the voice.

You ran her down... left her to die.

His eyes popped open, but not from the pressure on his temples. From recollection.

You ran her down.

Ran her down.

He shook his head. "No... can't be..." Mental images of his car assaulted his mind's eye: hitting the bump, the icy sweat from snapping awake while driving, his hands gripping the steering wheel.

Prepare yourself, Edson Doherty.

He was haunted by the image of the rain that made it hard to see; the blood and chunks of hair and scalp being washed away by that rain. No evidence, no crime. Snuffed out. Just like that....

Edson... Doherty...

He was shaking. A deep voice shouted in the distance.

Edson!

The shaking wouldn't stop.

"Edson!" Bogdan gripped his shoulders and shook him. "Snap out of it."

Glossy-eyed, he looked up at the Russian. "It's my fault."

Bogdan glanced over his shoulder at the barricaded door. "I believe they found us."

"All my fault."

Again, Bogdan yanked on Edson's arm to get him moving, but he wouldn't budge. "Nonsense, my friend. But we must now go."

"I thought it was just the curb or a pothole." Edson's eyes welled up. "I was so tired. Only closed them for a second. One second!"

Bogdan finally got him to his feet and pulled him towards the exit. "You can tell me all about it later, but for now we must go!"

Edson jerked his arm back. "You don't get it, you big retard. The phone call, the birds. She said *I* killed Anusha." He began to shake, tears streaming down his cheeks. "I fell asleep driving, and ran over her daughter!"

"Oh." Bogdan's face went slack. "Well, you made real bad fuck up then." His face turned cold and he scowled. "You have a curse on you! And you have taken me downtown with you."

"I know. I'm sorry. It was just an accident."

Bogdan huffed. "Sorry...? *Pizda ti jopoglazaya!*"

The woman walked through the fog; it seemed to part for her as she approached the offices. Higher in the sky, well above the building, the sunlight struggled to pierce the dense clouds hanging over the property. The grayness swirled with each step as she traversed the field of dead birds, crunching the shells of dead bugs under her feet.

She rolled three smooth, tumbled stones between the fingers of her left hand while clasping onto the ornate amulet around her neck with the other. Her lips moved, working the chant she barely knew and had hoped she'd never have to speak. Though her words were inaudible, the magnetic resonance fluctuated with her intended inflection.

Layers of leaves, feathers, and fallen insects flittered away on a ghostly breeze. She looked up, mesmerized by the sound waves that only she could see swirling around the building. The magnitude of the spell she had cast to exact vengeance on her daughter's killer left her not only stunned, but despotic.

"Edson Doherty!" Her voice ricocheted off the fog until it joined with the funnel of magnetic interference. "I know you're still in there... alive. Have you made your peace?"

Enthralled by the terrifying power she never thought possible to harness, but which she now felt coursing through her, she twirled the smooth stones in her hand until they rose from her palm. All around her, the fog joined the churning magic and grief emanating from the center of her soul. She quivered, her whole body blinking in and out of focus.

And then the three smooth stones shot from her palm into the building.

"You hear that?"

The Russian nodded. "Of course I heard that."

Edson paced. "She knows I'm still in here. She knows who I am and what I did." Fear and guilt painted his face, his cheeks burning with shame. "I'm dead... and she's gonna kill me."

His voice echoed onto itself in the closed quarters of the unfinished room. His words melded into each other, forming nothing more than incoherent gibberish. The fullness of the sounds pushed on their ears as if they were rising to the surface from a great depth.

The structures around them vibrated to the point of blurriness. "We must escape," Bogdan mouthed. "Now!"

Edson allowed himself to be pulled and guided, letting the Russian act as momma bear protecting her young. Through fading mental faculties and crippling exhaustion, his adrenaline dump cramped his brain. All around, exposed metal studs rang like tuning forks, shaking dust throughout the abandoned work zone.

Edson Doherty...

The syrupy tone of the voice rumbled as the words crawled closer. Around one corner, was possible escape. Around the other— perpetual madness and unknown doom. Doom for them both now, surely.

Edson felt terrible for unintentionally involving his friend, let alone the countless employees who'd most likely fallen prey to some form of the witch's vengeance. Beleaguered, he succumbed to his pitiful uselessness, content with relying solely on Bogdan's strength and will.

Edson... Doherty...

The voice got closer.

Killed my Morningstar...

They were right around the corner... coming for them.

Vengeance is mine...

A hand breached the turn, gripping on until the whole wall trembled. From the shadowed corridor, a pulsating group of shapes appeared. Barely recognizable as the women from his office, he swallowed hard when he realized the writhing mass at the front was most likely Veronica.

"Ronni?" he said. "Please, no. What's happening?" The shambling figures lurched forward, each weaving through the other until almost forming one congealed voltaic mess.

"Stop! You don't have to do this," Edson begged, as the Russian ran to check around the far corner. For all his insight and perceived strength and bravery, Edson knew Bogdan was just as terrified. The formless thing continued forward, shifting in spectrums like television interference.

"*Please...* I'm a good person. Tell her I'm *sorry*."

Bogdan's scream split the air loud enough to cut through the electric din of the witch's messengers. The scream faded fast, ending with a cracking thud.

When Edson allowed himself to tear his eyes away from what was in front of him, he raced down the hall, almost meeting the same doom as Bogdan who had fallen through the floor and into the office below.

Edson grabbed an exposed beam just in time. Not as lucky, Bogdan's husky size had contributed to speed of the fall. The force of the impact split his skull open and twisted his neck enough so that his dead eyes stared at the backs of his legs. Edson shook from fear and nausea.

He couldn't look away from the nebulous mass of static; he knew his death was in there somewhere. "I'm begging you," he said, between wet snorts. "I'm sorry! Tell her!"

"Tell me yourself...."

Three stones rocketed out of the center of the spectral flux, sending the bodies rippling in diverging circles. In succession, they slammed into Edson's shoulders and abdomen, propelling his body backwards and pinning him to the wall. Struggling was little use. He watched a form step out from the chaos. The mass of bodies violently flickered before separating and falling to the floor as lifeless individuals, around the witch.

As she stepped out of the ring of bodies, she looked just as mortified as Edson assumed he must. Yet, he detected a spark in her eyes. She seemed genuinely surprised at what just happened, but her face also offered him a glimpse of madness. He knew only bad could come of this." Her eyes became an afterthought as the dull drill bit sensation of the three stones pushing into his flesh set his nerves on fire.

"Tell me *how* sorry you are!" Her voice boomed.

Edson grimaced through the hot pain crushing his body and his vision sparkled, the salty taste of tears in his mouth. He knew he was speaking, mumbling more useless apologizes to the woman stalking closer to him, but he heard nothing. He just felt his jaw moving, soundlessly.

The woman released the amulet and the stones released their pressure, rushing back to her palm but sending Edson slumping to the floor. She smiled, pleased with herself in ways she'd never imagined. Why had she never pursued this path with her gift? Why had she always stuck to the *white ways* of her family's coven despite their meager place amongst families darker and more powerful? Now, with the thrilling ache of untapped potential and authority, she would exact revenge and walk towards legend amidst the great mystics of her culture.

Edson fought for focus. Even with all her flickering pawns now motionless behind her, the magnetic whirling didn't dissipate, as if she was the source of it all. He watched the three stones spin in her hand as she gripped her amulet again and grinned. That maniacal expression made him feel weak and pathetic.

"I said, tell me!"

Edson jerked. "Yesyesyes! I'm so- so... sorry. You have *no* idea." If he could've pushed himself inside the wall behind him just to get farther away he would have. "I swear, if I could switch—"

"Don't you *dare* say you'd switch places with her!" One of the stones shot from her hand into his stomach, knocking him back down, windless.

Through his violent coughing fit, he heard her mocking him, ranting about the beautiful life he had taken from this world. He noticed a small hunk of two-by-four behind his feet, and reached for it. He was careful not to alert the witch, fumbling, refusing to take his eyes off her while he formulated his plan.

The woman chanted louder now, the harsh tongue of her native dialect accentuating the key phrasings. As the stones swirled in her hand and a gray mist wafted behind her, she clenched the talisman. Her cadence and volume increased, rising over the static din. Edson finally had a sure grip on the hunk of wood and waited for the perfect time to strike.

Her sneer faltered mid-chant and for a fleeting moment, he spotted panic and uncertainty in her face. The words—or her memory—failed her, and the smooth stones slowed their rotation, wobbling and clanking together. Edson, not squandering the moment, launched the block, side-arming it with all his might.

Lost in her confusion as she struggled with the phrases, the witch couldn't avoid getting clobbered. The chunk struck the hand that was clutching the talisman, gouging her skin and cracking the charm in half. She roared as the pieces fell and broke into even smaller shards of crystal.

Edson dared not move. He stared, waiting for her reaction, and wondered if he'd just made things worse. The whirring sound and foggy mist intertwined, thumping and contorting the air into a living thing, hemorrhaging from every fracture in the building. The air turned thick, and Edson felt as if he was stuck in quicksand.

The building shook, rattling worse than ever. A staticky boom filled Edson's ears, covering the whole Earth with its deafening howl for all he knew. His skin tingled, and all his body hair stood to attention; more waves of nausea seized his innards. He covered his ears, hoping his drums wouldn't pop, as he balanced against the wall.

Frantic, the woman dropped to her knees, ranting through tears as she tried to scoop up what remained of her talisman. In her rancor she seemed oblivious to or unfazed by the surrounding calamity—including her wounded hand—and failed to notice how her blood sizzled and seeped into the dirty, uncarpeted floor.

Edson swiveled as he searched for an escape route. To his left was the deathtrap that had taken Bogdan, and to his right was a pile of construction material concealing a fire door.

"Shit! Shit! *Shit!*" he shouted, barely noticing the background noise diminishing, becoming more of an intermittent zapping or revving sound. He turned back to the witch and her current state of confused despair. She was mumbling, declaring that she spoke the spell correctly as she played with the puzzle pieces that were her amulet.

The only way out is through her....

Edson skidded to a stop.

Despite the uncertainty he saw in the witch's face, she still held a rage in the glowing embers of her eyes. Edson knew nothing about witches or spellcraft. Hell! He was dumbfounded such insanity even existed. But he felt certain something was amiss—he knew the look of terrified bewilderment, no matter how brief it was. He knew it well enough to be able to tell she had fucked something up.

Enraged, she stood before him, screaming her infernal words. In each hand were the two biggest halves of the bloodied talisman, and as she pushed them together against their magnetic resistance, light erupted from the space in between.

He saw movement behind her through a curtain of sparks. His coworkers' bodies (or what had become of them) were gone. No corporeal traces remained. Some clothing, some hair, and stains—that's all—as if they had dissolved into the floor to become one with the structure.

Their surroundings took on that disorienting in-between-television-stations sensation again. As everything pulsated, the two halves of the amulet sucked together and disappeared into an orb of blackness, dark unlike anything either had ever witnessed before. It hovered between them, emitting a hot wind before imploding in on itself into exquisite brightness. Then a horrible rumble, like that of a detonation, tore open the floor beneath them, giving way to a jagged hole through the center of the building.

The woman plummeted into the breach but snagged her shirt on a sharp beam, managing to grab hold before falling deeper. Edson dropped to his stomach as the building around him swayed and shimmered. Perhaps out of guilt—or instinct—he reached down into the pit to help her.

"Grab my hand!" He shouted over the noise, anchoring his foot against some fallen beams. "Please! I'll help you!"

The orb-light intensified. Murmurs whispered from nowhere and everywhere at once, indecipherable to his ears, bouncing off the trembling walls.

"C'mon! Stretch!"

She strained to hoist herself up higher, her lips quivering and her eyes full of fear.

"You can make it!"

The light brightened.

The voices coalesced, mimicking the light's growing potency.

Their hands finally touched, fingers interlacing at their tips. "I got you." The building rattled, almost breaking his weak grasp on her. He was having trouble seeing her now, as his eyes would no longer adjust to the increasing brightness. "Hang on!"

In an instant, the blinding whiteness shifted in color, turning red, then blue, then back again. Oscillating. Strobing. A stiffness overtook his body and his hand seized, releasing his fragile grip on her fingers. Yet, he didn't hear her fall or scream... just a distant wailing. As the light pulsated—red/blue/red/blue—he felt nothing but pain in every part of his body, and tasted the blood that was trickling down his throat. He tried to cry out, but nothing happened; he felt asphyxiated.

Hang on buddy... We'll get you out of there...

He heard the other voices more clearly now, panicked with a sense of urgency. And the wailing grew louder. A woman crying, shrieking in a foreign language he didn't understand. As the white light faded, pain sharpened his vision, and the scene came into view, almost triggering an anxiety attack. And with his difficulty breathing, he was on the verge of going into shock.

He was in his car, the front of which had hugged a conjoined pair of telephone poles; steam hissed, and smoke wafted from the engine block. Blood—his blood—was smeared all over the steering column and dashboard. The radio was spitting out nothing but weird static and fuzzy squawks and buzzes. Surrounding him were a number of emergency vehicles all with their lights blazing—red/blue/red/blue. A paramedic was standing by as the firemen pried open the door.

"Hang on. You're gonna be okay."

He was fighting for words, something to say—to ask—about what had happened, but the howls of sadness gave him pause. In the dangling rearview mirror, he saw a woman kneeling over a white sheet steeped in red. She held a bloodied hand in hers as she screamed the dead one's name.

The firemen had to tear the door off its hinges before the medic could wrap a collar around his neck. Then they gingerly pulled him out of his seat. Though he was able to stand on wobbly legs, his knees buckled, and he vomited all over the orange spine board waiting for him on the sidewalk. The rescue workers did their best to calm him down, offering soothing reassurance as they called for someone to bring the gurney.

Edson looked back to the crying woman. The swirling lights danced off something crystalline hanging around her neck. Everything slowed to a crawl. She looked up from her dead daughter's body to Edson with laser-focused anger and contempt assaulting him like a physical blow.

"No, no, n—no. This can't be happening!"

"Calm down, sir," said the paramedic holding him up. "We need to get you to the hospital."

"It's... It's her..." Edson shook his head and started shivering. "No!" he repeated, getting louder each time until he was yanking himself out of the medic's grip. "It was a fucking accident!"

You bitch!

Edson shoved the medic, sending him tripping over the stretcher. Despite his injuries, he snatched the fireman's Halligan bar leaning against his car before anyone could react. Gripping tight, with the axe blade on the business end of the tool shimmering in the police lights, Edson snarled and took off running towards the woman and her talisman... determined to get to her first this time.

SYBARITES OR THE ENMITY OF PERVERSE EXISTENCE

"What can I do ya for?" asked the man through his unhygienic grin.

Jim anxiously thumbed through a pamphlet. Despite already knowing the purpose for his being there, the reality of the situation—in the form of colored images jumping off the brochure—solidified the knot twisting and tying in his gut. "I'm interested in, um, room three-fifteen and possibly three-eighteen, as well," he admitted in a hush, even though no one else was around.

Mr. Halitosis' smile broadened, showing off half a mouthful of pumpkin-colored teeth. "Solid choices, m'friend." He spun around on his beat-up stool to a pegboard lined with keys, almost falling off the wobbly thing in the process. He caught his balance and said, "This ol' thing needs to be put out to pasture, one too many years of duct-tape triage." He chuckled. "Haven't seen you 'round here before, pal. Gotta name?"

Jim's anger boiled, but he forced a smile, answering, "Yeah. It's been a while. Name's, uh, Jim."

"That an interesting forename ya got there, Uh-Jim. Well, irregardless, we're gladta have ya back. Name's Buxton, but my friends call me Buck." He looked down his nose at the pegboard. "Ah, let us see then… el numero tres-fifteeno y eighteeno." Buck glanced back to Jim with a sly wink. "That's Spanish."

With another chuckle, he turned to the board, but stopped and shook his head. "Whoops." He tapped the empty spot under the peeling 315 label. "You are outta luck, Uh-Jim. Looks like that one's been scooped up for the foreseeable future." He next scanned for 318. "Same thing, I'm afraid." The proprietor spun back to the counter with a giddy *"whee"* for added effect. "Sorry 'bout that. Don't seem to be your lucky day, friend. Coupl'a those rooms in that price range been kinda popular these days, if ya catch my drift." Perversity glinted in the wink of his hooded eye.

Jim searched the room. The door behind him, marked "PRIVATE - EMPLOYEES ONLY" on the opposite side, led back to the crappy backwoods half-outpost, half pawnshop called Mountain Buck's General Store. Jutting up to the side of the mountain, it was your one-stop-shop for shit beer, bait and tackle, *and* beef jerky. Maybe even grab an old, beat up pink bicycle for the kids while you're at it.

This room, though, was nearly empty, save for some overstock merchandise. Nothing gave off any outwardly sleazy vibes or lent credence to the rumors that had circled the place for decades. On the other side of Buck's setup, he saw the entrance that led down below, to the place with the doors those hanging keys unlocked.

Behind Buck, a key labeled "MASTER KEY" dangled from a hook. Jim reached into his jacket, quietly thankful that the general store beyond was no longer open.

"Didja have any others in mind? Shame to waste a trip," Buck asked, flipping through the pamphlet, trying to be helpful. "We got all sortsa—"

Click!

Jim's hand shook as he cocked the hammer of the SIG Sauer P220 he had pulled out from under his jacket. The last thing he wanted was for this to go sideways, to come in here all guns blazing. Apparently, it wasn't going to be that simple. "Where's my daughter?

"What in the name of holy fuck now?"

"H-how many are down there now?"

Buck stared cross-eyed at the barrel pointed at the middle of his face. "Um, shit… let's see," he started, cautiously looking over his shoulder. "Looksta be 'bout five'r six at the moment, give'r take."

Jim glanced at the board, memorizing the spots with missing keys before glancing down beyond the stairs. He took a deep breath, bothered that this was now the only solution. In his periphery, he saw Buck reaching for something. "Probably not the best idea you'll have today, *friend*."

Buck popped off his stool and backed away, hands in the air. "What the fuck you thinkin' you gonna do down there, huh, Uh-Jim?" he said with a smirk. "That shit down there'll fuck you up good."

"Shut your fuckin' mouth! I'm just here to get my daughter away from this sick, filthy place."

Buck's creepy sneer slid from his face, his pupils nothing but pinholes as he stared.

"What're you staring at?" Jim shook the gun for effect.

"Thinkin' I'm starin' at a dead cocksucker that don't know *shit* 'bout evil." Buck jumped for his stashed gun under the counter, but Jim's bullet rifled down the barrel faster, ripping through Buck's face before lodging into the crumbling wood paneling.

Jim froze, relatively certain no one had heard the shot, but leery nonetheless. Buck slumped forward with a wet slap before collapsing beneath the counter, leaving a smear of brains and jowls along the laminate.

Since people did occupy those other rooms, he'd have to make damn sure he kept his shit together. He thought about what might be happening beyond those other doors, the rooms that didn't harbor his objective, but in the end, they weren't his concern. The room *she* was in—that was the *only* room that mattered.

His gun hand trembled as he pointed it forward, creeping down the steps into the deathly quiet hallway, conscious that some form of depravity was happening nearby.

Ominous black doors lined the walls, each numbered—odd on the left, even on the right. Even the lechery happening behind them couldn't rattle the unsettling quiet. His mind spun at the sheer number of rooms that ran deep into the mountainside. The situation's enormity terrified him. After months, his search for Cassie had finally led him here, and, as he stood at the precipice of definitive iniquity—the door to room 315—he knew he couldn't turn back.

His sweaty hand gripped the doorknob as he inserted the master key into the tumbler. He paused to listen, pistol ready, before easing open the door. When the stench hit him—the damp, goatish odor—his nose crinkled. He felt deep rumbles below him as if something large was squeezing through a tight space. As he peered into the dank, candlelit room, weird, droning music filled the air. The flames seemed to dance in time to the ambient soundscape.

A large canopy bed was the centerpiece of the room. Strange wet markings on the walls reflected in the flickering light. Misty shadows within the bed's netting caught his attention. A sudden light breeze from down the corridor infiltrated the room, rustling the veil.

Writhing on the bed in a perverse coital tangle of limbs, three naked forms groaned. Deeply engaged and enraptured in one another, they were oblivious to Jim. Their heavy sighs and moans were a sure sign of money spent wisely. The male component of the tryst, positioned and fixed purposefully on his knees behind one of the females, thrust into her with pneumatic force and pumping rhythm, gripping her hips hard enough to break the skin. Blood dribbled down her thighs.

The other female, a blonde, sat spread-eagled with her back against the headboard and her hands tangled in the feminine locks of the head buried in her crotch. Through the canopy, Jim watched as the blonde's head snapped back, savoring the bliss of it all, her throaty groan rising over the music's repetitive melody. All the while, the male's pelvic assault never wavered. A sweaty sheen glistened over their bodies, mocking the air's chill and the puffs of breath escaping their lips.

A gasp froze in Jim's lungs when the middle girl pulled her face from between the blonde's legs. As she came up for air, crazed sparkles of lust *and* awakening danced in her eyes. Jim breathed, relieved and revolted, yet still distressed his Cassie was still out there. And as he watched this young girl, mouth caked with blood and dripping with the blonde's juices, arch up and kiss the other, his anger roiled with a newfound urge of aching determination to not only save his daughter, but also make someone pay.

His stomach churned and his head ached from a surge of adrenalin. Jim slowly backed away and let the door close as if he were never there, yet knowing that someday, somehow, those miscreants would get their due. He could see it in his mind's eye….

However, what Jim didn't see—*couldn't* see from his perspective—was the opening in the mattress that led down into a deep pit. As the young girl suspended herself over the empty space, held up only by the man's thrusting loins and her death grip on the blonde's legs, two mucousy tongues of incredible size and girth, covered in pointy barbs and papillae, lapped hungrily at both their crotches, tongue-fucking them.

With room 315 ending up a dead—albeit disturbing—end, Jim stood uneasily at the door of 318, almost unwilling to discover what visual onslaught might be waiting inside. He psyched himself up, smacking himself in the head to clear the confusion and doubt. "Relax," he demanded, rubbing his eyes with his palms. He took a deep breath and put his ear to the door.

Nothing.

Still anxious, he unlocked the door and pushed it open with the barrel of his gun.

A high-back leather chair sat in the center of the large room, positioned on an ornate throw rug. It faced a massive hole in the wall that peered out to the granite of the colossal mountain. On either side of the opening, metal shackles were bolted into the ceiling and the floor. Dried fluids in a myriad of different colors stained the hardwood floor in front of it.

Numerous candles lit up the room in ceremonial flashes of white and yellow, each at a different state of melting and becoming one with the floor. They encircled the chair on the outer fringes of the rug and burned in all corners of the room. A waxy semi-circle sat aglow around the large opening.

Jim sensed he wasn't alone; a strange, moist *thwapping* sound reached his ears, with the intermittent jingle of metal hitting wood. Gun thrust forward, he ventured closer, stopping short when he heard soft moaning coming from the other side of the chair.

"Cassandra, I'm getting all hot and read— Hey! What the fuck you doing in here, man? Where's Mistress Cassandra?"

Startled, Jim jumped and nearly pulled the trigger. He stole his attention away from the gaping breach in the wall and set it on the pissed off, middle-aged fat man that nearly bounced out of the chair. His pants hung around his thick ankles. With his cock still clasped in his meaty fist, he ranted, "Excuse me, dickhead. I'm talking to you."

Jim just blinked, eyeing him in disgust.

"What the holy hell? I'm getting Buck down here!" the big man complained, still not seeing Jim's weapon as he skirted around the candles. "This is unacceptable. I paid good money to get this room, and I wanna know what the fuck you're doing here!" The floor rumbled as something under the building's structure shifted again. "Shit, man! You're gonna ruin all the fun."

Jim, with his faculties back in check, leveled his sidearm at the man's ruddy face and cocked the hammer. "Shut up!"

"Whoa, partner. No need to get all serious." The man's eyes converged on the barrel's sight.

"Where is she?" asked Jim, all business.

"What're you talkin' about? Where's who?" answered Fat Man, now aware he was half-naked. He went to pull up his pants.

"Don't fuckin' move." Jim stepped closer. He reached into his pocket, taking out a worn Polaroid of a young woman in her twenties. "Cassie, my daughter," he said, shoving the photograph into the man's face. "I know she's here." Jim saw a glint of recognition in the man's eyes and it was enough to make him see red. He raised his gun, threatening to strike.

"Hey! Hold up! I have no idea." Fat Man started shivering as his deflated penis slinked back into his unruly patch of pubic overgrowth. "Can I please pull up my pants, for Christ's sake?"

"No! You can't, you lying sack of shit!" Jim pressed the barrel against the man's forehead. "I heard you say 'Cassandra'."

The man scrunched his eyes tight, bracing for the worst. "Okay, okay! Relax," he begged. Jim lowered the gun an inch, leaving a bright red indent in its wake. "That's Mistress Cassandra. I'm one of her regulars."

"Her *regulars*?" Jim's face burned. The vein in his forehead throbbed with rage. He raised his gun again.

"Hey! Hold on, friend. It's not like I knew she was your daughter. Listen. My name's Todd. I'm sure we can discuss this like rational adults. Okay?"

Again, something vibrated the floor, shaking the room and knocking over some of the less melted candles. The wall with the opening swelled. When Jim noticed something enormous—something fleshy—had filled the hole, squeezing into the space between the man-made room and the ancient rock of the stony giant, he fought for his bowels not to release.

Though he had heard the rumors, the strange reports about the quaint general store and beyond, Jim couldn't comprehend that something so colossal dwelled within the mountain. He now understood the cold facts of his dilemma—shit just got worse, and he was more terrified than ever.

"Goddamn it!" shouted Todd. "It's here... and it's gonna be pissed that your—"

Jim stood transfixed by the rippling surface of reptilian skin that filled the entire gap in the wall, not hearing a word Todd was uttering. "Wait," he gasped, turning back to Todd. "Pissed about *what*?"

Todd flinched, almost expecting a pistol-whipping. "It was summoned, and Mistress Cassandra wasn't—"

Jim scowled.

"Sorry, Cassie, your daughter, wasn't here for the ritual."

Jim's mind flashed back to his innocent Cassie sitting in her bedroom playing with the dollhouse he had made for her so many years earlier, yet the slow trudging pulsation of the room reminded him of the monstrosity residing within its walls and the task, now ever more complicated, at hand.

"What *kind* of ritual?" Jim struggled to control his anger as the twisted circumstances escalated. "The kind that involves you jerking off in front of my daughter in some dungeon while that, that fucking *thing* does what, huh?"

Before Todd could even try to explain this madness, the building shook again as if the beast were everywhere all at once. That atrocious notion made his head spin. How could he fight what he couldn't understand? He couldn't fathom how something so colossal had remained hidden for so long from everyone—save for a lecherous few.

A deep, guttural growl, alien to Jim's ears, pierced the tumultuous vibe within the room.

The rippling and stretching of the creature's skin as it slinked through the tight space proved more than Todd could handle. A lascivious moan escaped his parted lips; his eyes lost focus on everything around him except the horrid, undulating beast-flesh. He stepped out of his pants and rushed over to the body of the passing giant.

"Hey!" yelled Jim. "Get back here, you fucking lunatic!" But Todd, completely entranced, ignored the command, opting instead to rub himself all over the creature's filthy, moss-colored skin. Jim could only watch as Todd caressed the thing, licking and savoring it as if tasting it for the first time.

Yet, denied Cassie's ritual, the beast was angry still. Another foundation-shaking roar filled the air.

"C'mon, man. Get away from it," ordered Jim.

Yet, the big man refused to listen or budge, content with lapping up and slathering himself with as much bestial grime as he could, seemingly oblivious to the multiple boils rising on its flesh. The growing, ochre bumps silently ruptured, revealing fiery red eyes devoid of pupils.

Jim choked back a sour gag as he watched putrid tears of mucus drip from every eye, covering Todd, melding with his skin until he started becoming one with the beast. Another huge blister formed under Todd as his gyrating pelvis rubbed against it. The corrosive tears completely bathed Todd, digesting him within the liquescent cocoon. The newly formed boil split open to reveal a massive lamprey-like mouth lined with teeth and fangs like the gears of some organic meat grinder. A phallic, barbed tongue darted in and out of the cavernous orifice, groping and prodding Todd's melting form until he was no more.

Jim stood panting in the hallway, reeling from the chaotic chain reaction that had just played out in room 318. His resolve evaporated, quickly turning into a mire of hopelessness—and terror... terror beyond all bounds of his imagination. What he had learned from Todd, before his demise by the horrible gaping maw of that perverse creation, sent him over the edge. He burst into tears, sliding down the soundproof barrier of wood and sheetrock that separated him from the hellish thing within, before collapsing into a defeated puddle of a man.

More images of his daughter rattled his thoughts, stinging him with the promise of loss. How in the world did she end up here? What unfortunate circumstance had led her down this path?

The distant pitter-patter of bare feet slapping against the hard floor ripped Jim from his reverie. He hopped up, wiping his tears, readying himself for anything. The darkness of the endless corridor swirled to life as if the blackness were smoke caught in a breeze. Someone approached—fast—and he raised his weapon.

A young woman erupted from the shadows, plunging headlong down the hall. Freshly carved arcane symbols decorated her naked flesh. Makeup around her crying eyes ran in rivulets down her flushed cheeks, making her look like a devilish raccoon.

"Cassie?" Jim ran towards her, recognizing her instantly, closing the gap between father and daughter. His heart missed a beat before it started its gallop. Despite the tears, her eyes were vacant of everything except terror. She rushed by him in her need to escape, not even seeing him, yet almost bowling him over. "Cassie!" he screamed, reaching out, but she continued her hasty retreat past the closed doors of the abominable place, oblivious to his voice.

Jim gave chase with renewed purpose. He extended his hand, mid-stride, snatching her arm before screeching to a halt. Cassie struggled to break free, still not aware of who had a hold of her. Jim whipped her around and pushed her up against the wall. He locked eyes with hers, but there was no calming her down.

"Cassie, please," begged Jim. "It's *me*! *Daddy*!"

Terror locked her tear-streaked face in a snarl while her eyes darted about, unable to focus—perhaps tormented by everything they had seen, or were still seeing. She trembled as Jim cupped her cheeks, forcing her to look into his eyes. "It's okay, baby, I'm here now." Momentary recognition twinkled in her eyes and she seemed to relax. "I've got you now. You're safe." He took his jacket off and draped it over her naked, shivering body.

Then, like some hell-borne freight-train whistle, a roar sounded, funneling down the corridor towards them. Cassie stiffened; shock and despair collided, souring her expression further.

Everything quaked again.

"No..." she muttered, after the reverberations stopped. "No. We're not safe." Her eyes turned rabid again. Her mumbling escalated, evolving into booming declarations. "We'll never be safe! They're gonna kill us!"

Jim's eyes welled with unshed tears. What had they done to his little girl? He pulled her close, embracing the daughter he thought he had lost forever. "I'll get you outta here. I promise." He held her at arm's length, trying to instill in her some hope, some of that remaining strength he had left. "Please! Cassie, you need to calm down so we can figure out how to get out of here--"

"NO!" Cassie shouted into his face as she twisted from his grasp. "There's no calming down and there is *no* escape! I tried to get away, but they got me. I made him angry, Daddy. Don't you understand?"

"Made *who* angry, honey?"

"No. Let. Go... of me." As hard as Jim held on, she wriggled free and bolted down the hallway. "I can't let them get me again!"

Jim was certain they *would* get her, unless he intervened. He rushed up behind his daughter, pulling her close and muffling her cries in his chest. She fought, but Jim's embrace proved no match for the weakened girl.

A piercing ring resounded through the corridor, followed by sporadic static chirps.

"*Cassandra...*" A cold, deep voice boomed over the PA. It drew out her name, stretching the syllables and letting the vowels ring out. Her name was repeated two more times in a sadistic singsong.

Father and daughter, caught frozen in mid-embrace, looked up at the speaker; Jim covered Cassie's head and ears with a father's protective instinct.

The voice boomed again. "Cassandra, our sweet, you can't get away from us. We are your family. We can't let you leave. You know this."

"Fuck you, Mordecus!" shouted Cassie. "I'm not yours anymore, you sick bastards!"

"You tried to leave us once. But now you belong to Him... eternally."

Cassie wept. Jim could only clutch her tighter; worried that his defensive shell of flesh and bone would be quick work for whatever new insanity the situation delivered.

"Mister Clarke, leave us the girl and you will be unharmed," the voice echoed. "She is part of our family now and must atone for her transgressions against us."

Jim was incredulous. "Cassie's my daughter! *Mine*! Not *yours*!"

Doors all around them opened, reacting to the commotion. At the thresholds stood men and women of all sorts, in varying stages of undress and rapture. Jim stared into each lustful face; their breathing was shallow and their eyes teary, glazed over as if on the verge of sexual climax. A voice from behind caught Jim off guard.

"I'd suggest you do what he says while the decision is still yours to make."

Jim spun around with his pistol aimed, but stumbled back a step. "Senator Weir?"

The politician smiled, naked and unabashed. He glistened with a sweaty patina; a redhead embraced him from behind, fondling and kissing his body. "Even before she broke the rules, son, she was theirs. She's gone, no longer yours, but ours to corrupt and be defiled by." His grin widened. A teardrop collected in the corner of his eye as he moaned, his body quivering in the onset of orgasm. "She's His... Ours..."

A sudden movement from the doorway behind the Senator alerted Jim. Another monstrous tendril slid its barbs down the doorframe, leaving a syrupy trail in its wake. Jim fired before it disappeared. The bullet ripped through the vile muscle, leaving a jagged crater. The beast inside the mountain bellowed as not only the injured tongue-thing, but also the multiple smaller appendages, withdrew from the orifices of their hosts and recoiled into the darkened rooms.

"That's possibly the worst thing you could've done, son," clarified the Senator, no longer carrying any hint of desire on his face.

A larger man clawed at Cassie, pulling her away from her father. As he turned, clocking the Senator in the face with the butt of his gun, Jim pulled the trigger again, shooting her attacker through the throat. The closeness showered Cassie in more blood, painting her fresh wounds redder, but the man collapsed.

Jim cursed for not arming himself heavier in case this shitshow went south—and south it was heading, quicker than he had imagined. If another one of those deviants decided to make a statement, he'd better take proper aim. One clip was all he had.

Then—darkness.

Everything went black. The intercom squawked again. A throaty chuckle echoed. *"You belong to Him now, Cassandra."*

Something slimy and wet squirmed between Jim's legs, sweeping them out from under him. His breath caught in his throat as he reached out, grasping for a handhold before gravity pulled him earthbound with a cracking *thud*.

Deep within the mountain's core, a horde of hooded proselytes stood around a stone well at the chamber's center. A distant *swoosh* came from deep underground, getting closer every second until water, viscous and colorless, filled the well, bubbling over the edge and flooding the ground.

Jim's vision slowly returned; his head throbbed. A wet surge doused his face as he lay slouched over on his side. He righted himself out of the shallow tide's path when its odor started to sting his nostrils. *Methanol?* Attempting to wipe the blurriness from his eyes, he realized his captors had bound and secured him to an iron ring in the ground. Against a rock wall and half-soaked by tainted groundwater, he spotted a closed steel door to his right. Where it led, he didn't care to learn—perhaps to another twisted path of deprivation and madness.

All around, kerosene torches peppered the chamber, casting an eerie battle of light versus shadow. Jim twisted his body to look around, to assess just how fucked they now were.

His heart froze.

Cassie hung above the mouth of the well. Splayed helplessly, four pikes rising from its base skewered her through each limb—between the tibias and fibulas and between the ulnas and radiuses. Blood dripped anew from fresh carvings in her flesh.

Before an altar of dark stone stood Mordecus, the shadows within his hood distorting his features and adding ferocity to his timbre. When he spoke, his speech was riddled with phrases in an unearthly tongue. *"We give this body to Osmodai, Prince of Lechery,*

Preacher of Lust. We give this soul to Osmodai, The Grand Adulterer." He raised a chalice over his head; the torchlight flashed brighter. *"This flesh is His Flesh. This blood is His Blood."*

"Cassie! No!" His daughter's life rained down from her wounds into the open chasm and into Mordecus' chalice.

Yet, the zealots ignored Jim as they repeated the lines of the litany in faithful unison.

"You motherfucker, I'm gonna fucking kill you." Jim clenched his teeth, yanking on his tethers. Mordecus glanced in his direction and Jim could almost sense a sneer from within the man's shaded hood. "You hear me?!"

Unfazed, the priest continued the invocation. *"Osmodai, accept this, our sacrifice, to be wholly devoured and baptized. Great Lord of the Abyss, we summon thee. Come forth and drink of the blood. Eat of the flesh of this temple."*

As Cassie's life drained, spiraling down into the fathomless depths, Mordecus drank from the full cup before passing it to his left. After each had sipped the blood and passed it along, they removed their hoods, revealing their crimson-smeared grins, their crazed eyes rolling up into their heads.

Jim watched in defeat as Cassie twitched, dangling there naked and abused. Dying. "It's okay, baby," he cooed, stifling tears while hoping to portray even the minutest bit of strength and comfort to his daughter. "Daddy's right here. You're not alone." He swallowed hard, unable to sustain the façade. "It'll be over soon," he reassured her before succumbing to wracking sobs.

Altogether, the congregation chanted, invoking Osmodai as one.

They raised their hands high as they turned their eyes down into the well. Monstrous roars rattled the chamber; dust and loose debris shook free from the walls and ceiling. Cassie's eyes rolled open and she gazed into the swirling dark of the well beneath her. Her scream ripped through the air, rivaling the beast's demonic howls.

The chanting escalated, reaching inhuman levels. The harsh consonants of the ancient dialect finally shifted to a language Jim could understand. *"We have opened the Abyss. The Abyss is open within us. For Lust in the Kingdom of Power is Yours. Come forth, Osmodai. Manifest thyself."*

Everything quieted as if a vacuum sucked all the air out of the chamber. Jim's eardrums popped right before hot, fetid air exploded out from the well. A wet, slopping noise—akin to the sound of peeling a raw steak from a countertop—followed the stink, repeating and getting louder.

"Help m-me!" cried Cassie. "I-I want my dadd—" She fell silent, slipping into catatonia.

Over the well's edge, thick reptilian tongues, each barbed and covered in horrid snot, stretched and pulled something up from below. Through the meaty slaps sticking against the walls of the well, Jim heard the familiar sound of something gigantic worming its way through a tight space.

Drunk with desire, rapacity washed over the worshippers. They disrobed, displaying their symbol-scarred bodies to their rising Lord. And they smiled broadly as they chanted, swaying to the volatile rhythm of their hymn, hands interlocked and held high.

Mordecus shouted over the din. "Rise, Osmodai! Rise and bask in our sybaritic lust."

The constant rumbling was unbearable. The torchlight flickered from the steady vibrations. Despite being bound, Jim dodged more than his fair share of crumbling rock breaking off the chamber walls. A sharp chunk landed by his side and his eyes widened. He reached for it, stretching against his shackles and beyond his physical limits, praying the throng of demon resurrection enthusiasts would pay him no mind.

Osmodai's terrible head crested the top of the well. Like a horrid combination of amphibian and elephant trunk, its gray skin, scaly and marbled, sprouted errant patches of coarse hair. Its primary mouth yawned, expelling a cloud of hot breath and revealing rows of deadly teeth similar to those he'd seen earlier.

The tentacle-like tongues that it used to grab and pull itself to freedom from within the core of the mountain moved around under its thick, meaty neck-skin like a wreath of squirming and morphing worms. Again, pus-filled blisters rose on its skin, bursting and forming the lids that protected its sinister red eyes. The worshippers cheered and reveled in Its rising.

Jim wasted no time with the fallen rock. He toiled vigorously, holding the makeshift tool between his bound fists and sawing through the hard plastic strips, occasionally glancing up to take visual inventory of the situation. Cassie still dripped blood, but coagulation finally seemed to stem the flow. "Hang on, baby!" Seeing her hanging there ignited so much anger, more rage than he was prepared for. "Daddy's coming for you, Cassie," he said, each word accentuated by a hack of his makeshift tool.

In his rush, Jim sliced himself open. His hands felt wet and he bled onto the bindings. Feeling the tension on his wrists loosen, he yanked out his left hand, ignoring the squeezing pain. With a hand free, he cut through the rest. Once he'd cleared his right hand, Jim bounced to his feet. Everything spun and his knees went slack, the concussion swarming in on his consciousness.

Osmodai groaned, shifting inside the confines of the well, saliva dripping from the corners of its gaping mouth. Every burning eye locked onto different targets. Its tendril-tongues latched on and enveloped the worshippers, crudely molesting their bodies and exposed genitals. From out of its huge mouth, a sickly tongue wagged through the air towards Cassie. The thing released a contented moan as its antenna-like papillae licked the fresh blood oozing from her wounds.

Everyone shut their eyes tight in the midst of some demented ecstasy. Jim made his move. He circled around, hoping the moans and groans would mask his rapid footfalls as he headed straight for Mordecus' back.

The beast began to rise higher towards Cassie, preparing to devour her in some diabolical sacrament of matrimony. Its mouth widened as its tongue smacked at its foul opening.

Jim launched himself over the stone altar. With pinpoint accuracy, he rammed his shoulder into the small of the mad priest's spine. Knocked off balance, Mordecus yelped, and fought to remain standing. In a desperate effort, he snagged Jim's shirt and arm, holding on tight as he fell.

The demon's gullet churned and salivated. It wrapped its tongue around Cassie as it continued to bathe her in spit. Seemingly ambivalent about who or what landed in its hungry mouth... aroused only by the thrill of the feed and bloodlust.

More ragged tendrils swam in Osmodai's frothy gorge, slowly making their way up its esophagus to latch onto Mordecus' kicking legs. The worshippers finally opened their glossed eyes and came to their senses. They hurled obscenities at Jim, but they were powerless in the debilitating grip of Osmodai's tongues.

The more the cultists squirmed and struggled to break free, the tighter the tongues constricted. Putrid sludge oozed from the papillae and the caustic mucus burned their flesh, melting them into vermillion putty. Their rapturous groans turned to peals of agony that erupted from their liquefying faces. Mordecus howled as he watched his flock disintegrate into puddles of human offal. He yanked hard on Jim's shirt, trying to overtake his position on the well's rim with no success.

The worshippers had dissolved and were absorbed through Osmodai's pores. The tendrils retreated into its body, writhing under its skin like maggots through rotting meat, as the suffocating stink of the bile rising in its gorge gagged Jim to light-headedness. Its main tongue, still curled around Cassie, pulled on her lifeless form as it descended into the abyss. Jim knew Cassie was dead. Either from the pulverizing fear or from the massive blood loss, but dead regardless—enslaved, tortured, and, ultimately, sacrificed by the hands of this immoral sect. He had failed.

Osmodai started closing its mouth, having rendered Cassie into nothing more than blood-red pudding. Jim wept as he watched the liquefied remains of his only daughter sliding down the beast's tongue into its waiting mouth. Mordecus seized the opportunity to claw at Jim's face to gain a foothold on escaping Osmodai's closing maw. Jim reeled back, his shirt ripping apart with Mordecus' weight, and crashed into the altar.

The stone shrine wobbled.

Mordecus struggled to climb out from within Osmodai's mouth. The beast's back teeth sunk deep into his legs as its mouth closed. Shrieking in agony, he yanked and twisted to free his shredded appendages from the vice-like grip of its jaws.

Jim noticed the altar had lurched when he slammed into it. He jumped to its opposite side, dug his feet into the muddied ground, and pushed. He grunted, smashing his shoulders into it to loosen it from its spot. With a growl, he reached deep into that reservoir of resources, that place where all his anger and anguish congealed into pure hatred for that perverse creation descending back into the earth's crust.

The altar's legs collapsed, tumbling sideways, as the table shifted and dropped. A deadlift and a mighty heave propelled the stone over the edge and down towards Osmodai's toothed chasm. It bounced off the inner wall, tumbling as it chased the sinking monster. The altar smashed through a barrier of Osmodai's gnashing teeth, and vaporized Mordecus' head on impact.

"Fuck you!" cursed Jim before spitting into the well. As he leaned over the edge, he laughed, watching the demon choke, trying mightily to chew the slab in half. The deeper it descended, the more thick water it displaced in its retreat. Watching the water rise, Jim, not content with just hoping the beast would choke to death, had a final surefire idea. His eyes lit up and he ran around the chamber collecting all the flaming torches.

Jim remembered methanol was flammable. And somehow, whether happening naturally, by fracking, or caused by the giant creature dwelling for eons within the mountain, a fissure was opened, releasing gases into the ancient river flowing deep underground.

Standing at the lip of the well, arms full of incendiaries, he pictured Cassie in his mind once more, recalling her as she used to be, as he remembered her—and he smiled. Eyes closed tight and arms opened wide, he dropped the torches into the well and waited for the fiery inevitable.

END_GAME (DEMENTIA PRAECOX)

```
Greetings…

Welcome to Kill4Coin, the Dark Web's
finest. If you need someone killed
you've come to the right place.

Standard asking price is 10,000 USD
paid in Bitcoin. An additional 2,500
USD is required for multiple kills on
the same contract, up to 3.

Example:
Two hit contract = 10,000 USD + 2,500
USD = 12,500 USD
Three hit contract = 10,000 USD + 2,500
USD + 2,500 USD = 15,000 USD

Other factors will increase the base
fee. Here are some of them:
```

```
Political Targets              +8,000
(no major figures)

Law Enforcement                +5,000

Clergy                         +3,000

Minors under 16
(you're on your own, psycho!)

Extended suffering     +2,000
per hit

Photos/Proof of Death          +1,000
per hit

Disposal of remains            +2,000
per hit
```

Want someone to suffer? We can make them suffer. Need to make an example? We can arrange that. Need to make it look personal or like suicide? Custom methods of execution available upon request on a case by case basis (for an additional charge per contract).

We require half payment upfront with the rest to be paid immediately upon proof of completion.

We are currently accepting contracts from North and South America.

For someone to be eliminated, we will need their name, age, address, description, and a current photo. Additional details such as habits, pets, and tendencies are helpful but not required unless pertinent to the contract.

It can take 2-4 weeks to complete a contract. You will be contacted once it's done.

Thank You.

You are now logged in to HitChat. Log Out | Return To Index

Connecting to server...
Connected, please wait...

[02:16:37] You are online
[02:16:38] You are a participant in this room

--X-- Welcome to HitChat, a murder-for-hire contract request room. This is a private room. If you haven't already, please read the channel rules and FAQ before chatting. Thank you and who can we kill for you today?

[02:17:01] Kill4Coin_One (admin) is online
[02:17:02] Kill4Coin_One (admin) is a participant in this room

[02:17:12] Left_4_dead1: Hi? Read the FAQ... willing 2 pay all upfront but has to b done this weeknd.

[02:17:33] Kill4Coin_One (admin): Apologies. But that is not enuff time 2 prepare n execute.

[02:17:58] Left_4_dead1: Ill add an xtra 2000 per hit.

[02:18:01] Kill4Coin_One (admin): up front?

[02:18:07] Left_4_dead1: yes. Very important it happens this weekend.

[02:18:33] Kill4Coin_One (admin): how many?

[02:18:50] Left_4_dead1: 2. My parents… in their home.

[02:19:04] Kill4Coin_One (admin): any bells n whistles?

[02:19:29] Left_4_dead1: huh

[02:19:52] Kill4Coin_One (admin): add-ons custom ways 2 do it.

[02:20:10] Left_4_dead1: o ya srry. Messy n personal, like a home invasion gone wrong

[02:20:55] Kill4Coin_One (admin): no kids right?

[02:21:34] Kill4Coin_One (admin): hello?

[02:21:57] Left_4_dead1: no. no kids. Im the only one…

[02:22:21] Kill4Coin_One (admin): need disposal or POD?

[02:22:55] Left_4_dead1: no thx. I have a plan for that myself.

[02:23:44] Kill4Coin_One (admin): Ok. Ur party.

[02:26:09] Kill4Coin_One (admin): Alright. With the extra custom charge for the mess itll b 18,000 USD. Please send Bitcoin payment to this wallet: 15rt59ip0Fwft4SQTYUklp9T5 followed by contract info for the individuals to this secure email:

k4forKoyn321@gmail.com.

Once it clears it's on and ull be contacted afterward.

```
[02:26:33] Kill4Coin_One (admin): any
questions?

[02:27:00] Left_4_dead1: no. all set.
You will have payment & details within
the hour.

[02:27:57]   Kill4Coin_One    (admin):
Great! Enjoy the rst of ur day and
thanks for choosing Kill4Coin for ur
murdering needs.

[02:28:03] Kill4Coin_One (admin) has
left the chat

[02:28:11] left_4_dead1 has left the
chat
```

A dam wondered if it was always this easy.

It took him longer to get the nerve to go through with it than it did to complete the order. Order? How callously casual, the dichotomy of condemning someone to die by contract.

Aside from scouring the dark recesses of the Internet over the years for just the right provider, he found the whole thing almost as simple as ordering a pizza on Grub Hub. Judge, jury, and executioner (by proxy) all with the electronic *ding* of a Bitcoin transaction. As he took a final swig of his rotgut bourbon, his lips pulled taut at the liquid sting. He smiled, almost hearing the metaphorical sound of a quarter sliding down the chute into the bank.

"Are you sure we should go through with this?"

He leaned back in his computer chair and kicked his legs up on to the bed. With his hands clasped behind his head, he glanced up at his sister. *She hasn't changed in years*. He considered her question. "Well, Lissie. I thought we came to terms with what had to happen— what *needed* to happen. After all, this has been a long time coming."

"I know. But don't you think it's gonna be more trouble than it's worth? I mean—"

Adam's feet dropped off the bed with a thud. "And living *this way* is worth it? Living with all this *shit*—" He twirled his index finger in the air around the side of his head. "Up here? Sorry, but I don't fucking think so. They deserve what's coming. Every bit of suffering..." He stood up in frustration and circled his computer chair. "You of all people should get it." He looked into Lissie's eyes. "You *do* get it, right?"

Lissie held his glare for as long as she could before dropping her eyes to the floor.

"Yeah. That's what I thought. They need to reap the consequences of the life they have created for us." With that, he snatched his empty glass off the desk and stormed out of the room. He found sentencing people to death made him thirsty and he'd had enough of Lissie and her negativity. Though he did consider her a sort of moral compass for him—damaged, but understanding—he knew with no doubt she felt the same way.

He knew the time had come to move forward with the next phase of his life. But what was *after* that? He hoped and prayed that no longer coexisting with the crippling sense of worthlessness would close the wound. The timing couldn't have been more perfect, either, and they both knew what he just set in motion was a foregone conclusion—even if only *he* needed it to happen.

Adam returned to his room positive he'd find Lissie still standing there with that defeated look on her face. Yet, he knew she took his side, probably even agreed with him on some level, but time and again she spouted her warnings that it would change him—forever. When he rounded the corner, ready with a quip to challenge her logic and doubt, he found the room empty. All for the best, really. With her off in her own little corner of the world, she freed him to prepare for the next stage.

For Xavier, the night felt perfect for a mock home invasion. After such a long drive, he was itching to give their client his money's worth. If the party that hired Kill4Coin's two-man team hadn't tried to negotiate and held out just a little longer, they would've done the rush job for the invoice price. Yet the client was adamant and who was he to turn down all that extra cash? However, his partner in crime didn't feel the same way.

Turner, cautious to a fault, had his own set of reservations about working this job with barely a week's notice. If it wasn't for Joey Migs breathing down his neck to pay his gambling debts, he would've made Xavier turn down the job. He also wasn't feeling all warm and fuzzy being back anywhere near his home town. In essence, Turner had started Kill4Coin here and he learned a quick lesson decades ago not to eat where you shit—or murder people for money.

But with money being money and work being work, he'd adjust. And it wasn't as if he'd planned on hanging around afterward. Get in, check everything off on the list, and get the fuck outta Dodge. It also not being an intricate gig set him somewhat at ease. His home invasion package was a tried-and-true method to get shit done quickly—and one of Xavier's specialties. Turner had always chalked it up to the guy's deranged ninja fetish; he even had his own katana for Chrissake!

They sat in the car a block down from the address the client had supplied. Not far enough away that they couldn't see the main egress route out of the house, but also not close enough to stick out or tickle some nosy neighbor's curiosity bone. No overhead streetlamp, obstructed on one side by a high fence, and enough room to vacate the scene if need be—or when the time came.

In the two hours they sat there in the car waiting for a sign that it was go-time, nary a soul ventured near the property and not one interior light turned on. The neighborhood was a dead-zone save for the mangled, one-eyed cat that ventured near Turner's rented vehicle.

"Aw, dad! Can we keep him?" Xavier rolled down his window and made kissy sounds to the wandering feline. "I can feed him to Osmodeus."

Turner didn't divert his eyes from the house—just in case. "There is something not right with you."

"I am who my parents made me," Xavier said, rolling up his window. "I'll tell ya what... There's something not right with this job. Like, is anyone even home? You sure you got the right place, man?"

"Of course, I'm sure. This is where the email said to go. What am I, the new guy?"

"Just askin'. You never know."

"Before you came along to enrich my meaningless existence," Turner began, turning to his partner, "I had my first contract in this town."

"No shit?"

"Yes shit. Not a neighborhood this fancy or anything but, yeah, kinda where it all started. That's why I wish you had talked to me first before finalizing this job. Just feels... weird being back here."

"Bro. No way I could've turned down that money," said Xavier. "And you know it."

A light on the second floor illuminated the blinds in a pale yellow and Turner perked up. He backhanded Xavier. "Hey, get your game face on. Shift's about to start."

Xavier reached through the space between his knees and grabbed his satchel of gear. "About fuckin' time. There be murder afoot."

"Remember. We're professionals. Messy and mean... just like the client wants."

Adam smiled as his watch's alarm chirped. He ignored Lissie and her long face as he grabbed a framed photo off the shelf and looked into the faces of his parents—as they were—one last time. "And so it begins."

"You can still call this off, Adam," Lissie said. "I understand how you feel, but this is not going to end well."

Getting her to shut up seemed next to impossible, but ignoring her got easier with each day. And now that the time had come for his plan to see fruition, her words just bounced off his eardrums as if she'd never said a word. Adam dismissed her once more before turning off the light and leaving the room.

Hidden by the darkness of the tree-lined street, Xavier and Turner made their way towards the client's parents' house. Even with no one out at this hour, they still used caution and the swirling rise of the neighborhood's shadows to mask the commencement of the hunt.

Employing hand signals, Turner instructed Xavier to go around the house and enter through the back door. He took off with his satchel slung over his shoulder and a pry bar at the ready in his mitts, obedient and happy as a puppy.

Turner shook his head. He knew someday Xavier's overzealousness might destroy what he had built—the man enjoyed this work a little too much and may soon come to find he had fulfilled his purpose. There was a fine line between taking pride in one's work and being too psychotic for even other psychopaths to handle.

With his trusty cattle prod in hand, his straight razor tucked in his back pocket, and hammer-ended utility bar hooked to his belt, Turner snuck up the front steps, aching to satiate his own bloodlust that, at times, surpassed even his love of money.

The house was still, not even shadows moved within its confines. After all these years, he still felt the thrill pumping through his veins, filling his cock with life. *Relax, little buddy. Gonna need some of that blood to think.*

On the brink of breaching the threshold, Turner found the home deceiving in size and depth, bigger than he'd originally estimated. He wondered if Xavier had the same feeling as well—or if he had already jizzed his shorts from the excitement.

An uncharacteristic sensation—bordering on anxiety—gripped his mind as his hand rested on the door handle. He pressed on, suppressing that sudden overwhelming stir of emotions. *Cut that shit out! You're a fucking professional.*

Locked.

He wished he had pressed the client for more intel about the residence as he put the utility bar to work. The crunch of the doorjamb as the tool popped the lock made him pause. With it so unnaturally quiet, he knew even the slightest of sounds could make the loudest of noises. Satisfied by the returning silence, he continued into the foyer, the dim ambient glow from outside illuminated a small pathway into the house's interior.

The living room was empty. Turner's trained ears heard Xavier making his entrance through the back door into what he assumed was a mudroom or enclosed porch. His finger hovered over the cattle prod's power button just in case.

Xavier stood on the porch facing the solid back door. He wished he could just kick it in and make a grand entrance, raise some hell, scare the shit out of his victims—anything to instill even greater fear in his prey and have fun while he was at it. But he resisted; there was a method to this work and a method to working with Turner—even if he *was* becoming some kind of soft pussy in his later years. Still... rules were rules and he was the boss man.

He forced the end of the bar into the doorframe and pried it open with the practiced ease of a career criminal. *Easier than an oyster.* After slipping in through the breached entryway, he found himself in a small area with benches and coat racks lining the walls. Tucked out of the way under the benches were shoes of all sizes and styles, yet most appeared out of fashion. He scoffed at a pair of stubby, wide orthopedic shoes caked in a layer of grime. *Wonder what mongoloid* those *belong to.*

The house on his end stood quiet—almost *too* quiet. Xavier hated silence. Even as a tool of the job, it made his skin crawl. Thankfully, the noises in his head kept him even-keeled. He expected at least some evidence of life meeting his ears, but the home's size and layout masked even Turner's movements.

In the kitchen area, it was more of the same. He inwardly cursed; his thrill-kill erection withering away with every actionless second. But there *had* to be someone home! They saw lights turn on. Despite having already mentally spent the client's money, he still needed to kill—the urge demanding satisfaction now that his senses came online.

Turner crossed the expanse of the living room, walking over the lush carpet in the center of the room to further mask his footfalls. Ahead, he honed in on a sprawling staircase with only the weak light coming in through the windows now that he realized no one currently occupied this floor of the home. Perhaps they were upstairs asleep, he thought.

He stepped off the carpet at the edge of its thick, retro shag and onto the hardwood floor. Mid stride his foot wouldn't budge. Before he could course-correct his other foot landed and immediately cemented in place. Turner yanked on his left leg, trying in vain to dislodge his foot from whatever had him stuck as worry creased his brow. With one final tug, he yanked his foot out of his shoe. His momentum tested his balance and his socked foot planted into more of the sticky substance.

"Mother of fuck," Turner mouthed as he steadied himself before making another ill-fated attempt at freedom. *Challenge accepted, shitheads*. He estimated his distance from his sticky situation to the base of the staircase and peeled his feet out of his shoe and sock, standing on them to stay clear of the stuff. His adrenaline pumped as his mind worked this unprecedented situation. With a quick leap, he landed on the first stair, grabbing the rail to steady himself.

As he stood there, listening to the silence for anything other than his stifled breaths of frustration, he thought about calling out to Xavier, but decided otherwise, hopeful his partner was faring better. He wrestled with his right brain for reasoning, wanting to take a moment to assess the path of his dilemma. But the game was on.

Lights and sounds from a room at the top of the staircase alarmed him; the flickering and faint echoes filtered out into the second floor's gloom. A television! Turner took a step careful not to make the wood creak in his ascent. *Got you, fucker*.

The searing pain of his skin splitting open rocketed up his body. He clenched his hand over his mouth to suppress the cry of agony from the razor embedded in his instep. His blood careened around the trap and cascaded over the edge of the stair. Tears threatened to fall as he choked back a reflexive sob. Slowly, he lifted his foot off the mounted blade; the slick sound of his own flesh sliding from the metal punched him in the gut. His years of training and discipline allowed him to calm down, to find his center, and think three steps ahead.

He peeled off his remaining sock and tied it tight around his wound to stop the bleeding. The sights and sounds from the television upstairs persisted. *Someone* was *home after all*. Someone who had set traps—someone who expected their imminent arrival and had prepared a welcome. With the double-cross evident, he felt the rage building inside, yet he knew giving into it would make the situation worse. He'd been doing this too long to get completely outsmarted, but now he saw red. It had become personal—and that pissed him off.

Turner made it to the landing, having traversed a path up the steps through the deadly maze of razors. The TV room was up ahead to his left, so he gripped the prod's handle, sensing its powerful potential to subdue any pending threat. *Whoever's in there is fuckin' dead!* He moved toward the room careful not to slip in the puddle of his own blood as his drenched sock made spongy sounds with each step.

The room sat empty. Even with the old TV set in the room's far corner casting flickering shadows across the walls, he still could sense he was alone. On the screen, a family sat around a kitchen table covered in wrapped presents and desserts, the centerpiece a decorated cake lit with candles. The quality of the home video had succumbed to age and multiple viewings. Through the analog distortion, he made out few details: the faces of the four family members, a teenage girl decked out in late 80's Hot Topic accouterments, a young birthday boy of about eight or nine sporting a pointy, paper hat, and the parents....

The parents.

Their faces stared into the mounted camcorder as if looking back at him through the screen. Turner recognized them immediately, and chills prickled the back of his neck as he broke out into a cold sweat. Pieces were falling together for him... because he now realized what was possibly happening.

Various shades of green swathed his field of vision as he watched out of sight through his night-vision goggles. At least *one* of the intruders fell victim to his "inconvenience" downstairs. When the trespasser stepped onto the razors it took all he had not to burst into fits of laughter. Yet, he remained quiet and omniscient, commanding discipline in the darkness. He knew the TV gag—and the images on the screen themselves—would trigger the man's internal alarm. Hopefully, for his own amusement and satisfaction, they would also pique the man's curiosity.

As the intruder entered the room, spotting the home movie playing the television, his black clothes registered a pale green through the goggles. As he lurked in the shadows, he trod across the second-floor landing with a metal pipe in hand.

The man watched the screen, seeming to absorb all the details as they flashed by. The hunter savored the game, welcoming the moment recognition reflected in the hitman's face. He stepped closer and pulled the VCR remote from his pocket.

The image of the two parents paused on the screen; their loving smiles and happy eyes stared back at Turner through the wavy distortion of the old VHS tape. He heard a shallow creaking behind him and it was enough for the visceral knot of tension to clench his belly. The cattle prod suddenly felt heavy in his hand. He spun to face whoever was standing there, but before he could react his vison exploded into bright lights, blocking out everything else. As he crumpled to the floor, unable to alert Xavier downstairs, he heard his attacker snicker before everything went black.

Xavier was leaving the kitchen area on his way over to a door that stood ajar when he heard a loud *thump* coming from the second floor. Whether that was Turner or the marks, he couldn't tell. The last thing he wanted to do was risk the contract if nothing was wrong. Maybe Turner found one or both of the parents and, at any second, will call for him to come to join the fun.

But as he waited for any sign of things progressing, staring into the churning darkness of the narrow staircase on the far wall, he could've sworn he heard a floorboard squeak. Against better judgment, he whispered, "Yo... that you?"

No answer. No more squeaks either.

Xavier stepped back the way he just came, zeroing in on the darkened staircase, forcing his eyes to adjust. Through that opened door behind him, he heard quiet voices—hardly noticeable whispers really—permeating the air. He strained to make out the words, but regardless, they were words... and that meant people. At that moment, the creaking floor became nothing more than a memory.

Fuckers are in the basement!

Turner's attacker raced down the back steps and clicked play on a second remote. He slid it into his pocket and waited out of sight in his shadows of the stairwell. He heard the second intruder step softly to the basement door and knew the ruse worked. Any second now, the man's curiosity would bring him to the threshold and eventually down the stairs.

The lurker smiled as the basement door hinges squealed and the intruder mumbled a curse at the disruption to the silence. Yet, his smile faded. The trespasser was taking too long at the top of the stairs, just looking down into the gloomy basement, listening to the recording of family videos playing over a speaker.

Impatience set in.

The plan was risky. If intruder number two took any longer, intruder number one in the den upstairs could wake up, spoiling his entire plan. He weighed his options: wait for the bastard to fall victim to the trap in the basement and chance the asshole upstairs coming to, or just charge over and smashing him in the skull, shoving him down the stairs.

Then the intruder decided for him and he smiled, slinking into the shadows of the kitchen.

With the practiced grace of a cat burglar, Xavier pressed on. Each step brought him closer to obtaining his goal—*pure fucking murder*. His bread and butter. Self-aware enough, he could admit that getting paid for this was secondary to the thrill and the quench of the thirst. He'd end up doing this stuff anyway.

His eyes adjusted to the dimness as he stepped with care onto each wooden step. No longer concerned with what they were saying, he was ecstatic he found them first. *Suck it, Turner!* As he advanced, he felt something under his foot and heard a snapping *tink*. His mind raced to place the peculiar sound, but as his internal gears were turning a waterfall of thick liquid from above doused him before clobbering him with the empty—but heavy—bucket.

He tumbled down the rest of the stairs, his skull hammering against each step. The spill seemed endless until one final crash onto the bottom landing sent him spiraling into borderline unconsciousness. Xavier ended the fall in a bent mess, landing on a sheet of fiberglass insulation littered with tacks and shards of broken glass. Dazed, the pain of his cuts barely registered above his throbbing head. The noxious resin-coated his clothes and clung to his skin, mixing with his bloody wounds. It smeared across his face, clogging his ears and stinging his eyes. He attempted to move, to untangle his brain from the pain of the fall as well as his body from the odd mesh sticking to his moistened form. Only, his struggling made it worse.

Xavier muttered something incoherent as he lay face down in his fog of agony and confusion, tacks and glass dust penetrating the skin of his forehead like some medieval crown of torture. A shard of glass had sliced through his cheek. Visually impaired, he still sensed somebody nearby and called out. "Turner... Help..."

Footsteps creaked down the stairs towards him.

"Who's there? Help..."

In the murky basement, Xavier saw nothing but the floor and the tacks inches from his eyeball. The resin felt thicker now that he had unwittingly wrapped himself in the itchy mesh. He heard a loud click followed by an even louder hum. Overhead, a large bulb buzzed to life, casting a pale pink hue over him. As the heat from the ultraviolet lamp reached his body, he could feel the resin hardening... feel the tacks and glass press into his flesh as his cocoon stiffened.

He screamed, fighting for his semi-conscious brain to remain on-line, to keep struggling against his quickly setting binds—to do anything but lay there and get stabbed to death under that pink light of hell. Through the breaks in his hollering, Xavier heard the staticky chorus of voices continuously looping in the background.

Turner's eyes parted, slowly at first with eyelashes like cobwebs obscuring everything into a misty swirl of grays and blacks. He was thankful that the waking world wasn't as black as the one from which he'd just returned. His head spun and, when he reached up to the sore spot, his hand came away sticky. *How long have I been out?* Then he remembered the fleeting glimmer—his reflection ever so brief—in the night vision goggles of his attacker.

He sat upon his haunches as his head throbbed, but the searing pain in his foot as he flexed it reminded him of his dire situation. Through a grimace, he focused on the flickering light of the TV, momentarily lost in the garbled image of the family staring back at him from another decade.

The floorboard creaked, alerting him to more possible danger. *Praise Jesus for old houses!* He climbed to his feet with the aid of an armchair for balance trying to ignore the pain in his bleeding foot. His cattle prod and utility hammer were gone. Panicked, he went for his back pocket and found his trusty straight razor. *Still there.* The brush of the metal against his thumb as he opened it filled him with relief. If anything, he could still defend himself.

He had no doubts that the job had gone awry. His brain hurt. *What the* fuck *is going on?* Some details made a fuzzy kind of sense, while other pieces of the puzzle were just bat shit absurd. The neighborhood, the faces on the old video—they meant something. If it wasn't for his concussion, he'd be able to connect the dots. Again, the floor in the hallway squeaked, a forewarning that someone was moving.

Turner peeked around the corner of the door half expecting to see Xavier standing there. Empty. His wounded foot throbbed, but he needed to continue ignoring it so he could figure out just what the hell was going on. He lurched out into the hallway with the blade ready to strike. No one there. He crossed the threshold into the room opposite the den.

The pure and unforgiving blackness played tricks on the eye, creating even darker shadows that danced around him with a kind of corporality. He couldn't see a thing, but he refused to turn on a light—he needed *any* advantage against his enemy.

With the room void of answers, he returned to the hallway. At the end of the hall, near the top of the stairs, stood an indistinguishable form. Though his eyes still adjusted, Turner assumed it was the same asshole who attacked him earlier. Turner saw the silhouette of *his* cattle prod in the shadow's hand, which confirmed the suspicion. Running on pure adrenaline, Turner rushed down the hallway towards his enemy, his razor held high with deadly intent. The shadowy form remained still.

By the time Turner realized it, it was too late. His awkward, high-speed limp carried his momentum forward. As he fought for the balance to stop, his adrenaline dump turned to desperation and searing pain spiked up his leg. Now off-kilter, Turner crashed into the wide, full-length mirror, losing his blade and crashing through the railing rigged to break on impact. He had nothing to catch him as he went airborne, and in a split second of sheer necessity, he thrust his arms out and grasped onto the chandelier.

The fixture shook and swung, spinning against its anchors in the ceiling. Light bulbs exploded upon his impact, kicking up dust and showering him in tiny glass particles. Turner felt the wires pull taut and heard the cracking of the plaster as he clung to it for dear life.

He glanced over his shoulder to the landing. A night-vision-goggled man stood at the precipice laughing. Turner reached out to grab him and was rapped across his knuckles with his own utility hammer. His assailant—his tormentor—wiggled his index finger disapprovingly before pointing down. As Turner followed the man's finger, his eyes adjusted. Below him, a net crafted out of barbed wire filled the space. The chandelier's anchors gave way some more, dropping him down another foot.

"You motherfucker!" spat Turner, his face burning hot with anger. "I'm gonna choke you to death with your own intestines." His cattle prod sparked, creating a hot blue arc when the attacker struck the metal frame of the demolished mirror. Turner felt sweat dampen his palms, making his grip on the light fixture falter. "Don't you fuckin' dare, asshole."

The man chuckled, his amusement making him twitch with giddiness.

Turner heard a low mumbling somewhere in the bowels of the house. "Xavier! That you? Get up here, man!"

A weak and muffled cry for help returned his own call for aid.

"Xavier's a little *wrapped up* at the moment." The figure laughed again. "Ha! I've always wanted to say a badass movie line like that!"

Turner felt his hands slipping, and with nothing under him for leverage, his fingers were losing grip. The continued rocking motion of the chandelier tripled his nauseating fear. Every swing towards the broken railing brought him closer to the asshole with his cattle prod. With one simple touch, the prod's electrical current traveled through Turner's body, scorching his nerve endings. His muscles seized and his fingers uncurled, releasing the chandelier and dropping him into the waiting barbs of the metal net.

Turner stirred, aware that he was bound with something metal and sharp. Wholly concussed now, he knew he couldn't take another hit to the head. At first, he thought he might have gone blind. Blackness covered everything and he felt a heaviness over his eyes and head. It wasn't until he heard the click of a switch and the buzz of fluorescent lights that he realized he was hooded.

Through the open bottom of the hood, he caught a glimpse of a pair of black sneakers. While Turner could only make out very little detail, he knew they belonged to a male... and more than likely, the same one who put him here. The sneakers, short in length and squared off in the toes, threw him off, reminding him of specially-made orthopedic shoes.

A musty odor permeated the material's fabric and entered his nostrils—the smell of old dirt. Turner raised his head to get a better angle through the opening but was popped on the head with something hard. "Do that again, cocksucker, and see what happens." His captor yanked off the hood and fluorescent light stung his eyes, engulfing everything in yellow radiance.

"What's going to happen," a feminine voice said from beyond the light, "is that things are about to get unpleasant."

The voice sounded peculiar. Completely unexpected. Off.

Turner tilted his head to avoid the glare. Next to him in a lump on the floor, Xavier struggled inside a sheath of fiberglass-like fabric slathered in an amber gel. A heat lamp blazed above him, appearing to harden the caked-on substance. Xavier's blood had leaked through, creating a leopard spot pattern all over the material. His raw skin, which had adhered to the gel, contorted, looking painfully taut in some spots and bunched up in others. Glass and tacks stuck out of his partner's wounded flesh, forcing Turner's own skin to crawl and go cold.

Acid burned his esophagus when he saw Xavier's mouth, now realizing why earlier he only barely heard his cries for help. The gel had glued his bottom lip to the mesh, pulling it into a horrible shape as his dry tongue struggled to stay clear of the sticky mess. Xavier's exhausted mumbling oozed from his mouth along with puddles of drool.

Turner thrashed about, unconcerned with the barbed binds piercing his skin. "You fucker...." He looked at his partner. "Relax, X-man. This cunt doesn't know who she's fuckin' with."

From out of Turner's compromised periphery, Adam's fist smashed him in the face. "Watch what you call my sister, asshole!"

However, the blow didn't even register. Turner had already fixed his gaze on the two desiccated corpses—one male and one female—displayed in open, dirt-stained coffins. They were propped up against the wall in front of an old table adorned with a primitive memorial of melting candles and framed photographs. Some of the photos contained images of a loving family, while others were of a violent crime scene, a grisly diorama splayed out in vermillion detail.

The old and brittle bodies inside the caskets had seen violence in their previous lives. Turner could tell they had been mutilated and violated beyond repair, surely indicating a closed casket ceremony had been necessary. He stared into the distorted faces that death and time had altered, yet, even after all these years, he still knew who they were, and the crime photos confirmed his suspicion.

"Can you still recognize your handiwork?" the female said still somewhere behind Turner.

Adam's voice replied—colder and crueler. "Of course, he does."

"Fuck you *both*!" He spat a glob of blood onto the cellar floor.

"Spoken like a true professional." Adam stepped out from the backdrop of shadows and stood in between Turner and Xavier. "You shouldn't talk to your customers that way."

Turner's brain kicked into overtime, clicking over as thoughts raced through his memory banks.

"Certainly not to those who paid in full," Adam continued. "*And* in advance to boot. After all... isn't the customer always right?"

Turner smiled as all the pieces thudded into place. Xavier, with his frozen expression of fright, looked on with terror in his burning eyes. "Don't sweat it, X. I know what this is about."

Adam leaned into Turner's face and scowled. "You don't know *shit*."

Turner grinned in defiance. "So you're the little puke that got away that night. Mommy and Daddy were *so* scared for you. *Run, Adam! Run!* I should've realized something was up when I saw your crippled, mutant feet standing in front of me. You sure had me goin' up to now. Must be slippin' in my old age." He chuckled. "How *did* you manage to get away on crutches with those two potato feet of yours?"

Adam sighed. "You wanna know what the lost opportunity of this whole ordeal has been? Once I turned eighteen and finally inherited my share of our parents' estate, I had enough money to buy back the ole homestead. If it was still standing, that is."

He snatched a handful of Xavier's hair and yanked his head back. Xavier groaned. His flesh tore away from the resin, leaving a permanent grin on his face and his bottom lip still stuck to the fiberglass. "Wouldn't that have been somethin'?" Adam continued. "Tricking you right back into the house where our nightmare all started."

Traces of his instability twinkled in the blacks of his eyes.

"But instead... I had to buy this here fixer-upper." He waved his arms out wide to imply the grandeur of the place, twisting Xavier's neck to painful angles. "Because some little twerp burned down his house after he saw..." He smiled. "Well, I'm sure you catch my drift."

The flash of Turner's razor was as dazzling as it was immediate. "If I only knew then what I know now. Yet, I'm still glad the ruse worked." Without missing a beat, Adam carved a vicious path through Xavier's throat, severing his carotid and slicing through his windpipe. Blood pumped out of the breach in sporadic bursts as the crimson rainbow arched through the air. Choking gags echoed throughout the basement as Xavier gasped for air, slamming back and forth in his struggle to live.

Turner refused to let the fear show—an emotion he'd spent years learning to deny—and gave his captor his bravest fuck-you-face. At the end of the day, Xavier was expendable and empathy was a weakness as far as he was concerned. "I got paid a shit ton of cash to do your parents. Even by today's standards. Somebody wanted them dead as shit! But...," he paused, "I seem to remember making the acquaintance of another youngster that night. A hot little piece of high school trim, if I remember correctly." Turner winked. The lascivious twinkle in his eye raised Adam's ire. "Lissie was it?

Adam's face dropped at hearing the name.

"Yeah, that was it." Turner smacked his lips together. "Damn, she was *f-i-n-e* fine. Tasted *so* sweet, too, if memory serves. Catch *my* drift?" He chuckled. "But, I don't have to tell you. You had front row seats. *Didn't ya?*"

"I'm two seconds away from cutting out your fucking tongue, you son of a...." Adam held up his hands, his anger subsiding long enough to smirk. "She's right behind you, actually."

Turner strained to peer over his right shoulder to the darkened corner of the cellar. He could finally make out the vague silhouette of a woman sitting in a chair. He turned back to Adam. "So *that's* who your little lady friend is back there. Hey, sexy. Miss me?"

"She didn't think this was a good idea at all. Didn't think you were even worth the effort." Adam paced as he talked and ended up behind Turner. "Fucking morality and shit. Fought me tooth and nail, even though she swallowed a bottle of pills after what you did to us.

"But our parents deserve vengeance! And you deserve every–*fucking* –thing that's coming to you. And I think she finally sees things my way." He squeezed Turner's shoulders before giving him a reassuring pat on his back. "Isn't that right, Lissie?"

Lissie sighed. "I'd rather be with you than against you if that's what you mean."

Turner's blood froze in his veins when he heard Lissie's voice come out of Adam's mouth. His captor's whole demeanor had changed, all the way down to the way he stood.

"What's wrong, tough guy?" Lissie's voice asked. "Don't like it when a lady's in control?"

And just like that, Adam's natural voice returned. "Not so cock-sure now, are ya?"

Turner glanced over his shoulder at the silent and still figure sitting there in the dark. He knew now it was just another corpse. "Oh, I fucked you up good, huh?"

Adam, confused, looked down at Turner. "You slaughtered our fucking parents! Not to mention what you did to us. Of course, you fucked us up!"

"Us? I don't mean to burst anyone's bubble or nothin'," Turner said, "but there are only two of us here, champ." He spat another glob of blood, which landed on Adam's shoe. "You. And me."

Adam scowled and stomped over, clocking Turner in his jaw. "Quit your fucking mind games! You lost. We won."

"How hard did he hit the floor when he fell, Adam? Geez! I'm standing right next to you for God's sake," the voice that wasn't Adam's said. "We should just hurry up and get this over with. I'm still not feeling too sure about all this."

Like a switch. "Relax already. But you're probably right. See? I *do* listen to you sometimes." A weird, hybrid laugh erupted from Adam, like two sets of vocal cords emitting the same pitch but with two separate voices.

Adam spun around, his attention suddenly elsewhere. He made a bee-line for the nearest coffin, which contained his mother's corpse. He leaned in awkwardly as if huddling up to talk to someone—both childlike and terrifying at the same time.

Finished, Adam bounced back over to Turner. "Good news! I think it's time to get down to business." He pinned Turner's hand down onto the armrest and switched open the razor, slicing across its index finger at the second knuckle. Turner spasmed as the pain rocked him.

Adam worked the blade as it wobbled to and fro, its sharp edge embedded halfway into the cartilage between the knuckles. He reached behind him to snatch a hammer from under the table and with a fierce blow to the top of the razor severed Turner's finger.

Tortured by the agony, Turner finally relented with a howl as blood surged out of the stump. Adam bent over and scooped up the appendage. "You're lucky I only need the finger or else I'd keep on going," he said, tapping the dull side of the razor on Turner's head.

"You better put something on that before he bleeds to death," Adam spoke in Lissie's voice.

"Suppose you're right." Adam ripped off a strip of Turner's shirt and cinched it around the gushing wound. "I wonder if he still feels his finger there like we felt Mom and Dad still there after he *butchered* them!"

Turner's dizzying shock fogged his vision. Adam then cut off an excessive clump of Turner's hair. In separate hands, he carried both the clipping and the finger to the table in front of the coffins. "You better fucking kill me, 'cause if I get out of this—" Again, Turner pulled at the wire tethers.

Ignoring the outburst, Adam set to work. As if following a detailed recipe, he reached under the table again, this time pulling out a stone bowl and a carafe of deep-red liquid. Next, he grabbed an old book and set it down on the tabletop. Bound in mahogany-colored leather, the tome looked antiquated and world-worn; at some point in its history, archaic symbols had been engraved on its cover and spine.

Turner looked away and ended up gazing right into Xavier's dead eyes, blood no longer pumped from the savage hole in his neck. So many warning bells, so little judgment due to money, ego, and bloodthirst. *I fucked up* real *good!* Corpses, booby-traps, schizos, and blood-fucking-rituals. *I picked one hell of a way to go out.*

Adam/Lissie mumbled incoherent words as they read from the old tome. In his reverie, Turner overheard the siblings start arguing over the pronunciations of words so foreign and archaic, he knew he'd never heard them before.

"...I know what a glottal stop is, Lissie!"

"Are you sure? Seems to me you didn't practice hard enough...."

"For someone who didn't want me to even do this, you're sure giving me a lot of shit about it." A mixed bag of garbled vowel sounds and coarse consonants stabbed at the air between them as Adam struggled with the chant or a spell of some sort.

"You really are just one step away from full-blown mongoloid, aren't you kid?" He snorted as he giggled, and that made everything that much funnier to him. At that moment, amidst his fit of laughter, he found himself more curious than scared as to his immediate future.

Adam sliced the hunk of finger lengthwise like he was readying a hot dog for the grill before he squeezed out its remaining blood into the bowl. He peeled off the flesh and muscles and removed the bones. After a few more throaty verses, those items, too, went into the bowl. Eyes filled with intent, he poured a hefty serving of the red potion and went to work with a pestle, crushing the bones into fragments and grinding the ingredients together into a ruddy mush.

Satisfied, Adam shook the tension and soreness from his arm. "Probably go a lot smoother if I had a blender or something. Huh?" He scooped up the lock of Turner's hair and tied a knot in the center of its length. After inserting the hair inside the boneless finger, he left an inch of it exposed to create a macabre paintbrush.

"You've *gotta* be fuckin' kidding me." It took Turner had, but he burst out laughing again anyway at the absurdity of it all.

Adam did his best to ignore Turner, but his eyes told the truth— he was nervous and unsure about it even working in the first place. He dipped the finger-brush into the bowl, making sure to saturate the hairs with as much of the concoction as possible for adequate coverage. He paused, uncertain.

"Just do it, Adam," Lissie's voice blurted. "Just get this over with."

"Yeah, Adam," mocked Turner. "Gitter done, you crazy bastard!"

With the brush and bowl in hand, Adam turned to his parents' coffins. He painted delicate symbols on the pale foreheads of each dead parent before exposing both of their torsos to paint more symbols over their hearts. "Sorry, Mom," he said, blushing as he guided the hairs over her withered breast. He continued his barely audible mumbling.

The painted marks sizzled and smoked. Turner's laughter caught in his throat. His eyes widened. Adam's chanting quickened, getting louder as he neared the end of the incantation. The symbols darkened, searing and scarring the dead flesh until they became one with the skin. An acrid mixture of burnt meat and sulfur saturated the air.

As the brands cooled and the smoke cleared, the corpses' eyelids cracked open, revealing empty, mottled pits. The taut, ashen skin of their faces stretched and contorted in the throes of reanimation. Horrible gaping maws snapped to life, expelling decade-old breaths and gases. Their remaining teeth clicked together, chattering as deep guttural moans escaped their once useless esophagus. The remnants of their lips parted to reveal blackened, recessed gums. Their shriveled tongues darted in and out, cutting through the mucus of mouths unused in years.

Terrified, Turner's heart raced, skipping beats. On the verge of potential arrest, all of his veins felt on fire. Pain coursed to the tip of every nerve in his body as he watched his inaugural victims come back to life. The corpses writhed in their death beds, their stiffened joints popped. Bones in their sockets scrapped together as the dust of cartilage long gone ground them into further collapse.

With a broad smile, Adam cackled, proud of his success. "See, Lissie? It worked!"

Turner's guts somersaulted from the crunching and crinkling sounds of Adam's dead parents resurrecting. The clicking of teeth, the hollow, dry groans, challenged his constitution until he retched.

When Adam's parents finally gained awareness and spotted them, their gnarled mouths pulled back into snarls. They hissed and lurched, gripping the sides of the coffins to propel themselves forward.

Adam's eyes welled up at the sight of his reawakened parents. His smile beamed. "Lissie, they're back," he said with a sniffle, looking off to the side where only he saw his sister. "Mom. Dad." Both of their heads turned as if understanding their son's words. "We missed you *so* much. It's time for your revenge."

The resurrected lunged from the confines of their burial coffers, lumbering into the living world like newborn babes on fresh legs. Yet, their interest in Adam didn't waver. Rickety and uncoordinated, they shambled towards their son, need punctuating their ghastly wails.

Adam dropped the bowl and brush, sending them crashing to the floor. "Lissie? What's happening?" He snatched the old book from the table and flipped through its pages looking for answers. Backpedaling away from the gnashing, eyeless horrors, he cried. "Lissie! Help me!"

Turner watched it unfold in a placid combination of awestruck curiosity and pants-shitting terror. In delirium, he chanted, "You fucked up! You fucked up!" interspersed with bouts of chuckling like an idiot. He so wanted this madness to end.

"Lissie!" Adam cried. "I translated it wrong." His eyes scoured the pages hoping for a passage to right the wrong, but he found none. The lumbering corpses staggered closer. "Shit... my hair. Not his... *Mine!*"

"Mom! Dad!" Lissie's voice yelled from Adam's mouth. "Please, stop! He's the one you want." Adam pointed at Turner, but they wanted nothing to do with the hitman, not now that they had their eyeless sockets on him. "No! Him! *He's* the one you want. *He's* the bastard who killed you."

The pleas fell on unhearing—uncaring—ears. Adam swung the old book out in front of him in feeble defense until he just chucked it at them. The echoes of Turner's laughs filled the void. He continued backing up and stumbled, tripping over the emaciated body of his sister sitting in the dark. Together they fell in a mess of tangled limbs, crashing to the cold, stone floor. Mom and Dad closed the gap and pounced, slumping over their son with mindless conviction.

Adam screamed for them to stop. He cried for his sister's help, but he was, at that moment, alone—alone with the horror he perpetrated. His cries turned to gurgles as his mother tore a hole in his throat while his father gnawed on the flesh of his arms and neck.

The wet, slurping sounds, the sticky peal of muscle ripped from bone, sent Turner's empty stomach into acidic turmoil. As he gagged, he continued to laugh, uproarious guffaws of a broken mind between bouts of heaving whatever else he had left in him. At that moment, his vacant belly rumbled with its own hunger. And no, the irony was not lost on him. He knew he was next on the menu.

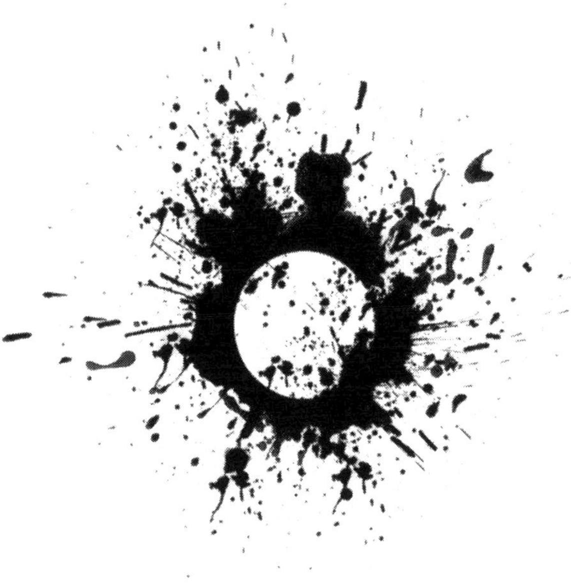

A DIFFERENT KIND OF SLUMBER

Thomas Isaac Griffey

"The Master is feeding me my dreams," Thomas answered in growing aggravation, the words spewing from his mouth.

"What does that mean, though?" she asked—again.

Repetition... the strength of foundation... but as she repeated the question despite his answer, mimicking her own words into oblivion, he couldn't help but grow less tolerant of her by the second. This routine had become stale. She asked the question, and he answered, and every time, he said the same thing.

"The Master is feeding me my dreams."

Her apparition moved like smoke, dancing on the musty current flowing through the old abandoned warehouse. Yet, it hadn't truly been abandoned, for her spirit still roamed freely through the crumbling hollows of the structure. The wispy contour of her face fell into a frown. Her eyes, one bright green and the other deep blue, appeared to well up with tears.

Why did she have to frown?

He gave her no reason to be sad. Despite the fact he had murdered her—had taken her life in this very same building—her sadness became an unwelcome distraction. Yet, that had happened so long ago she should've been over it by now, damn it!

What more did she expect from him? He had no more to offer. Why wasn't the release from her unchaste life enough? However, that did not seem to be the case. Her ghost haunted these halls, hanging about them like an ancient shroud never to be removed from the sacred walls.

"Who is your Master?" Her voice rang in his ears.

The answer carved a smile across his face. The Master. Just the thought of what that meant made him tingle. He continued to clean and organize his collection of knives, blades of all devious shapes and sizes, the instruments of his trade; he would need them later. "You're dead. You shouldn't bother yourself with the business of the living," He didn't look at her, his voice cold and distant. "Especially *my* business."

"I still love you, Thomas. I died loving you. There is nothing I can do to change that now."

"Don't say that!" Thomas had only himself to blame for that, though. He knew that when a person died suddenly and at a height of emotion, they would forever harness that feeling in the afterlife. He turned back to the vision of his first love hovering next to him. "Don't ever say that to me again!"

"It's okay, Thomas. I know you still love me," she replied with a smile. "And I'll always be by your side."

From his deadly collection resting on the cracked tabletop, he drew a blade and threw it at her. She rippled like a stone-tossed pond and the knife vanished within her foggy form. "No, I don't love you. I killed you, for fuck's sake! Now leave me alone! You're dead...." His voice trailed off. The thrown knife reappeared back on the table, slick and wet.

It had become an exercise in futility, the arguments he had with his dead lover. And as many times as he had seen her, either floating about or talking to him, he still couldn't believe it possible. She wouldn't go away, no matter how much he begged. Despite his efforts, the ghost of Jane remained, because, deep down, he did still love her.

Thomas left the building at dusk with his satchel of blades. He checked the alleys and windows to see if he was alone, before jumping into his car and speeding off. Exhaustion pressed hard on his eyes and that meant the Master would soon call. Only when his eyelids went heavy did he feel the desire to sleep. Sleep. When the Master—*his* Master—worked magic.

His little car moved along just above the posted speed limit. At home, his bed awaited him, soft downy pillows to lay his head upon, satiny sheets to feel against his warm skin. Once asleep, his world became more. He could do anything, be anything. That was when He came in—the force behind his bloody masterpieces.

When he had first met the Master, he'd had no desire to be a part of the twisted perversions he had to offer. At first, he'd chosen to stay awake, blindly walking through his day dead on his feet but refusing to sleep. However, the Master possessed the virtue of patience.

After months of convincing, Thomas succumbed to the invigorating power of his dreams—the dreams sponsored in part by the alien force of the unseen entity and by the deep-rooted evils his mind had not harvested until then. The power, the surge of emotion, left him breathless and invigorated. To kill and kill again, to taste the life's blood dripping from his hands, made all the sense in the world to him.

In his dreams, he would talk to the Master. "Why can't I do this while I am awake? How does it work if I'm sleeping?"

"It is a different kind of slumber. Only with me can you make your dreams a reality. Only in sleep will the magic work."

At first, Thomas had thought that they were, in fact, just dreams. Until the one day, he caught a glimpse of the nightly news—the savage murder of a college woman in the park—did he finally believe in the reality of the Master in his own dreams. He had dreamt about her, dreamt what the reporters had said was done to her. With that news, he shook with sickness and guilt. Yet, he couldn't avoid the excitement creeping inside of him and, eventually, felt guilt no longer. His dream had given him sensations that he could not ignore—feelings of power, of immensity. And the Master—shapeless and mysterious—had been pleased.

He smiled to himself. The memories remained fresh in his mind; the sounds of tortured screams as he took lives away, aroused him so. His erection fought against the material of his pants. *Tonight's dream will be something special*, he thought... *no one will be prepared for what I might do*.

Lost in his reverie, his knuckles burned white from his tight grip on the steering wheel. He had boosted his speed noticeably past the speed limit.

"Where are we going, Thomas?"

He almost lost control of the vehicle. Jane sat in the backseat staring back at him through the rearview mirror. No longer did she smile; she looked sad and concerned—concerned for him.

"I told you to leave me alone," Thomas said, keeping one eye on the road.

"I'll never leave your side, I said. Remember?" Hazy swirls of mist swam around her form. She looked as if she had been crying.

"Why do you look so sad?" he asked, before he could stop himself.

"I am worried for you, Thomas. Something bad is going to happen to you, I fear."

"What the fuck do you know? For the last time, you're dead. Don't you remember?" A block away, his apartment stood waiting for him—waiting for him to go inside and sleep. He pulled next to the curb and put the car in park. In the back seat, he found no trace of Jane.

As anxious as he was to get to sleep, Jane's warning poked at the back of his mind. He couldn't shake the feeling. Could she be right? But why should he believe anything a ghost would say? Then again, before she arrived, he'd never believed in ghosts.

Outside his car, the air had grown stagnant and warm. Above, the clouds covered the sky and distant moon. The smell of rain hung in the air. He reached the front door of his building and looked back at the car. Jane sat in the back seat again, silent and still, regarding him with deep worry in her ghostly eyes.

To this day, he regretted killing her, but it was unavoidable; the Master had requested it. She could have come to know too much. Thomas had no choice but to oblige... even though he loved her more than anything or anyone in his world. He had dreamt her demise, a demise at his hands—his blades.

He shivered, her stare penetrating his soul. Once inside the lobby, he shut the door behind him, out of view of her mournful gaze.

The neglected apartment building was all that he could afford after Jane's funeral. He had lost his job and had to rely on government assistance—a severe breach in his pride. Options he had no choice but to live with.

At his door, he fumbled with his keys. A sense of relief washed over him–again—when he found she wasn't waiting for him. He made a straight line for his bed at the opposite end of the one-room apartment.

He left his clothes on, he felt more comfortable that way. In his dreams, he could be wearing anything, and look like anyone he could imagine. Yet, he always remained himself save for the clerical shirt and collar he wore to spite the Master's enemy—an added touch that seemed to please his Master. He would leave no witnesses to point their finger anyways, so why expend the extra mental energy on something as frivolous as appearance?

Under his pillow, he set his wrapped kit of knives for later use. He regulated his breathing as he relaxed. His head felt secure against the soft downy pillow. The satiny texture of the sheet as he rolled the corner between his thumb and forefinger, sent him deeper into his coming world. In moments, he would be asleep.

And at his Master's disposal.

Detective Cindy Norton

The victim hung nude and spread-eagled between the lampposts by razor wire and industrial cabling. Someone had woven her intestines around other threads of wire hooked to her body as if attempting a spider web design. The ligature marks around her wrists and throat had turned her skin the color of a bruised plum. Her eyelids had also been removed; her lifeless eyes stared blankly back at Detective Cindy Norton.

She surveyed the scene and the crowd of onlookers just beyond. Perpetrators tended to take the chance of hanging around the crime scene like morbid spectators admiring their work from afar. No one seemed suspicious or overly excited, so she turned her attention back to what used to be a living, breathing, human being. She called over to the officer in charge of securing the scene. "Deputy? Do you have kids?"

The detective's question confused the deputy. "Um, yeah. A seven-year-old daughter. Why, Detective?"

"I'm going on a hunch here, but I'm assuming you'd never want her to see something like this." Cindy hooked a thumb back to the gruesome display behind her.

"Not at all," he replied, still puzzled by her questioning.

"Then why would you think that some other parent would want their child to see it as well?"

The deputy's face dropped in embarrassment. "You're right, Detective. My fault."

"Get those people back and get up the privacy curtains. Now!"

"Right away, Detective."

Cindy walked up to the crime scene, shaking her head. *Fucking dolt.* As she took in the entire grisly aftermath, she sighed. "Do we have TOD?"

"I'd say with the current temp from the heat of the day and the lividity... roughly four to six hours." Dave, the medical examiner, bent the victim's arm at the elbow. "I'll know for sure once I stick her liver."

"You do that," Cindy teased, while taking a long sip from her coffee. "You find any ID on her?"

"Not yet, haven't found it. You don't look so good, man. Rough night?"

The Detective laughed. "I wish my life was that exciting. It's this goddamned insomnia. Can't shake it."

"You should try warm milk with two shots of bourbon, Detective. Hold the milk. Works like a charm." Dave nodded to a crime lab intern to hurry over. "Help me cut down the body."

They clipped the razor wire and lowered the body to a plastic sheet. Her face and torso had been severely beaten and slashed. Amidst the carnage inside the body cavity, coagulated blood started oozing out from the wounds, revealing the woman's purse, which had been lodged in there. The sticky sound of innards peeling off the purse pushed the newbie intern over the edge and he ran, without shame, to vomit in a nearby bush.

The medical examiner shook his head. "That's great; just contaminate the crime scene a little more while looking like a professional." He grabbed the purse and fished inside for the victim's wallet before handing it over to Detective Norton. "Where's your other half, by the way?"

"Who? Steve? He's stuck dealing with that mess over at Halloran's Funeral Home on the other side of town," she answered, as she pulled the driver's license out of the victim's wallet. "Meet Heather Conrad. Twenty-seven. And she's local, lives about a block from here."

"Look over there." Dave nodded to a lamppost with a security camera pointed right at the scene. "Maybe the killer didn't realize he was dead center in a neighborhood watch zone. You're on Candid Camera, asshole."

"Hey, Jenkins," the detective called out.

A young and eager officer ran right over. "Yes, Detective?"

"I need you to find whoever runs the neighborhood watch around here and see if you can get your hands on the video for that and any other camera in a four-block radius."

"Got it, ma'am."

She turned back to the dead Heather Conrad. "From the positioning of the body in relation to the wounds, I don't think this is the primary. She was strung up here, obviously, but not killed here."

Dave inspected the body for any immediate clues or evidence. "I would have to agree with you on that one. I found some trace. Looks like a little metal shaving of some sort. It's a bit rusty, too."

"I don't see any rusted metal around here," she said. "Do you?"

"That would be a negative."

After the crime scene photographer finished his last shot of the victim, Dave gently moved her upper body to lay her flat. Her head rolled lazily around as if filled with ball bearings. With his gloved finger, he opened wider the skin around her eye sockets. Lifeless eyes, one blue and the other green, stared coldly back at nothing. "Uh, Cind. Looks like we got another one."

Jane Davies

Jane's mist-like form hung unseen amidst the throng of bystanders at the crime scene. With Thomas having murdered her in similar fashion, Jane more than felt the victim's pain and the void she had left in the living world. Thoughts of regret and despair clenched her ghostly heart, for she knew of no way to stop the killing of innocent women, no way to prevent her former lover from continuing his sick deeds.

In the distance, she spied Detective Norton and prayed for a way to intervene and help stop the murder spree. She felt for the detective and the weight she was carrying by investigating these crimes. It all felt hopeless… a solitary tear slid down her cheek and vanished into the ether before it could hit the ground.

Thomas awoke refreshed; he always rose from these slumbers vibrant and full of energy, satisfied with completing his Master's task. Looking around his simple apartment, he smiled, realizing he was now a step closer to his Master having fulfilled his promise. His feet touched the cold wooden floor as he stood and stretched. He found no trace of Jane's ghost or any evidence she had been there— the telltale sign of a potentially good day.

He flipped on the television before heading to the kitchenette to brew a pot of coffee so he could start his day. Like clockwork, the network had a breaking news story. As he expected, the vicious murder of Heather Conrad was the topic. Video from the scene, interviews with bystanders, and photos of the victim flashed across his screen. He beamed from a job well done. He'd pleased his Master again, for sure.

The coffee maker's timer rang and he equipped himself with his favorite mug in anticipation of the first warm beverage of the day. The steamy black liquid flowed out of the pot. The aroma tantalized his nose, making him smile. He had nothing specific on his agenda today except for savoring the memories of the previous night's magical events. Eventually, he would have to make it back to the warehouse to prepare for the next time his Master would beckon.

"You sure seem proud of yourself."

Thomas jolted, dropping the mug and sending it crashing onto the floor. Shards of porcelain and boiling drops of coffee exploded all over the place. He scrambled to avoid the sharp slivers and hot liquid, but they had already inflicted their damage. He groaned in pain as his skin burned and bled.

"God damn it!" Jane remained silent and still as Thomas hobbled over to a kitchen chair to tend to his wounds. His glare towards Jane was nothing less than life threatening. "I am beyond sick of this, Jane. I wish I could kill you again just for this." He carefully extracted pieces of the mug from his foot with one hand while putting pressure on the bleeding wounds with the other. "You knew that was my favorite mug, too. You bitch."

"Only serves you right for what you did," She hovered above the floor and glided on her ghostly mist about the room.

"What I did?" he asked. "What I did and what I do is a miracle. It's beyond yours or anyone else's comprehension. One day the Master will grant me life everlasting and powers far surpassing any of my dreams." That mere thought alone soothed his pain. "I can't expect you to understand."

"You're right, Thomas. I will never understand. But we are bonded. Bound by death and by what you did to me." She vanished from view only to reappear behind him and whisper in his ear. "I love you, I have no choice. But if you don't listen to me and stop now to save yourself from what is going to happen, *I* will stop you from what you are going to do to others."

Her ethereal hair tickled the nape of his neck, sending chills throughout his body. Thomas spun around, but she disappeared again. "I will not stop! I cannot stop!" He hollered at the air, knowing she was still there, somewhere. He stood up despite the pain. "This is my destiny. The Master promised me, and I will not let you jeopardize that!"

Bobby Montgomery

Bobby Montgomery spent his eleventh birthday just like every other day—alone. It wasn't that he didn't have any friends—he had one or two, perhaps—he just enjoyed being by himself. And, to him, this day was no different from any other.

He walked down the earthen path with the deftness and purpose of someone who had travelled it many times in the past. The deeper into the woods he went, the quicker his problems at school seemed to disappear. Above, the sky threatened to open up and drop rain from the low hanging clouds. Despite being autumn, he found it unseasonably humid and warm. With a natural sure-footedness, he traversed the uneven plane of the forest floor. Memory had served him well. Either from years of playing along these old paths or from being out in the wild, hunting with his father, he knew his way around.

Even though his hyper-vigilant mother told him to stay out of the woods for a while, Bobby could not resist the call of Nature's calm quietness. His eyes and ears took in all the sights and sounds the earth offered. Not even the frustration of losing his lunch money again could break him from this joy.

The wind picked up force. It funneled down the path toward him. Old dead leaves lifted off the ground and marched in his direction as if on some daring mission from Mother Nature herself.

Feeling chilly, Bobby zipped up his coat and continued down the path, avoiding the spinning tempest of leaves sharing it with him.

As with every other time he had ventured into the forest on his way home, he walked past the chain link fence that separated the old abandoned warehouse from the woodland, and, each time, he marveled at the majestic wreck of a building standing just past the fence with its fields of overgrowth and boarded up windows. Its lone smokestack reached up from the bowels of the place and high into the air.

Bobby ventured to the edge of the wood and stood at the metal barrier that kept the two worlds apart. With the sun shining through regardless of the low clouds, he laced his fingers together for a better view before covering his eyes to look up at the ancient chimney. He rejoiced in his adoration of all things. On one side, he had nature's reserve, a fertile and breathtaking forest alive with so many wonders, and on the other, a concrete miracle of man's desire to build and create.

The difference this day, however, was that Bobby didn't intend to let the chain link barrier keep him from exploring. After all, it was his birthday. He found an opening cut into the fence some yards away and squeezed his little frame through it, only to snag his coat on a burr. His mother would be upset, for sure, but he didn't let it spoil his journey.

Through the overgrown field, he marched towards the concrete and asphalt that surrounded the warehouse. Once on the pavement, he immediately missed the feeling of the soft ground beneath his feet. Yet, he was on a mission and knew he didn't have to choose one over the other, they each held their own magic for him to appreciate.

He enjoyed the solemn quietness afforded him by the forest, but the stillness surrounding the old building held a stark difference, an eerie sadness he was unable to decide if he liked. Avoiding deterrence, he continued his exploration. Atop a set of rusted metal steps, he noticed a dented and defaced metal door ajar. The darkness just beyond the gap in the entrance gave him a shiver.

Nevertheless, he climbed the steps and walked down the ramp, not with the sure-footedness he displayed on the rocky trails of the forest, but with an awkward and hesitant pace that belied his previous enthusiasm. If his mother knew he was here, about ready to cross the threshold into the unknown, she would surely tan his hide. At the door, Bobby took a deep breath in preparation to breach the abandoned keep.

The Heterochromia Killer?

Detective Norton entered the autopsy room through the set of double doors. On the cold metal table, the body of Heather Conrad lay covered up to her navel by a simple white sheet. The intense light of the lamps, which separated the examination area from the sterile and unwelcoming ambience of the rest of the room, shined on the body's pale blue skin. All over the victim's body, a multitude of vicious stab wounds decorated her skin. The familiar stitching of the Y incision on her abdomen and torso sealed her back up.

"The count stopped at forty-five stab wounds," said Dr. Jordan McKee as she stepped out from the shadowy corner of the room into the lamp light. She held a specimen jar full of formalin solution. Floating in the preservative was the weighed and dissected brain of the victim. "Just like the others. But I have a feeling you already knew that."

No matter how many victims Cindy had seen laid out in front of her, and no matter how hardened her job made her, she was never comfortable with this stage of the process. There was something about the color of the skin, the barren stare in their eyes, that made her shudder and break into cold sweats. She did her best to conceal this from her colleagues, but sometimes the reality of the situation got the best of her, and Dr. McKee just happened to be one of those few individuals that knew her secret.

"Yeah. I figured as much," Cindy said. "Once I saw the eyes." She reluctantly looked the dead girl in her mismatched eyes. "Who knew there were so many people with that condition?"

"I'm not too keen on the nickname the media has given this psycho," McKee said. "The Heterochromia Killer? Doesn't exactly roll off the tongue, does it?"

"Not really," Cindy replied. "And what about the back? Same thing as the others?"

"Indeed. Carved in the small of her back, 5:9," the doctor answered, putting down the brain jar on the counter. "This time, the cuts weren't as haphazard. Looks like the same type of blade, but with more finesse, I guess you could say, than the others."

"So, again, we got a young woman, early- to mid-twenties, stabbed exactly forty-five times, with the same cryptic carving on the back."

"Well, the only correlation I've been able to surmise that makes any sense is that five times nine equals forty-five." Dr. McKee looked over Heather Conrad's chart. "The only other thing I can think of is maybe the 5:9 denotes a date or time, or is some kind of Bible passage, but which book is anyone's guess."

"Never read it," said Cindy.

"Read what?"

"The Bible. I was never big on organized religion once I was able to form my own opinions." She stepped closer to the autopsy slab and forced herself to look into the dead girl's eyes again. There was something odd there—a wrongness. "Jordan, did you look at her eyes?"

"Of course, I did. That's how I knew she was one of our killer's before I even saw the stab wounds."

"That's not what I meant," Cindy said.

"Well, since she has no eyelids, I skipped over examining her conjunctivae at first," the doctor admitted. "Was just about to suck out some of that good ole vitreous humor as you walked in. Why do you ask?"

"There's something not right."

Dr. McKee chuckled. "That's an understatement."

"Again... not what I mean," Cindy said, leaning in closer. "Once someone dies, do the eyes continue to change or get deader? If that's even a real word."

"Not usually. Once there is brain death, the pupils don't react to light stimulus and become dilated and appear to have a bluish haze," the doctor explained. "That change in color and fogginess you see in a dead person's eyes is due in part to the opacity of the cornea and the lens, brought about due to the lack of oxygen. Once dead, the eyes stop blinking and producing tears, and blood stops circulating. To keep absorbing oxygen the cornea must be moist."

"I see," Cindy said. "Can I see your flashlight?" She grabbed the light from the doctor and clicked it on. Back and forth, she went to each eye, studying the differences. The light reacted differently when shined in the girl's green eye; it still seemed to have a luster that the blue one no longer had. "See? Why is this eye reflecting brighter?"

"To be honest with you, I'm not quite sure." Dr. McKee probed the dead girl's eye with her fingers and gently touched the iris. It moved. She recoiled.

"You gotta be shitting me," the detective blurted.

"Hold on." Dr. McKee took her pair of tweezers to the green eye and with careful precision peeled off a green contact lens, revealing a matching blue eye underneath.

Cindy looked up at the doctor, awestruck. "Doc, what the hell is going on here? The killer's *making* them fit the profile now?"

The Warehouse

Bobby squinted to see through the dusky haze covering everything inside the abandoned warehouse. Even as the shadows of the distant corners seemed to ebb and flow, he bravely stood his ground. With both feet now planted inside, he looked around in wonder at the interior of the massive industrial shrine.

High up in the rafters, taped-up and weathered windows allowed in a minimal amount of daylight to cast a glow upon the ceiling. Skylights, dirty from years of neglect, didn't offer any more brightness either. From there, it was a gradual shift in darkness all the way down to the murky floor where he stood. He walked slowly and softly, yet his tiny steps still echoed and kicked up dirt and dust.

Rows and rows of empty metal shelving lined the walls and floor, stretching high up into the air where only a man with a machine could reach. Bobby, as he investigated, thought the rows of shelves resembled a looted library in some distant dystopian future. Whatever the owners of this place had used it for in the past, there was no evidence left behind. He let his imagination run wild with images of shelf upon shelf stacked with replacement robot parts and weapons for fighters and protectors of the human race after an alien invasion, with visions of huge industrial machines toiling away under the control of men and women fighting for humankind.

A fluttering sound ripped him from his daydream. He spun around looking for its source. Overhead, fit snugly between intersecting rafters, a mother bird fed and guarded her young. She let out a caw, a warning to Bobby for his intrusion. He just smiled and continued on the path deeper into the warehouse.

At the end of the section marked on the wall with "2-A", he saw a solitary wooden table in the center of the space. Despite all the aged cracking and warping on it, he still could make out strange symbols and carvings all over its top. The only things he was readily able to discern were the words "sleep" and "master." He tried to ignore the chill and the creepy sensation that swept over his body as he scouted around the room looking for more weird symbols or clues to what the words meant.

Another sound reached his ears and he smiled again thinking that the momma bird was watching him and being over-protective of her hatchlings. When he gazed up, a swirling mist danced high in the air. As he stared, he thought he could make out features like hair and a dress. *That's impossible*. The mist didn't seem to acknowledge Bobby as he watched from behind a pillar. More and more, as it swam in the murkiness, it began to resemble a woman. He blinked and tried to rub the nonsense from his eyes, but it was still there.

He took a retreating step and kicked a scrap of metal that screeched across the concrete floor. He stopped and stood stone-still, hoping his blunder had gone unheard. His eyes returned to the floating form that now stared back at him, drawing closer. The immediate flood of fright and panic assaulted his stomach, sending waves of pain to his adolescent brain.

As the mist took shape and swam closer, Bobby stepped backwards, unable to run and gripped by fear. The smoky form seemed to smile at him as its wavy and translucent hair whirled about its head. Soft hazy eyes bore into his as he continued his slow and unsteady retreat, unaware of the ledge he was about to walk off. The ghostly vision reached out its arms toward him. Terrified, he finally mustered enough energy to run from the thing that was coming for him, but as he turned around he failed to see the edge of the floor vanish from beneath his feet and he plummeted six feet to the hard ground below.

The ghost of Jane vanished as if sucked into a vortex. Immediately, she reformed right next to Bobby's fallen body. In her ethereal form, she could do nothing to help the hurt little boy. She hovered next to him just an inch from the cold floor. The fall had knocked him unconscious and now a trickle of blood was making a puddle, matting his soft hair to his head. It was her fault the boy had fallen, and she felt every bit as guilty for it, too.

In his unresponsive condition, she listened to his ragged breathing while his mouth released little grumbles and moans. Even though she couldn't physically touch Bobby, she ran her vaporous hand over his head, trying to do anything to comfort the boy and soothe her own remorse for frightening him so. As his eyes moved under their lids, she hoped he would at least have happy dreams.

The blood finally stopped leaking out from the head wound and she noticed his breathing had steadied itself; he now appeared to be in a deep sleep. She let herself smile; hoping Bobby was over the worst of the immediate danger. Nevertheless, with no way to check, nor a way to go for help, she still knew he wasn't completely out of harm's way.

Everything around him seemed muted, softened, like looking through very fine cheesecloth. It struck Bobby as odd; he found he wasn't too concerned seeing his own body lying motionless on the warehouse floor. He noticed a faint ringing in his ears but couldn't place its source until he realized the sound emanated from within his head. In addition, he found no trace of the "ghost" that had chased him over the ledge.

Was he dead? Did he die in the fall? Questions he had no answers to. Yet, he felt more vibrant and aware, more alive now. He wandered through the warehouse unaware of, and unconcerned about the time. The passage of time itself felt sluggish. The setting sun hadn't moved an inch since he'd woken.

At a set of rusting metal stairs, he paused to look up. A door marked 'Office' stood closed. He skipped up the steps without regard for the shaking and squeaking noises, for he felt impervious to danger now. Even with the racket he was making, he still put his ear to the door, listening for any movement or sound coming from the other side.

He heard nothing but silence over the ringing in his head. The handle turned freely, and the door opened on its old hinges with a screech that echoed through the concrete building.

In the center of the room, a metal desk sat covered in folders and papers, and a computer monitor flickered on and off. Filth dripped from the walls, which were decorated with pictures and certificates, and the linoleum floor was dirty and stained. From his vantage point when he'd first walked in, he didn't see the woman seated in the chair on the opposite side of the littered desk. Her head rested on her forearms as she slouched over in a deep sleep. Bobby couldn't make out any details of her face; her long brown hair covered her features.

He scanned the room. It didn't feel like a normal warehouse office… but what did he know? As he tiptoed in, he could make out more features of the office: chairs against the wall, filing cabinets, and a cup of coffee, still steaming.

The place was supposedly abandoned, so who was she? What was she doing here all by herself? Too deep in his thoughts, he kicked a hunk of something and froze. It skidded across the grimy floor until it hit the desk with a bang.

Revelation

The loud and sudden bang yanked Cindy from her desktop nap. Her elbow knocked a reference copy of the King James Bible to the linoleum, which didn't help her awakening nerves. She broke out in an icy sweat as her stomach churned from the fright. As she scanned her office, she found nothing out of the ordinary or out of place, save the puddle of drool on her desk calendar. The fuzziness of sleep and the peculiar dream about a lost and hurt boy quickly dissipated. Little sparks of light, those tiny explosions that dance in your eyes after you wake or stretch, replaced the fleeting images of the dream.

Cindy snatched her trusty mug from its ring-stained spot on the desk and peered inside, unhappy about its lack of hot coffee. She grumbled all the way down the hallway to the coffee maker that held the piping hot and freshly brewed elixir of her profession. Burning her upper lip—like usual—on the steaming liquid, she blew on it to cool it off on her way back to her desk.

She placed the mug back into its default spot and spied the stack of folders all marked 'Confidential'; all labeled with the same case number... The Heterochromia Killings. While all the previous women they'd found butchered with the same M.O. had the same genetic anomaly, this current one, Heather Conrad, seemed different. She couldn't quite put her finger on it, but something about it was off; it felt forced. All the other women had the mismatched eyes, but Heather had one green contact, which only simulated the irregularity. Aside from that detail, she ended up the same way as the others—butchered.

What was she missing? She knew this case was beating her—and she hated it. With all her years doing this job, all those solved cases under her belt, she still felt defeated, inferior to the person, the madman, committing these heinous and calculated murders. Everybody left evidence, even the minutest trace that they were there, but here, it was like she was dealing with a ghost. She couldn't wait for the killer to make a mistake, and she needed to do what she knew was impossible—be everywhere at once.

Cindy's frustration built into a crescendo. She threw Heather Conrad's file across the room and hammered her fist onto the desk with an angry thud. Through the window of her office, her partner noticed her outburst and popped his head in.

"Hey, Cind, you doin' okay?"

"No, Steve... Yeah, I guess," Cindy said. "I have no idea. This case is messing with my head."

"Maybe you should give it a rest for the day and go get some sleep. You look exhausted."

"I know. Maybe in a bit. Just want to finish up some stuff first."

"I'd love to help you, being your partner and all, but the Chief's up my ass to put this funeral home fire scandal to bed as quickly and quietly as possible," Steve said. "Some sick shit was going on in there. Some big names in the wrong place at the wrong time. It might go all the way up to the Mayor, too."

"Sounds juicy," Cindy said. "Well, good luck with that."

"Gee, thanks." He knocked on the doorframe with his ring finger.

"Just kidding with ya, sport."

"I know." Steve turned to leave, but stopped. "Oh, yeah. Your lab geek boyfriend wanted me to tell you... he finally found out some info on that cabling your killer uses to bind his victims."

Cindy glared at her partner. "He's not my boyfriend. We went out once and all he talked about was his cats."

"Sounds like love to me," Steve teased. "Anyways, he said it's really old and antiquated network cabling, like dialup AOL chatroom old."

"Yeah, I remember the days."

"While it wasn't manufactured in the states, there was a facility in the county that warehoused it, but the company folded years ago and the place has gone to shit."

"Well, that wasn't helpful."

"Sounds like one of those dead ends we detecting folk love," Steve quipped.

"Yeah. Thanks for the info." She sighed in resignation. "I think I'm gonna take that advice of yours and go home." She grabbed her mug and downed the now lukewarm coffee.

"Alright, then. Take it easy and I'll see you tomorrow."

Cindy barely heard Steve when her eye spotted something in one of the folders that lay open, the result of her earlier tantrum. "Yeah, good night." She didn't even look up. "See ya."

She pulled a witness statement out of the file of the first victim, Jane Davies, and mouthed the words as she read. Her jaw dropped and she immediately got angry with herself. "How the *hell* did I not see this before?"

She gathered up all the folders and files and bolted out of the room and down the hall to the Chief's office. He sat at his desk staring at his monitor and cursing the upgraded software the department had installed. "Save time and money, my ass." The Chief grumbled as he henpecked his keyboard.

"Chief," Cindy said, with a simultaneous knock on the door. The old cop looked up. "I can't believe I missed it, but I think I found the clue we've been looking for!"

Slumber

Thomas sat at the foot of his bed in anticipation of another task. Rarely had the Master asked him to perform again so soon after a previous outing. *The Master must have His reasons.* And he hoped those reasons would be wonderful. He fixated on a framed photograph of he and Jane sitting on the shelving unit next to his bed. Those long days when he preached and taught at summer bible camp, praising the Almighty while falling in love with Jane, were over and gone. Despite his disdain for those same words he'd preached, he remembered them all and could recall every passage with fluidity and ease. His favorite was Mark 5:9.

And Jesus asked him, 'What is your name?' He replied, 'My name is Legion, for we are many.

The words rolled off his tongue with practiced effortlessness. Oh, how he knew the Master had chosen the proper student to do His work. It was that passage alone that guided his disdain, and began his fixation against the very religion to which he'd once chosen to devote his life. And in line with his Master's perversions, he was granted a modicum of his personality to shine through as he added to his victims' flesh a mark that made his work all the more personal and meaningful.

Behind his dusty window shades, the sun had set and the last vestige of light sunk below the horizon. His Master needed him again and he, without hesitation, heeded the call. Who his next victim would be, he did not know, and that missing detail always excited and aroused him no end. He lay back on the bed, his head sinking into the soft pillow, feeling around for his wrapped set of knives, making sure everything was in its proper place.

His eyes grew heavy and his lids closed. He didn't fight it, he welcomed it with open arms, the warm sensation of being needed and cared for by his Master, the fulfillment of doing something with his life that mattered.

Jane felt hopeless and useless. Every attempt to intervene became a futile effort almost immediately. Foggy tears fell from her phantom eyes onto the floor where they exploded into tiny fireworks of shimmering light. Not knowing what to do with herself, she hovered quietly over the concrete floor of the warehouse.

Just beyond the storage room lined with shelving units laid the little boy's comatose body crumpled on the cold ground. With nighttime fallen, she knew Thomas would be in his special place to do his special and perverse deeds; it was only a matter of time. She had been there as he prepared in his apartment, but she refrained from making contact... it would do no good any longer. Demons had driven Thomas—or the man he used to be—too far from rationalization. At any moment, he would appear here at his altar-like slab with his newest victim, only to dump the body, lifeless and defiled, wherever he deemed appropriate.

The Chief

"So, whaddya got for me, Cind?" the Chief asked. "The boss upstairs is breathing down my neck 'cause of this friggin' case."

Cindy dropped into one of the chairs facing her chief's desk and opened up the case file. "Like I said, I can't believe I overlooked this, but I think it's the missing piece of the puzzle. Talked to McKee down in autopsy, she thought the carving and number of stab wounds in each vic was religious in nature." She pulled out a color photo of the latest victim's wounds. "If that's true, then our perp thinks he's some zealot or something, leaving us a holy message of sorts on his victims. So I did some digging."

The Chief leaned in closer. "What's so religious about it?" He grabbed the photograph.

"Glad you asked," Cindy said. "Almost makes all the stupid research I had to do worth it." She smirked at her own sarcasm.

"No Sunday school for you growing up, I take it?"

"Anyways." She gave her chief a sidelong glance. "The 5:9 is a passage from the bible. Book of Mark to be exact." She grabbed her notepad. "It goes... 'And Jesus asked him, 'What is your name?' He replied, 'My name is Legion, for we are many.' Creepy, huh?"

"But what about the forty-five stab wounds?"

"Five times nine equals forty-five," she answered.

"Christ on a crutch! I knew this guy was sick, but if you're right about this, it only makes it worse." He plopped back into his chair with a deep sigh. "What else?"

"As you know, the boyfriend of the first victim, Jane Davies, was cleared" Cindy began. "Even though his alibi was weak, we had nothing on him. But...!" She dug the statement out of the file. "According to this, Thomas Isaac Griffey was a bible retreat teacher and counselor. When his boss found out about the secret relationship between him and one of his students, he was dismissed immediately from his position."

"Let me guess, that student was Jane Davies."

"Correct," Cindy said. "Into religion, fired from his job, his girlfriend murdered. He was possibly unstable even before all that. It's starting to add up, don't you think?"

The chief's overgrown mustache rustled under his nose from his sharp exhale. "It's all circumstantial... at best. He was cleared. I can't bring this upstairs if this is all you got."

Cindy leaned in and smiled at her boss. "Chief, remember... Jane Davies had two *real* different colored eyes."

Thomas' Ritual

After he had scared the mysterious sleeping woman in the upstairs office, Bobby ran down the stairs and hid behind a stack of cable spools. From the space in between the spools, he spied on the office door, waiting for the woman to come rushing out looking for him, but she didn't. He listened for any signs of life even though he, again, felt all alone in the empty warehouse.

He regained his nerve to move; satisfied no one would storm out of the office, or anywhere else for that matter. Up and down the industrial-shelf lined aisles, he started taking a visual inventory of all the things the owners had left behind. On one of the metal shelves, a long metal pipe hung off the edge. He grabbed it with both hands; it felt as light as a feather somehow. He gripped it tight, taking the token knight stance as he held the pipe like a mighty sword.

Even though he walked through this dream-like mirror image of his normal world, without knowing how or why, he began to acclimate to his circumstances. He knew his real body still lay at the bottom of that concrete ditch, but his sense of wonder shielded him from the magnitude of his situation.

He heard a commotion. In an unexplored part of this dream version of the warehouse, someone or something moved around. The clang of metal-on-metal followed by metal-on-concrete reverberated down a corridor to where he stood. *Maybe it's the woman from the office.* With caution, he trod down the hall towards the source of the sounds. Around the corner, he stuck his head out until he could see inside the whole room.

A man dressed like a priest stood in front of a metal and stone table-like structure. Bobby didn't think he really looked like a priest, just a scruffy man playing the part. In the strange man's hands were all sorts of different-sized knives that he lovingly picked up one-by-one and put back down. The man smiled at his reflection in the lantern light shining off the blades.

Bobby fought not to move a muscle, not to breathe.

"We stand armed and dangerous before the bloody fields of history. Devoid of dogma—but ready to carve, to defy the transient. Ready to stab forth with our penetrative will, strain every leash, run yelling down the mountainside of Man. Ready and willing to immolate world upon world with our stunning blaze." Thomas recited the chant aloud as a man who had practiced the verses ad infinitum. He raised his arms high and wide.

"And let them all sing that we were here, as Masters among the failing species called Man. Our being took form in defiance to stand before your killing gaze. And now we travel from flame to flame and tower from the will to the glory!"

He looked upwards and his eyes glossed over with a muddy film. At the top of his lungs, his voice filled the cavernous warehouse, finishing the chant. "AGIOS O BAPHOMET! AGIOS O BAPHOMET!"

A violent wind kicked up from the floor, lifting dirt and debris into the air. Thomas' hair fluttered around like a flame caught in a breeze. The wind's crescendo peaked at a deep howl, almost like a roar, before all at once it stopped and all the junk floating around him fell to the floor. Once again, he stood in silence.

Then he vanished.

A Visit from the Dead

Cindy needed to sleep. As gung-ho as she was to get down to business with her new lead, she needed to shut her eyes something fierce. Her plague of insomnia finally seemed to break, which would be a good thing, but now she could barely keep her eyes open. She left the precinct as the moon reached its high point in the sky, and headed for her car so she could call it a day. A fresh start in the morning. She needed that, too.

She tossed her shoulder bag into the passenger seat and plopped down in front of the wheel. Exhaustion hit her like a sack of dirt to the face and she leaned back in the driver's seat, resting against the headrest. She felt her eyelids drooping as she melted into the comfort of the seat before finally passing out.

Her eyes bolted open as if something startled her. As she blinked the weariness from her vision, she dabbed at the dampness at the corner of her mouth. During her slumber, a fog had rolled in. She reached into her jacket pocket for her keys but stopped, her heart caught in her throat. Through the rear view mirror, she saw a pale woman dressed in white sitting in the back seat. The woman looked back at Cindy, with sad, mismatched eyes.

Cindy went for her gun, but it wasn't there. She spun around in her seat to face the intruder. "Who the hell are you?" Cindy blinked her eyes some more, thinking she was seeing things; she could see right through the woman.

"You know who I am, Cindy," the pale woman said. "You knew the moment you saw my eyes."

"Jane Davies?" Cindy fought to rationalize the situation. "How is this possible?"

"You're dreaming, Cindy. And you're in danger. He won't be stopped, and I fear you're next on his list." Her ghostly body rippled and waved as she spoke.

"Who?" she asked in rising concern. "It's Thomas Isaac Griffey isn't it?"

Jane nodded. A single tear welled up in her eye.

"I knew it. But how is he doing it? And why?"

"The Master is feeding him his dreams," whispered the ghost.

Cindy stared at Jane, even more confused than before. "I'm not even going to try to guess what that means. How is he doing this? Why is he killing all of these women?"

"To shame me and my memory," Jane said. "That's why all the girls had similar eyes. If they weren't that way naturally, like me, then he made them that way." The ghost of Jane sighed. "But that's *his* motive."

"What other motive can there be?"

Jane lifted her head to face Cindy, to stare her right in the eye. "Cindy, there are forces at work here greater than both you or I could ever understand. When Thomas lost his religion, he found another one. One that allows him special access."

"Special access?"

Jane spoke solemnly, her tone matter-of-fact. "Just like I am doing now, with you, coming into your dreams to warn you, he can enter your dreams and kill you or walk among us unseen as he dreams."

"This is just ludicrous! It makes no sense."

"Yet, here we are, in your car, talking to each other while you sleep." Jane caressed Cindy's face and the detective flinched. "Thomas is coming after you—and I can't stop him."

"How do *I* stop him, then?" Cindy's voice quivered with a nervous tension. "And why me?"

"Because his Master knows you are on to him," Jane said. "And he won't let you stop Thomas or his grand plan." Jane's wispy form dimmed as the fog outside the car swirled. "Our time is up, Cindy. Heed my warning. You have to stay awake and be careful. There is no telling what he'll do or how he'll come for you. I just know that he will dream himself into your life and when you're in his world, on his terms, there will be nothing I can do." With that, Jane Davies' ghost imploded and vanished.

Again, Cindy's eyes shot open. This time she was alone. The fog outside the confines of her car had dissipated, replaced by the normal shades of nighttime. Her mind was hazy. Slowly, the flashes of the dream came back to her, first in fragments, then in one swift rush when she saw the case file photograph of Jane Davies lying out on top of her bag.

Thomas stood at a distance, in a swirl of dream-mist, watching Cindy in her car, asleep and awake. He knew at some point Jane would attempt to intervene and that Detective Norton would be on to him. He admired her tenacity, her will and fortitude, when it came to her cases—especially this one—and for that, she now had to die. The Master wished it and so it shall be done.

His erection throbbed at the thought of the things he would do to her in the name of his Master and his own sickness. He knew at home—in his bed—his mortal body was pleasuring itself in its sleep. Soon, at the perfect time, he would come to her and whisk her away to his private sanctum. Cindy drove away, heading home, Thomas presumed. He smiled and vanished in a plume of fog.

The waiting, the hiding and scheming, made the whole experience much more fulfilling, even dramatic. The Master told him, as his vessel in the living realm, this was his most important mission ever and he could sense how close he was to completing his tasks and gaining his Master's prize, his majestic gift. The excitement made him giddy; it had been a while since he stalked his victims this way, outside of their own dream. Headlights shined through the windows and Cindy's car turned off. He heard her fiddling with her keys trying to unlock and open the front door.

Even though she couldn't see him in this form, his dream-mist hiding him from this world, he still lurked in the shadows only to reveal himself when he was ready—and when he wanted to. In his mind, he tinkered with when he would strike, how he would abduct her into his dream world. He could already visualize her stripped naked and bound to his altar in the warehouse as he prepared to carve his trademark into her flesh.

The Dream-State

Cindy tossed her car keys into an ornate copper bowl on the foyer table. Her house felt still, too still, as she replayed the dream conversation in her head. She took off her jacket, making sure to remove the photo of Jane Davies before hanging it up on the coat rack. As part of her ritual, she removed her gun and holster and placed it inside the table's center drawer.

In the kitchen, the unopened bottle of red wine called out to her, begging her to taste it. "What the hell, right?" she said, as she reached for the bottle and the corkscrew. "One glass then off to bed." She sniffed the cork, savoring the sweet bouquet, opting for a pint glass over a proper wine one. "Never said what kind of glass."

Parked right in front of the television was her father's old, beat up recliner. After he passed away, she couldn't bring herself to trash it. So, she held onto it and made it the centerpiece of her living room. She dropped down into the chair, slipping into its broken-in comfort. With a long sigh, she kicked off her shoes and stretched out, ready to relax. The wine smelled delicious as she took a hefty gulp before setting it on the coaster. Her head sunk into the soft cushion and her eyelids closed.

She jolted awake, her eyes reflexively scanning the room. She could feel a pressure, a heavy oppressive feeling, on her face and skin. Her dazed head darted around looking for anything out of place. Night had drowned her house in pitch-blackness and she couldn't see a thing at first until her vision adjusted. Yet, she could swear somehow the shadows in front of her swirled and moved. She thought she might be dreaming again, unable to tell the difference.

Cindy pinched herself, even though she never understood how or why that trick was supposed to work. Nothing happened except for a touch of pain, so she assumed she was awake. Yet, the shadows on the far side of the room still seemed to churn. Squinting helped a little as she noticed a shape congealing in the gloom. "Hey! Who's there?" No response. The shape became more obvious. "I'm a cop! You picked the wrong house to fuck with!"

A hazy form dressed as a priest stepped out of the dark as if passing through a membrane. Cindy reached for her gun, but she had locked it away for the night. "Shit!" The man-sized shape loomed closer. She jumped back, having recognized his face.

"Hello, Detective." Thomas' voice boomed in her ears.

With roughly fifteen feet between her and the table hiding her gun, she dashed for the foyer. Immediately after she turned, a stabbing twinge of pain radiated up her body. Behind her, Thomas grinned as he held up his bloody blade. She panicked, grabbing her side. Blood seeped through her shirt and covered her hands. The pain bolted through her and she felt dizzy.

"Don't worry, Detective," Thomas whispered. "You're not going to die, yet. The Master has such plans for you and I've dreamt them all."

After the man dressed like a priest disappeared, Bobby went back to where he had fallen. He still didn't understand why he could look down and see his own body but still felt perfectly alive. In fact, he felt great, and, if having lifted that big metal pole up was any indication, stronger still.

"Hello."

Bobby spun around, almost falling again. Floating an arm's length away from him, the pale but wispy form of a woman gazed at him with caring eyes.

"Oh, I'm so sorry for scaring you, again," the ghost said. "I mean you no harm. I feel terrible for causing your accident earlier."

"Are you an angel?" Bobby asked. "Am I dead?"

Jane softly smiled. "No, I am not an angel. Just a traveler stuck in this realm along with you. And, thankful you're still alive."

"But...."

"How can you see your own body?" Jane asked the question for him.

"Yeah. It feels so weird. I know I should be scared, but I'm not."

"You are between worlds. Caught halfway between the wakened world and the dream one," Jane explained.

"So, like I'm dreaming but walking around in real life?"

"Yes, something like that," she answered. "My name is Jane. What's yours?"

"Bobby Montgomery."

"Nice to meet you, Bobby Montgomery."

"You don't look real. Are you dead?"

"I am," Jane replied. "I was murdered in this very place by someone I loved." She made a sweeping gesture with her arm.

"Oh," Bobby mumbled, feeling embarrassed for asking such a question. "I'm sorry."

"No need to apologize. Nothing can be done about it now."

Bobby glanced up quizzically at Jane as if he'd just remembered something. "Who was that man dressed up like a priest then? Was he a ghost, or like me?"

Jane sighed. "That's Thomas. He's not like either of us. He's something else altogether… and the one that killed me."

"That's horrible. What does he want?"

"He wants to live forever and hunt us in our dreams," Jane explained. "He's a monster and is preparing to kill the only person who stands in his way of reaching his goal."

"Well, we have to stop him then. I feel so strong now. We can do it."

Jane smiled. "I'm sorry, Bobby," she started. "I'm afraid neither of us is that strong."

The air in the warehouse rippled around a center point in front of Thomas' makeshift altar. From out of nothing, Cindy stepped through, walking backwards until she bumped into the table. The skin of her face glowed as she finished morphing out of the ether and into the warehouse. Thomas followed her out of the rift with his blade raised and ready. Once he planted a firm foot onto the hard concrete foundation, his body absorbed the rippling air.

Cindy couldn't hide her panic or confusion. Thomas was unable to mask his excitement as a crude smile carved itself across his face. The coolness of her blood-soaked shirt touching her side reminded her of her wound. She applied pressure and winced in pain. Thomas' grin broadened. He reached down and gripped his erection. Cindy, feeling naked without her gun, looked around for anything useful to save herself from this nightmare.

"You have no idea how badly I've wanted this… how long I've waited for the Master to finally allow me this prize," Thomas said, sliding his tongue over his teeth.

"How is this even possible?" If she continued to ask questions, to feed into his ego and delirium, maybe she could find a way to escape. "What are you?"

"I am a tool to do my Master's bidding," Thomas explained. "He feeds me my dreams and promises me more than you'd ever be able to comprehend." He stepped closer, wiping her blood from his blade with his fingers.

"What would Jane think of you now?"

Thomas paused; his expression went cold. "Sh-she has noth-nothing to do with this." Anger returned to his eyes. "She's dead and in hell where she belongs! And you're going to join her, you fucking cunt!" His rage overcame his patience and the plan at the mention of his ex-lover. He threw his bladed hand high into the air, but stopped and softly smiled. "You almost made me ruin my plan."

As he grabbed Cindy's arm, a blur of movement appeared behind him.

With a thud, Thomas dropped to the floor. Blood pooled around his head. A little boy holding a steel pipe stood triumphantly over him. Cindy recognized him as the boy from her dream.

"This is not possible," Cindy blurted. "This can't be happening."

"Sorry, but it is. I'm Bobby Montgomery."

"Hi, Bobby. I'm Cindy. I'm a--"

"A cop. Yeah, I know. I was in your office, remember?"

"What's going on, Bobby?"

"I'll explain later. We have to go. This is his world; he won't be down too much longer."

"What does that mean?"

"We have to go. Now!"

Bobby yanked on her arm, pulling her along with him as he headed for his hiding spot amongst the cable spools. Cindy limped along, feeling woozy from her bleeding wound. Every few feet, Bobby looked over his shoulder to make sure Cindy was still following him and that Thomas was still out cold.

They passed by a manmade cut-out in the warehouse floor. Bobby reached back and grabbed Cindy's sleeve to hurry her along, but not before she looked over the edge and saw Bobby's unconscious form at the bottom.

Her face went pale. "Is that you?" She glanced back and forth unable to make sense of what she saw.

"Yeah, it is. But we gotta go before he wakes up." He tugged on her arm.

"But I've got to help you!" Cindy pulled away and readied herself to climb down to Bobby's body.

Bobby's little hand gripped her arm with unnatural strength. "Cindy, please. We don't have time for that now. C'mon!"

Cindy could see the desperation and need in his eyes, and relented. "Okay, Bobby. I trust you." Just up ahead were the massive spools. They sprinted and ducked behind them right as Thomas started to awaken.

As they both sat quiet and still, Bobby held his finger to his lips and Cindy nodded. Peeking through the gaps, they watched Thomas come to and get up. Even from that distance, they could see he was a bloodied mess.

Thomas' head spun as he looked around, but he saw no one. He howled, grabbing the table and flipping it over in his fury. "I'm going to kill you, you bitch! I'm going to swim in your blood and eat your skin! This is my world... you can't hide from me!"

"Boy, he's really mad now," Bobby whispered, spying the highly agitated Thomas.

"I take it you have a plan?"

"Sure do. The ghost told me how to beat him."

"Ghost?"

"Yeah. Jane. Thomas' girlfriend."

"Great. This isn't freaking me out, at all." Cindy waited until Thomas finished his tantrum and walked out of view. "So what's this plan of yours?"

"Well, remember that dream you were having at your desk when you were asleep?"

"Yeah. There was this loud bang at the end that woke me... wait." Cindy paused. "How the heck did you know that?"

"Um, 'cause I made that loud bang when I kicked something across the floor. I was in your dream."

"But how?"

"No idea. I just was." He pointed to the set of metal stairs that led up to the office. "I went up there while I was exploring after my fall. When I opened the door, there you were, drooling on your desk."

"So, let me see if I got this right. This big ole warehouse is like a train station for dreams and you can come in and out of them whenever you'd like?"

Bobby smiled. "That's kinda just like how Jane explained it, too. She said that's how Thomas moves around to kill people. He brings them here and then--." He stopped and sighed. "Well, you know the rest."

"Ah, I see." Cindy grimaced and shook her head. *This can't be happening.* "If Thomas is here, then that means he is somewhere else asleep and dreaming."

"Right on. I think if we go back to that office up those stairs, we will enter where he's sleeping, since we are kinda dreaming right now, too. And that way...."

"And that way, we can kill him and stop this insanity."

Bobby had been holstering a brave facade, but the idea of being involved with killing someone, even if that someone was the worst person alive, made that wall of courage quiver. Cindy recognized that look all too well. *The boy must be terrified.* "I know you're scared, Bobby. I just need you to be strong for a little while longer."

"Sorry," he said. "I'm trying."

"I know you are, and you're doing great."

"I just wish Jane was here to help us."

Cindy poked her head about, looking for any sign of Thomas' ethereal ex-girlfriend. "I guess we'll just have to do this ourselves. We got this. Right?"

"Yeah. And I'm gonna make it to see twelve."

As the sounds of Thomas' conniption faded and his wrath exploded on the other side of the warehouse in his hunt, Cindy held out her hand to Bobby, who immediately clasped onto it. In a concerted effort not to make any noise, they tiptoed across the floor to the flight of stairs that led up to the office. The aged metal steps groaned their discontent with the addition of their combined weight. Each creaking footfall brought them that much closer to ending this literal nightmare, but also brought Thomas closer to discovering them.

Cindy leveraged herself on the handrail mounted to the wall to displace some of her weight, but the decrepit plaster wall cracked and popped as the bolts holding it in came loose. She let go and stood stone still, hoping that the relief would settle the staircase. Nothing moved or squeaked.

"That was close," Bobby whispered, still afraid to release his grip on Cindy's arm. "You should try to be more careful."

"Yeah. No kiddin'." Cindy paused to center herself. "Come on, we're halfway there." They continued up, grimacing from every audible objection from the old metal steps, until they reached the door at the top of the landing. "Keep your eyes peeled for Thomas, okay?"

"Duh. I'm in sixth grade, not retarded."

"Fair enough," she said, turning the door handle.

Cindy was about to yank the door fully open when Bobby blocked its trajectory with his foot, startling her. "Makes a loud noise."

Cindy sighed in relief. "Good catch. Thanks." She went back to open the door just a bit so she could fit inside, but Bobby wouldn't move his foot. "Bobby?" His face was a pasty white and his quivering lips were chapped from panic. "Bobby... it's okay. Really. We need to get inside."

He still refused to budge.

"Bobby." She raised her voice above a whisper. "I won't let anything happen to you, but we need to get inside before he finds us." Color began flooding back into his face as his foot relaxed and moved away from the door. "This is almost over. I promise."

Beyond the threshold, the room was dark and menacing. With Bobby clutching tight to her shirt, Cindy entered the office space. The office around her swirled with life as if she was awakening from sleep. Misty drapes of color began covering the room before her eyes, circling out until the office was no longer the office, but a filthy bedroom in a seedy apartment.

The room finished coming alive; everything around them was unfamiliar and covered in dusty grime. Cindy scanned her immediate area, looking for any clues that might help, her knife wound the farthest thing from her mind at that moment. Bobby tugged on her shirt and raised a pointed finger to the other side of the room.

Set in a darkened corner of the bedroom sat Thomas' dirty old bed with him fast asleep nestled in the middle of it. His eyes rolled back and forth in REM sleep while his dry and cracked lips mouthed inaudible words.

It worked! Cindy's thoughts ripped across her brain. *This is really happening!*

Bobby looked up at her with sorrowful and scared eyes. "What do we do now?"

"We kill him in his sleep."

"Where are you? You fucking bitch!" Thomas shouted across the abandoned expanse of crumbling architecture. "I'm going to cut open your throat and fuck the hole when I find you."

Thomas stomped around, flipping old tables and spools of cable with ease in his search for the detective and her little helper. He stopped for a moment to listen to his surroundings. His ears heard a quick screech back the way he came, and he smiled.

"There you are. I knew the Master wouldn't abandon me now that I've come so far." His grin reached from ear to ear, slicing a ghoulish trench across his face, as he clenched his throbbing erection through his pants. He bolted down the aisles toward the sound. "This is my Master's world! *My* world! Not yours, you cunt!"

The warehouse walls raced by him in blurs. He sped back to his altar with the pinpoint accuracy of his purpose guiding him. As he approached the dock area where the ground was cut down to a lower level, he spotted something out of place. A small body, banged up and bloodied.

Thomas dropped gears to a halt and his momentum almost carried him over the edge into the sunken area as well. He stood with mouth agape, the synapses in his brain on overload. "How is this possible?" He recognized Bobby's body and realized with concern that he wasn't the only one able to traverse through the veil. "This isn't right!" He shouted up to his Master. "This is supposed to be my domain. Mine and nobody else's!" Rage burned his face red. "I rule here!" He jumped down into the pit, his hands balling into tight fists as he headed towards Bobby's fallen, unconscious form.

Cindy crept closer to the sleeping Thomas, afraid he might wake up at any moment. Bobby hung back against the door, not wanting any part of what had to come next. She paused. Mere feet away from the bed, Thomas shifted; his eyes rolled faster under his lids and his hands balled into fists.

As his head swayed to one side, Cindy caught sight of a rolled up, black satchel under a pillow. The stainless steel handle of a knife jutted out of the top of it. She looked around for any other possible weapon in the killer's ramshackle bedroom, but found none. The closer she got to him, the more her body shook in protest. She reached for the blade peeking out from under his head.

"What are you doing?" Bobby asked.

Cindy glanced over her shoulder and did her best to smile calmly at him. "It'll be okay. I promise." Yet, her trembling hand offered no reassurance as it grazed the metal handle.

"Please, be careful."

She put his voice out of her mind so she could concentrate on sneaking the weapon out from underneath Thomas' sleeping head. With her hand around the hilt, she pulled out the blade an inch at a time as every muscle fiber in her arm ached from the tension. She concentrated so intensely that she failed to notice Bobby's labored breathing behind her.

"Cin-. Cin-dy." Bobby fought to speak. "Hel-p."

"Shh, Bobby. I've almost got it." The sound of Bobby's knees dropping and hitting the floor forced her to turn around. The little boy's face was flush, and he grabbed at his throat as if he was choking or being choked. "Oh, shit! Bobby!"

She ran over to his aid but didn't know what was happening or how to help. The color of life began to drain from Bobby's face as the unseen force continued to strangle him. Each agonizing second that passed, he faded from sight, just as the room they occupied returned to the old warehouse office, until he vanished altogether.

Cindy's mind clouded over with confusion. As she stood up, she heard Thomas screaming obscenities in the main warehouse. Having been so close to ending this, she stormed out of the office, uncertain of what she'd find.

She stopped in mid footfall on the metal landing.

Thomas knelt over the unconscious little body down in the pit. He spat curses as he squeezed the boy's throat between his hands. Bobby, trapped somewhere within the dream shroud, lay motionless, unable to defend himself from the psychopath's rage.

"Stop!" Cindy stomped down the flight of metal stairs.

Thomas released his grip and glared up at her, his maddened sneer unwavering. Bobby's head bounced off the hard ground, rolling to the side as if joined to his neck with nothing more than a spent ball joint. The man stood up, looming over Bobby's body. He laughed—a smarmy chortle that echoed throughout the warehouse and made Cindy's skin crawl. "You can't beat me at my own game. There is no way you could ever fully understand the power I possess over here. On this side of the veil...."

"Get away from him, you monster."

Thomas ignored her, stepping over the boy and stopping at the waist high wall. "The Master made it so." He raised his arms up from his side and lifted straight up in the air before settling on the main floor of the warehouse.

"You're a psychotic piece of shit." With a trained instinct, she reached for her gun again, her muscle memory more astute than her mind's ability to recall the fact that her weapon still sat at home, in the real world. "Shit!"

Thomas continued to approach, gliding towards her on his toes.

She spun around, spotting a metal rebar caked in concrete, and lifting it with surprising ease. "Don't you come any fucking closer." She swung the stone-encrusted rod like a lethal pendulum. Thomas' smirk made her feel dirty all over, affecting her more than the fact he hovered over the ground in front of her. "I swear to God I will kill you."

"Detective Norton... you are here right now because my Master wished it, and I made it so." He stood stoic before her, but with a sense of self-righteousness. "No other reason. You're here because you came between me and my work... and that just won't do."

Cindy swung the rebar, but before it could make contact with Thomas' face, it vanished, sending her off balance and spiraling down to the ground, onto her knee. Thomas' grotesque laughter filled her ears. In his once empty hand, he now held the iron rod. "Now, that was funny. My home, my rules. Remember?"

A desperate groan made them both stop and look. Bobby, groggy and struggling to breathe, peeked up over the ledge. When he saw Thomas, he gasped and stumbled backwards, covering his throat with his hands.

"Bobby! No!"

Thomas turned to Cindy, who was nursing her wounded knee. "I'm sorry. I'll be back with you in a moment. Just need to tie up this annoying loose end." He waved his hand like a magician and the stone floor beneath her feet turned to sludge, trapping her. Satisfied, he glided back over to the cement canyon, spinning the rebar like a baton. "Bobby. So that's the name of this pain in my ass." Thomas glowered down at the little boy. "Don't worry. It's not you I care about, so I'll make it quick."

Bobby tripped over a pipe and tumbled with a thud. His tears only made Thomas' smile broader and his erection stiffer. Cindy pleaded in the background for him to stop and for Bobby to run and hide as she struggled to break free. Thomas stopped at the precipice, eager to move on to more important tasks—tasks that would solidify his place next to his Master.

The air in the space above their heads clouded over in gray fog and vibrated until a loud burst cracked the tension. Cindy covered her ears; the crackle in the air popping her ear drums. Out of the miasma floated down the misty form of Jane. Her ghostly eyes burned an angry red, enhancing her scowl. The rage she felt for Thomas, harbored since the day he had killed her, radiated off her in waves as she hovered over the gap and in between him and Bobby.

Unimpressed, Thomas snickered at the ghost of the woman he'd once loved. He felt just as much fear and anxiety towards her now as he did the day he took her life—none. "Jane. What's the point, really? You couldn't stop me before. What makes you think you have a chance now, all of a sudden?" He turned his attention back to Bobby. "I've got work to do."

Jane raised her arms protectively in front of Bobby. Through the translucent veil of Jane's form, Cindy could still see the little boy's terrified and tear-streaked face. "It's gonna be alright, Bobby. I promise," Cindy said, from yards away.

Thomas took another step, gently lowering to the ground.

Jane followed suit.

"You have no control here, Jane."

"We'll see." The glint in her smoldering eyes pulsed. Thomas sneered and lunged forward. Jane's ghost rippled from head to toe as a surge of power coursed from somewhere within her. She absorbed it all, focusing it outward at Thomas through her screaming mouth.

The steel-reinforced walls shook and cracked, and spider veins climbed up them in random arrays of violent lines and shapes. The force of Jane's banshee wail knocked Thomas backwards into a partition with a meaty thud, bouncing his skull off the concrete. Windows buckled and groaned in resentment as the sonic wave charged through, shattering them into millions of lethal daggers of glass.

Overhead, the skylights came loose. Bobby stood frozen as he watched the thick glass plummet earthbound—right towards him.

Thomas' power faltered, freeing Cindy. She shouted over Jane's unearthly howl as she rocketed towards Bobby despite her pain. "No! Bobby, watch out." She launched herself off the platform, hurtling through the air right before the hunk of skylight could come crashing down onto him. The force of her trajectory pushed Bobby clear of the impact, but her momentum failed and the glass struck her, its weight and gravity slamming her into the floor.

Bobby yelled, but his tiny voice couldn't break through the clamor. He ran to her side, scooping up her hand and holding it tight. Even though she was barely conscious, she still managed to give the teary-eyed boy a soft smile and his hand a reassuring squeeze. "Cindy. Please don't go."

"You... have to get out of here," she mumbled, between bloody coughs and the consuming pain of the inevitable. Nevertheless, she fought against the crushing weight of the skylight, even as it pushed all the air from her body. As her breathing came in ragged gasps, her eyelids fluttered and her body went limp. The corners of her vision began clouding over as her irises rolled up into her head yet her failing lungs pushed out three final words. "I'm sorry, Bobby...."

Bobby burst into tears. With all the strength his little frame could rally, he grabbed the skylight, pushing and fighting to lift the metal and thick pane of glass off Cindy, but he couldn't—he was no longer dreaming. Cindy, his only hope for safety, had passed on. Nothing would be able to wake her from this sleep, neither in the dreaming void, nor in the real world.

Faith & Fury

Ultimately, Jane's wrath had killed Cindy with her inhuman outpouring of rage for Thomas, the culprit. And as she burned in her anger, wraithlike tentacles assaulted him. She had succumbed to the fury consuming her, unaware of the calamity she had caused.

Thomas struggled to protect himself from Jane's attack, both in awe of the turn of events and the sheer power she somehow now possessed. In his twisting and turning, he caught sight of the child rushing towards him through Jane's transparency.

Bobby, steel rod in hand, lunged for Thomas. As he plowed through Jane's airy barrier, she exploded into ethereal shrapnel, evaporating into the nether. Their eyes met in that instant, anger and fright clashing with complete psychosis.

Yet, even as Bobby ambushed him, Thomas sensed his vigor returning now that Jane no longer accosted him. He intercepted the boy's timid swing and ripped the rod from his grip, sending the boy to the ground once more. Thomas stood over him and hurled the rod across the warehouse, his shadow engulfing the child. He chuckled, sensing final victory. That cop bitch was dead, Jane burst into dust, and soon he would turn this little creep into nothing more than a stain on the stone floor. Everything was falling into place—becoming what it should be.

"Please don't hurt me." Bobby began to sob. "I just wanna go home."

"Not so tough now without your cop bitch or metal rod to protect you, huh?" Thomas spat. "You little pain in my asshole." Bobby started shaking, dark streams of piss puddling at his feet. Thomas burst into laughter, deep belly guffaws that echoed through the building. "Now that's pitiful. Even for a little shit like you."

"Please…"

"Enough of this bull*shit*."

Thomas went to move in, but the stink of sulfur made him stop. Through the gap in the roof that once housed the fallen skylight, he saw the sky cloud up and darken in seconds. Following the smell, the ground beneath his feet vibrated, affecting his equilibrium.

In the confusion, Bobby scrambled up and away, hiding behind a pile of scrap metal. He stole a peek through a gap in the pile. He just wanted this to end, to be back at home safe with his mother and cursing his troublesome curiosity that had brought him into this twisted world to begin with.

Thomas stood confounded, yet almost amused. "Master? Is that you?" The soft rumbling persisted as the air inside the warehouse grew heavy and dank, almost as if it might rain. "I can feel you here, all around me." A burst of sound radiated off the ground, disturbing the humid air. "Master, please, I've done everything you've asked of me. Now show me what you promised would be mine."

No response.

"Master!" he called. "I'm begging you. Show yourself to me once and for all so I can rule by your side." The moist air circulated around him, creating a vortex within the old building. Invisible tendrils of air slapped the walls until the whole place shook. His beaming smile was almost childlike with anticipation; he had already forgotten about wanting to kill Bobby.

All around him, shapes appeared within the swirling wind. They spun at breakneck speed, coagulating into form with each revolution. White noise buzzed in his ears, turning to whispers, then murmurs. Faces appeared in the gusty static, and from these faces the murmurs became voices—all calling his name—a disharmonious crew of tormenting female voices.

The faces grew familiar. As they churned around him, each spitting his name and condemning him, he realized he knew every one of the faces. "This is not happening. Not now," he bellowed. "This is impossible!"

It is happening, Thomas. The voice of Jane whispered in his ear, yet seemed to fill the whole warehouse. *Your master has abandoned you. You weren't worthy after all.*

Thomas swung around, prepared for an attack. His legs buckled from the weight of failure and abandonment. "Master! You promised me!" He fell to his knees as all the faces congealed into form around him.

Poor, Thomas. We're your Master now.

The voice turned deafening.

We're your Master now.

More voices joined the chant, becoming legion.

We're your Master now.

They piled on top of each other, creating one cohesive declaration.

We are your Master now.

Their voices were cruel. They cursed him, berated him, and tormented him until he couldn't take any more. He cried out for it to stop, begging his Master for rescue. "You promised m—"

Bobby speared Thomas through the chest with the steel rebar, cutting his wail short. Blood erupted from his mouth. He gripped the rod, staring at it wide-eyed and dumbfounded. *It's not supposed to end like this*. His mind roared.

He turned to see Bobby standing behind him and breathing heavy, his little body coursing with anger. All around the boy, the phantoms of the women Thomas had killed, floated and smiled. His Master did not win today. They would soon find rest—eternal rest.

The last fleeting gasp of life wafted out of Thomas' mouth as he fell forward, only for the steel rod to prevent him from reaching the ground, propping him up in genuflection.

Tears filled Bobby's eyes; it was finally over. He felt a soft touch on his shoulder and turned to see Cindy behind him, smiling. She was nothing more than mist, but he could still feel her kind eyes. He smiled back. "I'm sorry, Cindy. I tried...."

She brushed his cheek with her hand. "It's not your fault, Bobby. You are the bravest boy I have ever met."

Bobby sighed as he watched gravity finally pull the impaled body of Thomas Isaac Griffey to the ground. "Nothing is ever gonna be the same again, is it?"

"No. But at least you saved us all from being stuck in this place forever."

"I guess."

"He will never be able to hurt anyone else. You are safe now."

Bobby's face saddened and he forced a smile back at her.

"So are you."

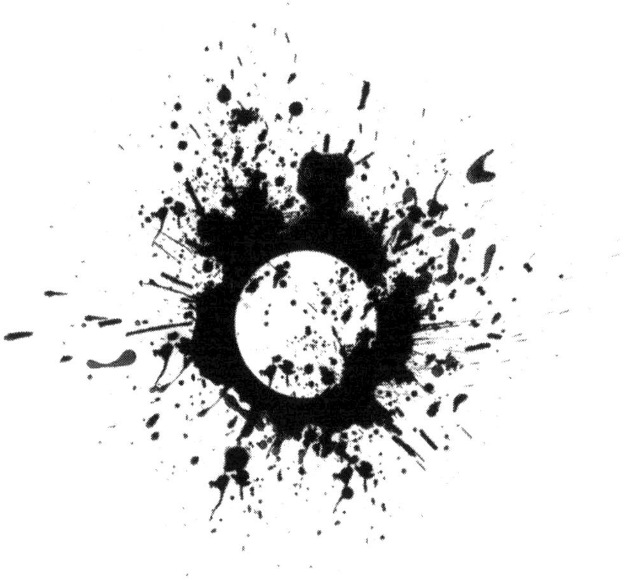

BIBLIOGRAPHY

"Unfurl" was first published in 2015 for Verto Publishing's *Gothic Tales* anthology.

"Osteogenesis" was first published in 2014 for JWK Fiction's *Bones III* anthology.

"An Incident in Central Village" was first published in 2015 for Sabledrake Enterprise's *Fossil Lake 2: The Refossiling* anthology.

"Bequeathed" was first published in 2015 for JWK Fiction's *Ghosts: Revenge* anthology.

"Alchemy of Faith" was first published in 2015 for JWK Fiction's *The Grays* anthology.

"The Yattering" was never before published and is original to this collection.

"Egregore" was never before published and is original to this collection.

"The Sickening" was first published in 2015 for JEA Press' *Undead Legacy* anthology.

"...And the Hits Just Keep on Comin'" was first published in 2015 for Smart Rhino Publications' *Insidious Assassins* anthology.

"Lotus Petals: Liminal Personae" was never before published and is original to this collection.

"The Jatinga Effect" was first published in 2016 for NEHW Press' *Wicked Witches* anthology.

"Sybarites (Or the Enmity of Perverse Existence)" was first published in 2015 for JWK Fiction's *Lovecraft After Dark* anthology.

"End_Game (Dementia Praecox)" was never before published and is original to this collection.

"A Different Kind of Slumber" was originally self-published as a standalone novelette in 2014.

AFTERWORD

So, *Fear of Free Standing Objects*. Pretty odd name for a collection of horror stories, huh? But have you ever been so frightened by something that your skin crawls? So unnerved your breath stops short, causing you to struggle for air and know fear—no matter how irrational or unfeasible? When the sweating and panicking make you so dizzy and faint that bile rises in the back of your throat? If you said *yes* to any of this then you know exactly what I'm talking about here.

Like many people, I have phobias. Some are common: such as the fear of spiders (arachnophobia) and stinging insects (spheksophobia and apiphobia), or the fear of small places (claustrophobia). Others are more random. Take the fear of vomiting (emetophobia) for instance. Throughout my life, I've always associated vomiting with pain and sickness. To this day I've only ever thrown up once from drinking. It's a personal statistic I'm not entirely sure I'm proud of. And don't even get me started on the fear of choking (pseudodysphagia). I once choked on a mozzarella stick and had to yank the hot, ropey cheese out of my gullet with my tiny little fingers. That experience screwed me up for years to the point I gave up cheese, carbonated beverages, and foods that were tough to chew—like steak. It certainly was an odd time in my life.

There are also other phobias that are more mental, which affect me on an emotional level. To illustrate, I am so absolutely terrified of a home invasion (scelerophobia) that I will lose sleep to the point of suffering panic attacks while lying in bed. Maybe it stems from a childhood incident when two men armed with shotguns stormed the bank my mother and I were in. She was at a desk talking with a financial advisor and I was in a waiting area on the opposite side playing with toys when they came in. To this day, I can still feel their guns on me as I ran across the bank to my crying mother as she lay on the floor. The fear of abandonment (autophobia) is another deep one that has helped keep my therapist paid for quite a few years now.

But on the flipside, I have other more non-traditional or uncommon fears that are, in some cases, combinations of phobias that the shrinks are just now coming up with names for. Bathophobia is the fear of depths; Thalassophobia is the fear of the ocean and unknown, watery places. Mix those two together and you get my most ridiculous and unfounded phobia, the kind of fear which, when I explain it to people, they inch away from me as if some of my crazy might rub off on them. This fear began as a recurring nightmare in my adolescent years. In this dream I would—for whatever reason—be dropped into the middle of the ocean, no land in sight, during a hurricane. Attached to my face would be a pair of water goggles that I couldn't remove, and every time a wave would crash down and submerge me, the goggles would allow me to see all the friggin' crazy sea monsters swimming underneath me. And wouldn't you know it? There's a name for that fear... more or less. Megalohydrothalassophobia: the fear of large things in the water.

The final phobia, the fear mentioned in the title of this collection, is a newer one for me—the fear of free standing objects. One day I just decided wind turbines creeped me out. Driving down a road while working, I saw a lone turbine breaking over the tree-lined horizon and it gave me the worst anxiety. That unease spread to eventually include gas and water towers, cell towers, and some bridges. Without warning or reason, these towering objects became my mortal enemy. It's fitting that this fear is called megalophobia and is the morbid and irrational fear of large objects. While that definition is rather vague and could refer to a multitude of "big" things—as well as hold millions of different meanings for millions of different people, my anxiety-inducing "fascination" is with giant mechanical objects (a type of *specific* phobia called—you guessed it—mechanophobia: the fear of machines). Also large, looming architectural structures, like solitary buildings rising like monoliths from empty acres tend to skeeve me out, too. There is no specific name for this combination that I'm aware of, but it's real and has affected me deeply enough to acknowledge it in the title of this collection, because to me these fears are horror stories in and of themselves.

At this point, I'm sure you're all thinking I'm some sort of lunatic, a posterchild for the benefits of psych meds. And perhaps you're right. However, I am how the universe made me. For better or for worse, these idiosyncrasies have made me who I am today.

I hope you've enjoyed these little peeks behind the gears of my noggin. Thanks for reading!

Doug R.

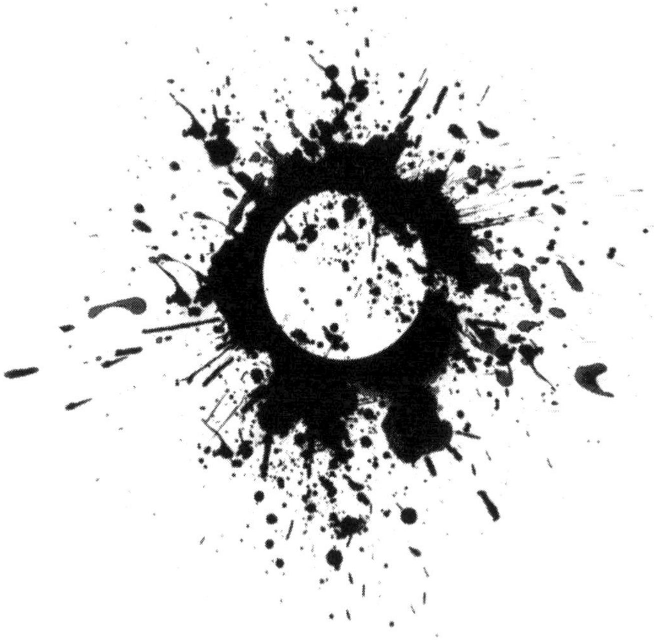

ABOUT THE AUTHOR

Doug was born and raised in the bowels of Connecticut. In the mid-90s he received his art degree in Computer Animation and Special Effects for stage and screen. However, writing dark fiction was his true passion. At the turn of the millennium, he joyously bid Connecticut a final farewell and relocated to Massachusetts where he continues to hone his writing and artistic skills. His work can be found in various anthologies from such publishers as Smart Rhino Publications, NEHW Press, and Scarlet Galleon Publications.

ALSO AVAILABLE
FROM DOUG RINALDI

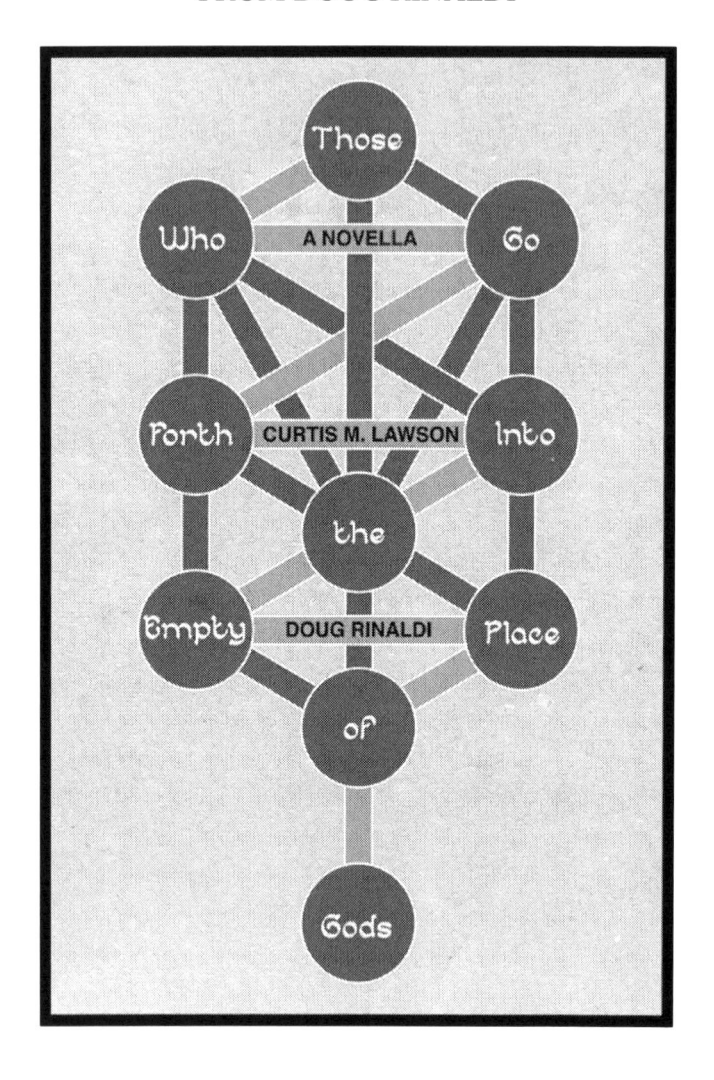

Those Who Go Forth Into the Empty Place of Gods

A NOVELLA

CURTIS M. LAWSON

DOUG RINALDI